Gabriel H

Murder
Mouse Trail Ends
Rattlesnake Brother
Chattering Blue Jay
Fox Goes Hunting
Turkey's Fiery Demise
Stolen Butterfly
Churlish Badger
Owl's Silent Strike
Bear Stalker
Damning Firefly
Cougar's Cache

Wolverine Instincts

A Gabriel Hawke Novel
Book 13

Paty Jager

Windtree Press
Corvallis, OR

This is a work of fiction, Names, characters, places, and incidents either are the product of the author's imagination or are used fictitiously, and any resemblance to actual persons living or dead, business establishments, events, or locales, is entirely coincidental.

WOLVERINE INSTINCTS

Copyright © 2025 Patricia Jager

All rights reserved. No part of this book may be used or reproduced in any manner whatsoever without written permission of the author or Windtree Press except in the case of brief quotations in critical articles or reviews.

Contact Information: info@windtreepress.com

Windtree Press
Corvallis, Oregon
http://windtreepress.com

Cover Art by Covers by Karen

PUBLISHING HISTORY
Published in the United States of America

ISBN 978-1-962065-89-4

Special Thanks to:

My beta readers and critique partner who help keep the story on track and give me input about law enforcement and medical issues.

This book was fun to write allowing me to travel the trails of the Eagle Cap Wilderness through Hawke.

Prologue

He'd finally caught the creature that would make him invincible. He stared at the cage he'd made to hold the animal. The stench of rotten meat and the spray the skunk bear had excreted in rage at being caught heightened his excitement. The male skunk bear snarled, baring white pointed teeth at him. A laugh rumbled in his chest and broke free into the pine and fir trees around them. As the sound died, he strolled toward the cage.

His trap had worked, just like he'd planned. The rotten deer leg hanging in the tree had lured the animal above the trap. As soon as more weight than the leg pulled on the frayed rope, it and the skunk bear fell into the trap and the heavy lid shut.

For years he'd wanted to catch a skunk bear but hadn't known where to find one. When he'd overheard one of the biologists talking to someone at Al's Café about finding tracks in the Eagle Caps, he knew what to do. That night he'd broken into the Fish and Wildlife building and found the coordinates of where the tracks were found. He didn't care that the animals were on the threatened list. He'd wanted a skunk bear since he saw one on television. Staring into the animal's eyes, he knew they would be good together.

This fierce small-bodied creature would be his mascot and give him the strength he needed to take down his enemies.

"Hey! Are you okay?" called a male voice from behind him.

Spinning toward the voice, he raised his rifle.

"It's not hunting season, what are you doing with that gun?" The man wore a large backpack and what he considered sissy clothes - shorts, t-shirt, and a floppy hat.

"This is none of your business," he ground out through his clenched teeth.

The skunk bear growled and the man's gaze landed on the cage.

"What are you doing with that animal? You can't cage up a wild animal." The sissy approached.

He raised his rifle, aimed, and shot the man in the middle of the chest. The sissy dropped faster than a buck.

"Hey!" came another shout, farther away.

What the Hell! This area rarely had hikers. He scanned the trees and saw someone. Raising the rifle to his shoulder, he set his sights on the man in the thicket of pines and pulled the trigger. The boom of the rifle echoed through the trees, bouncing off the other side of the canyon as the man dropped.

Son-of-a-bitch! This had become more complicated

than he wanted. It was supposed to be simple. Set the cage, catch the skunk bear, and get off the mountain.

He walked over and toed the body of the sissy. He'd witnessed dead many times. This man wouldn't tell anyone he'd captured a skunk bear. Staring at where he'd last seen the man in the trees, he headed in that direction, ignoring the tug of the brush on his canvas pants. He had to make sure his second shot had been a kill shot before he took his sought-after trophy home.

All he found was blood on the grass and lots of footprints. *More than one person.*

Double fuckin damn! Now he had to track these two and make sure they never talked.

Chapter One

Hawke swiveled his head as the second shot rang out in the Eagle Cap Wilderness. Dog started off the trail between Minam and Blue Lake, heading in the direction the original sound came from as a second shot echoed up the Minam River canyon.

This was Hawke's third day on patrol in the Eagle Caps. He spent most of his summers in these mountains. Mountains where his ancestors had roamed before the whites invaded their territory. Hawke always took as many assignments in the wilderness as he could get. He enjoyed being in nature, checking fishing licenses, and helping hikers and packers. This was his favorite time of the year. Summer in the high Wallowas was the same as he assumed heaven would be.

But today, with the sound of a rifle firing twice, he feared a poacher was taking down a trophy deer or elk. Or black bear. More had been seen in the mountains in the last few years. He reined Dot, his appaloosa gelding, to follow his canine companion. The sound had come from Brown Mountain. It wasn't a place most visitors to the wilderness usually accessed, making it the perfect place for a poacher to wait for a trophy to walk into his sights.

As he maneuvered Dot and his pack mule, Horse, through the pine and fir tree thickets and over shale slides, Hawke wondered how he would find the exact place where the shots were fired. All he had was a general direction.

After an hour of traversing the side of the ridge, he spotted ravens circling in the air farther down on the ridge. That was a pretty good clue to where he'd find what happened. Hawke reined Dot in a direct line to the large soaring black birds.

When they were twenty-five yards from the circling birds, Dog stopped, sniffed, and whined before running forward. Hawke urged Dot to move faster. He didn't want Dog confronting a poacher without him. Anyone who would shoot an animal out of season would shoot a dog running out of the brush at them.

Catching up to Dog, he found the animal sitting under a tree. Hawke sniffed and blew out the scent of rotten meat. His gaze followed the direction of Dog's raised nose. A rotten haunch of a deer lay on the ground surrounded by shattered wood and crumpled wire mesh. "Why would someone do that?" Hawke asked Dog and dismounted.

The grass and brush had been crushed and the wood had claw and teeth marks. Hawke crouched to check the ground for tracks. A track he'd only seen one other time in the Wallowas was scattered between the pieces of wood. He sniffed again, this time his nose close to the ground to smell less of the rotten meat. The musky smell emitted by wolverines still hung on the ground. "I think he was one pissed wolverine by the scent he left."

"Do you think that wolverine broke out of a cage and attacked the person trapping him?" Hawke asked Dog.

Dog whimpered and looked up at the ravens still circling.

Hawke raised his face to the sky and studied the birds swirling above. "They're looking to make a meal of that haunch." The torn-up cage didn't explain the two rifle shots. He stood and did a 360 scan of the area. He noticed what looked like a backpack lying about twenty feet away in the brush.

He walked over and realized the pack was attached to a man who was face down. Hawke hurried over, avoiding the set of footprints he spotted that walked up to the body and then away in the opposite direction of the trap.

Crouching on the off side of the footprints, he felt for a pulse and cursed. The man was dead. He walked over to Horse and pulled a small camera and a tarp out of the pack. Back at the body, he took photos and rolled the man over. Only one shot. Did the first one miss or the second one? He found the man's driver's license in his wallet in a side pocket of his pack. The victim lived in LaGrande. Rifling through the other cards in the wallet, he found a business card. The guy was a trail documenter. Had he been thinking a new trail could be put through here? If so, he hadn't known he'd come across a man with a gun.

Hawke glanced back toward the shattered cage. He walked back and looked around for a wildlife camera or marker designating that this was a cage set here by Fish and Wildlife. He didn't find anything. He marked the location on his GPS and walked over to cover up the body with the tarp and stake it down to keep the predators away, hopefully for as long as it would take him to contact the outside world and the investigators to get in here.

The direction the killer went would put him within a radio signal. He gathered up Dot's reins, called Dog, and led the horse and mule as he followed the set of prints away from the body. If he was lucky, he'd come across the shooter before he could call the shooting in.

Thirty yards beyond the body, Hawke found more footprints and dried blood on grass and bushes. "Shit!" He studied the blood and said to Dog, "The second shot got another person. Who the hell is this shooter?"

Hawke studied the boot prints and swung up onto Dot. It was nearing noon. With luck and the faster pace of his horse, he hoped to catch up to the shooter before he killed another person.

《》《》《》

Seth Finlay hurried as quickly as he could through the forest dragging his brother beside him. That lunatic who had shot the hiker for no reason had put a bullet in Alex's right thigh. They had to get away from him and get help. It was all Seth could do to haul his muscular athletic brother through the tangle of bushes. He wasn't an athlete. Not like his brother. He was the nerdy still in high school brother. The one who dinked around with electronics and posted monthly on a podcast about his nerdy ways.

He stopped and they both gasped for air.

"You can't keep hauling me around," Alex said.

"Leave me and go get help."

Seth's jaw dropped. "I can't leave you here with that lunatic after us." At that moment they heard something crashing through the brush behind them. They both dropped to the ground. That's when Seth saw their prints. He knew they had to get the man to leave so he could get Alex to safety. He whispered, "I'm taking your shoes. I'll draw the idiot away. You stay here under this brush."

He didn't wait for Alex to object. He pulled the sneakers off his brother's feet, brushed away their tracks leading to Alex's hiding spot, and put the sneakers on his hands. Starting from the tracks he left a good thirty feet from Alex, he dropped down onto all fours and moved as fast as he could in what they had called in grade school, a bear crawl.

Moving as quickly as he could through the forest, he thought about Alex, bleeding under a bush. They'd come on this backpacking trip as one last brother outing. Alex was headed to college in three weeks and he would start his senior year of high school.

Seth didn't know what direction he'd walked in. He just wanted to draw the shooter far away from Alex. Staring down into a deep ravine, he stood and stretched his back. He walked along the edge, making sure any tracks he made were brushed away by a stick he'd picked up off the ground. When he'd followed the edge about thirty feet, he headed back toward where he hoped he'd left Alex. As he crept through the forest, he prayed the man was lured away by his footprints and didn't find his brother.

Chapter Two

Hawke continued following the trail the man with the rifle was leaving. It appeared the shooter didn't think he'd be followed or he didn't care. He crashed through the forest like a bull elk in rut. Just enough ahead Hawke could barely hear the cracking of branches. Hawke had called Dog back several times with a sharp whistle when the animal tried to go ahead.

Stopping to get a better look at the tracks on the ground, Hawke dismounted and held Dog beside him as he listened and studied the ground. The shooter's tracks following the other two were clear. The shooter stepped with a purpose, leaving deep prints, trampling plants, and bending branches on bushes as he passed. It was a clear path to follow. The prints the shooter followed barely made imprints. It was clear that one person was dragging a foot. The same side that was dripping blood. While their impressions were lighter, they were clear enough for anyone who had ever followed any tracks to see.

Worry swirled in Hawke's chest. If he couldn't get to the two before the shooter following them, they could end up like the hiker he'd found.

The only thing that made sense was to catch up to the man with the rifle. He swung up into the saddle and urged Dot forward, picking up the pace to catch the man before dark.

《》《》《》

Seth heard the man with the rifle crashing through the brush ahead of him. That meant the man was between him and Alex. His heart raced wondering how he could get to his brother without the man finding them. Standing in the forest, the scent of decaying leaves and his own sweat filled his nostrils before he heard the rustling behind him. He was sure the man was ahead of him. He cocked his head to one side and listened intently. There was the swish of branches scraping against something. He wasn't going to stick around to find out what it was. This was the wilderness after all.

Seth checked the sun and made a change of direction. He'd try to come upon Alex from the upper side of the mountain. He struggled going through a patch of wild roses but used his brother's shoes, still on his hands to push his way through. Once he was clear of the bushes, he sprinted up the mountainside and then made his way along the slope, keeping an ear out for the sound of the man with the rifle.

《》《》《》

Dog stopped and sniffed the ground. He raised his nose in the air and sniffed.

"What is it? Are we getting close?" Hawke asked.

Dog started up the slope of the mountain.

Hawke called him back. "Why are you going that direction? It's clear the man we're after is headed around the side, not up." Hawke dismounted and studied the ground. Sure enough, a new set of tracks came upon the trail he was following and continued as if going up the side of the mountain. Hawke crouched, studying the older tracks and the new.

"I'll be damned. This is one of the people the killer is following." He rocked back on his heels and studied the scene. He needed to catch the person with the gun. He'd worry about the other person when the poacher was under arrest.

"Let's get this son-of-a-bitch," Hawke said to Dog and urged Dot to continue following the easy-to-see trail. As he followed, Hawke's mind wandered to what possible reason the second set of prints had for traveling up the mountainside.

Dog took off at a run and Hawke hastened Dot, but Horse picked that moment to decide he wasn't going any further. Not wanting to waste time dealing with Horse, Hawke dropped the rope and urged the gelding forward. He knew that Horse would either follow on his own or be in that spot when he returned.

Dodging the pine and fir trees and scraping through the brush at a canter to keep Dog in sight, Hawke was aware of the noise he made. The poacher would hear him coming.

Dog stopped, the hair on his neck and shoulders standing up.

Hawke pulled up on Dot, whistled for Dog, and bailed off. He led the gelding behind a rock outcropping and pulled his rifle out of the leather scabbard on his saddle. Dog stood beside him, his hair bristled and his lips curled back.

"What is it, boy?" Hawke whispered as he crept around the side of the rocks.

A gun boomed and a bullet zinged off the rock.

"Fish and Wildlife with the Oregon State Police. Drop your weapon!" Hawke shouted.

No response. Not a shot or a shout. He waited five, then ten minutes before he eased around the side of the rock and peered into the trees. He didn't see a sign of anyone. Or hear a sound. The shooter had disappeared without making a sound. That meant he did know how to be stealthy. Great! Now he'd have to worry about the shooter coming up behind him.

Dog came around the rock and his ears perked up.

"What do you hear?" Hawke asked.

The animal started trotting in the direction they'd been headed. But his hackles weren't up and his ears were listening.

Hawke jogged after the animal, scanning the ground to see which direction the shooter went.

He crouched when he saw an oddity in the placement of the floor debris. Someone had tried to hide tracks. Then he heard the moan to his right. Dog stood at the end of a downed log, his tail wagging.

Hawke walked over and glanced down. A young man in his twenties, he'd guess, lay as far under the log as he could get. Two backpacks sat at his shoeless feet. His eyes were shut. The dark lashes stood out on his pale face. Blood congealed on the leg not shoved under the log. Hawke had found the second victim.

"Young man, can you hear me?" Hawke asked, placing a hand on the chest barely moving up and down.

Wolverine Instincts

The young man's eyes opened wide, his face twisted in pain and horror. "Don't kill me."

"I'm here to help." Hawke grabbed the chain around his neck and pulled his badge out from the inside of his shirt. He understood why the young man was frightened. When he worked in the wilderness he dressed in regular clothing and let his hair grow. It was the best way to keep a poacher from taking a potshot at him as he rode around. "I'm State Trooper Hawke with the Fish and Wildlife. I was tracking the guy who shot you but he got away."

The young man gripped his arm. "My brother, Seth. Where is he?"

Hawke glanced up the ridge. "It must have been his tracks I crossed a half a mile back before I caught up to the shooter." He reached down. "Let me help you get out from under there. I have medical supplies in my pack back at my mule."

"I can't leave without Seth." The young man became agitated. "I'm his older brother. I have to protect him."

Hawke studied the young man, "What's your name?"

"Alex. Alex Finlay."

"I'm going to give you a temporary bandage while I go get my horse and mule." He pulled out the tail of his shirt and used his knife to slice a slit in it. He ripped the bottom off and folded it in a square. He placed that over the hole in the young man's leg and untied the bandana around his neck. He used the bandana to cinch down the bandage and, with luck, stop the bleeding.

"Ouch!" Alex said through clenched teeth.

"Sorry, it needs pressure to stop the bleeding. "I'll

leave Dog with you while I gather my horse and mule. If Seth comes back tell him to wait here with you. I'll get you both out of here safely." Hawke motioned to Dog and said, "Stay."

Dog looked at Alex then at Hawke.

"Keep him safe," Hawke said, patting the dog's head and standing. He gazed down at Alex. "Don't go anywhere. I'll be back in twenty minutes if my mule hasn't wandered off." And that's when he wondered if Seth or the shooter might have circled around and tried to take Horse.

Chapter Three

Hawke found Horse standing next to Dot. The crotchety mule hadn't liked being left behind. He grinned and mounted Dot. Leading the mule, he arrived back ten minutes after he'd left.

"No sign of your brother?" Hawke asked.

"No. I don't understand why he hasn't returned. He said he'd come back for me when he took my shoes."

"You can tell me why he took your shoes while I bandage that leg correctly." Hawke knelt by Alex and using his knife, cut away the leg of his jeans.

"He was trying to lure the guy after us away." Alex sucked in air when Hawke used the antiseptic wipes to clean around the wound.

"Why was he after you?" Hawke had a feeling he knew why but wanted confirmation.

"We saw him shoot a hiker. We hollered and he turned and shot at us. We were already moving when the bullet ripped through my leg." He winced and said,"

I'm headed to play college football in a couple weeks. This was a last adventure for Seth and me."

"Well, you'll have to wait to start football practice but you'll get to the college on time." Hawke stood and held a hand out to him. "You can ride Horse."

"I'm not leaving until Seth shows up," Alex said, taking Hawke's hand, and rising only to plop his ass on the log.

"I need to call this in and I can't do that until I get to the top of this ridge." Hawke glanced up the side of the ridge. He could see the snowy top of Glacier Mountain beyond the ridge line. He had to make the call, to get a crime team up to investigate before predators made a mess of the crime scene, and to get back up if the shooter decided to take care of the people who saw him. He didn't like leaving Alex alone but he didn't have a choice if the young man wasn't going to come with him.

"I'll leave Horse and Dog here with you while I take Dot and go to the top and radio that there's a body up here and a shooter on the loose. That will bring in help." Hawke studied Alex. "When your brother returns the two of you need to wait here for me."

The young man nodded.

Hawke tied Horse to a tree where he could nibble on the grass and bushes.

"You said you were leaving the horse," Alex said, looking confused.

"The mule's name is Horse. I named him that hoping he'd act more like a horse and not a stubborn mule. So far, it hasn't worked." Hawke shrugged.

"And your dog is named Dog?"

"Yeah, I couldn't come up with a better name and

he comes to it."

Alex pointed to the appaloosa gelding. "And what did you say the horse is called?"

"Dot. Short for Polka Dot. A friend of mine named him that." Hawke smiled thinking of Kitree, the girl he'd saved several years ago in these mountains. He'd tracked her for days before realizing she was intentionally avoiding him. She'd thought he was the man who killed her parents while they were camping at Mirror Lake. She and her adoptive parents worked for his partner, Dani Singer, who owned Charlie's Hunting Lodge in the Eagle Cap Wilderness. If he couldn't get hold of anyone by radio, he'd take the two brothers there.

"Remember, you and your brother stay here until I get back. There's no telling if the guy after you left or is coming back to try and finish you off."

Alex shuddered.

"If Dog's hackles go up and he growls, hide. It means he knows there's something bad coming your direction." Hawke studied the young man. "Understand?"

"Yeah. Where do I hide?" Alex's head rotated on his neck as he scanned the area.

"Either get on Horse and make him go the opposite direction Dog is staring or get behind that rock over there." Hawke drew his shotgun out of the scabbard. "Have you shot a gun before?"

"Sure, Dad takes us hunting every year." Alex's eyes brightened at the sight of the weapon.

"Only use it if your life is threatened. Don't just shoot because you are spooked." Hawke held the shotgun out but didn't release the weapon. "You understand what I'm saying?"

"Yes. Only use the gun if that lunatic comes back to shoot me." Alex tried to pull the shotgun from Hawke's grip.

He held on, peering into the young man's eyes. "It's not easy to shoot a human."

Alex's eyes widened in his pale face and he nodded. "I understand. But I think my instincts to stay alive will kick in."

Hawke nodded. Just like the wolverine's instincts had given him the strength to tear his cage apart and get away. He handed the rifle to Alex. "I should be back in two hours. After that, if your brother hasn't shown up, we'll head to a hunting lodge to get you flown out for medical help."

"What about Seth?" Worry ringed the young man's eyes.

"I'll come back and look for him. But I'm hoping he'll show up here by the time I get back." Hawke swung up onto Dot and told Dog to stay.

As he turned Dot uphill, he scanned the landscape looking for movement. The brother had to be here somewhere. Unless he miscalculated and walked on by where his brother was hidden. With the two backpacks sitting on the ground next to Alex, the younger brother didn't have any food, water, or shelter. Luckily it was early August and the nights weren't below freezing.

«»«»«»

Seth stopped to catch his breath and try to figure out where he was in relation to where he'd left Alex. He'd heard a shot and hoped to God that the man hadn't caught up and finished Alex off. His heart stuttered at the thought of him coming home and his parents' disappointment in him for what his father would say, running when his brother needed him.

He wiped at the sweat trickling down his face. The last time he'd sweated this much he'd been trailing a wounded buck. Their dad expected them to kill, not maim the animals they hunted. He'd been tense and worried that day just like now. He wanted his father's approval and felt he would never measure up to his father's expectations.

He stared up at the ridge. He'd managed to get up above the tree line which wasn't that far above the river below. They'd been on the Minam Trail when Alex spotted the hiker going up higher on the side of the ridge. He thought there might be a trail up there that would give them a better view.

Now he wished they'd never followed the hiker. He stared down at the shoes still on his hands. "We did right," he said, acknowledging his conscience. They could help find the man's killer. His mind went to the scene that he couldn't believe had happened only hours ago. He pulled out his small tape recorder, sat on a rock, and started:

"My brother and I decided to follow a hiker who seemed to know of a higher trail off the Minam Trail. We stayed back, not wanting him to know we were following. It felt wrong to follow, but we were curious." He swallowed, thinking of the saying 'Curiosity killed the cat.'

"We were back about twenty yards when we saw the hiker confront a man dressed in camouflage who was laughing like a madman. When the hiker said something about it wasn't hunting season, the crazy man raised his rifle and shot him. You could tell the hiker was dead by the way he crumpled." Bile rose in his throat and Seth swallowed it down.

"Alex shouted and the man turned his gun on us. Alex caught the bullet in his leg. I slung his arm over my shoulders and we took off as fast as we could go with him dragging a leg. The man didn't start after us right away, but later we could hear him hurrying through the forest behind us. I told Alex to hide. I used his shoes on my hands, to make it look like we went a different direction." He looked around. "Now I'm on the side of a ridge and I'm not sure if I need to go farther before I go down to find Alex, or if I've passed where he's hidden. There is a lot of area up here and I'm not positive where I left him." He clicked off the recorder, shoved it in his pocket, and dropped his face into his hands. What if he didn't find Alex and he died?

He heard the clatter of shale and glanced back the way he'd come. A man rode out of the trees and onto the shale rock above the tree line. He stopped and scanned the area. His gaze landed on Seth and he waved, riding his horse closer.

Seth studied the man and the horse. They looked as if they were one animal, they moved together so well. This man wore a cowboy hat, boots, and a plaid shirt. No camouflage. His face and smile were warm, welcoming.

When he was within twenty feet of him, he asked, "You don't happen to be Seth, do you?"

His jaw dropped open before he snapped it shut. "Yeah, did you come across my brother?"

"I did. He'll be happy to see you. Worrying isn't good for that wound he has." The man dismounted and held his hand out. "I'm State Trooper Hawke with Fish

Wolverine Instincts

and Wildlife." After he shook hands, he pulled a badge out from under his shirt by a chain. "I found the hiker that was shot and followed the tracks. I caught up to the shooter but when I shouted who I was, he took off."

Seth's heart raced. "You left Alex down there alone? That guy could come back."

"He's not alone. My partner is with him. I'm going to try and get a radio signal so I can get someone in to investigate the murder and get your brother medical care. Sit tight and I'll take you down to him."

Seth nodded and watched the man hand him the horse's reins while he dug into the saddlebag. He pulled out a large satellite radio. Seth had taken one apart for one of his science projects in middle school. "That's an old way of getting hold of someone," he commented.

"Up here it's usually the only way to contact dispatch." Hawke was impressed the young man knew something about the satellite radio. He turned it on and dialed in Union County dispatch.

"Union Dispatch this is Hawke, come in." He released the button and listened. Nothing. "Union dispatch this is Trooper Hawke, come in," he repeated. The radio made crackling noises and a voice came on.

"Trooper Hawke this is Mad Milly. You're coming through on my ham radio. What can I do? Over."

"Mad Milly, I have a body at," he repeated the GPS coordinates for where the body was, "get that information to the State Police. And tell them I'm taking a wounded man to Charlie's Hunting Lodge to be flown to Alder for medical care. They can catch up with me there. Over."

"I wrote it down and will pass it on. Over."

"Thank you. Over."

Hawke smiled. It wasn't the first time Mad Milly had picked up his calls from the Eagle Caps. She'd get the message relayed.

He turned to Seth. "You want to ride or walk?"

"I'm tired but I'd rather walk." He handed the reins to Hawke.

"Suits me and Dot." Hawke started walking downhill. "Come on. We should meet up with your brother in an hour." He glanced back and noted the young man picked up a pair of shoes from where they'd been sitting on the ground.

"Your brother said you took his shoes. That was smart thinking to try and lure the shooter away from your brother." Hawke didn't look over his shoulder. He heard the young man's steps gain speed and soon Seth was walking beside him.

"Your brother told me what happened. Did you get a good look at the man who shot the hiker?" Hawke asked.

"Not a good look at his face. He had a bushy beard. Brown with some gray, I think, but his face was all scrunched up in anger and red when he aimed and fired at the hiker."

Hawke heard the tremor in the young man's voice. The sight had been something he'd never forget and wish he could. "What was he wearing?"

"Camouflage pants and shirt. Boots and a ball cap. I think it was camouflage too." He sighed. "I'm sorry, I'm not much help."

"You're more help than I am. He shot at me but I never saw him. I thought he wasn't someone who knew the forest, because he left such an easy trail to follow. I understand now, he didn't think anyone would come upon his kill before he could hide it. He planned to quiet you and your brother and go back to hide the evidence he'd done anything wrong." Hawke wondered if the man had gone back to the body and would hide it. That didn't matter right now, he had to get the brothers to safety, then come back and search for the body if the shooter did go back to cover his tracks. Not that it would do him much good, since Hawke had the photos and the victim's I.D.

"Do you think he will come back to kill us?" Seth's voice held fear.

"I have a feeling he went back to hide the body. By the time he comes looking for you two, I'll have you safe in Wallowa County." Hawke knew that when he told Dani what had happened, she would warm up the helicopter and transport both the boys to Alder.

Chapter Four

Hawke approached the area where he'd left Alex with care. Even though he'd told the young man not to shoot unless he was threatened when people were scared they could get trigger-happy. He found Alex sleeping behind the rock Hawke had told him to hide behind. The young man had moved the mule behind the boulder with him. Dog sat at the side of the rock staring downhill. The direction the shooter had disappeared.

Seth ran up and hugged his brother.

"Hey, what?" Alex was too weak to rise.

"Help me get your brother on my mule," Hawke said, seeing that the young man needed medical care as quickly as he could get it.

Within minutes they had Alex on the mule and Seth on Dot. Hawke and Dog strode ahead, keeping the horse and mule moving at a brisk pace. Knowing the shooter could be waiting along the trail for them, Hawke stayed on the opposite side of Minam River from the trail.

Wolverine Instincts

He glanced up, glad that the sunlight would be longer this time of year. He figured they'd get to the ranch in five hours since they had to navigate without a trail.

《》《》《》

It was 9:20 PM when he and Dog spotted the lights of the hunting lodge. Seeing all the lanterns lit on the cabins, the guest ranch was at full capacity.

Not wanting to scare her guests, he led Horse and Dot over to the bunkhouse where Kitree, Sage, and Tuck lived. "Help your brother down. I'll see if Tuck or Sage are here." He knew this time of night Sage and Kitree could be cleaning up the kitchen. He hoped it was only Tuck relaxing in the bunkhouse.

He knocked on the door and said quietly, "It's Hawke."

There was movement inside and the door opened. It was Kitree in her pajamas. She was now a teenager. Her skimpy shorts and thin strapped top showed off too much skin, in Hawke's opinion. Her face lit up and she started to hug him.

He held her off with a raised palm. "You need to put some clothes on. I have a couple of young men with me. One needs medical attention. When you're dressed, I need you to get your parents and Dani without stirring up the guests."

She glanced around him, nodded, and shut the door.

"Who was that," Seth asked, holding his brother up on the porch.

"Kitree. Her parents work for my partner. Her father is the wrangler and her mother is the cook and housekeeper."

The door opened wide and Kitree stood back, dressed in a t-shirt with an unbuttoned long-sleeved shirt over the top, jeans, and cowboy boots. She studied the brothers as they maneuvered into the lantern light.

"Go get the others." He stopped her before she headed out the door. "It's nothing to be worried about. I just don't want to upset the guests."

She nodded and hurried across the space between the bunkhouse and the lodge.

Where this had once been a bunkhouse that housed up to six wranglers, it was now a cozy home with two bedrooms, and an open floor plan of the kitchen, dining, and living areas.

Hawke went into Kitree's room which had changed since the last time he'd seen it. There were rodeo posters and fewer flower posters on the walls. He grabbed the cot they kept under her bed and brought it out.

By the time he had Alex lying on the cot, the door opened. Dani burst through first, followed by Tuck, Sage, and Kitree.

"Hey, you didn't have to run over here. It's not that kind of emergency." He gave Dani a one-armed hug and smiled at Tuck and Sage. "I came across this young man with a bullet wound after I found a body shot by the same man that did this to Alex." He pointed to the bandaged leg. He peered into Dani's eyes. "I hate to pull you away, but is there a chance you could take these two to Alder? Radio ahead for the ambulance to pick them up and take them to the hospital?"

"What are you going to do?" she asked.

"Go back and secure the murder scene. I called it in and there should be more people up there in the morning."

"You're not going back tonight, are you?" Seth asked, looking at him as if he were crazy.

"You know how we talked about how that guy could go back and try to hide the body?" Hawke studied the young man.

He nodded.

"I want to make sure he doesn't do that and if he has, the trail will be easier to follow the sooner I get there." He smiled at Sage. "But I'd love a plate of whatever you made for dinner tonight before I head back."

"Let me check his wound." Sage knelt next to the cot. "Kitree, go dish up a bowl of stew and a slice of bread for Hawke and both of these boys."

Kitree lit out of the bunkhouse as if it were on fire.

"Tuck, come help me get the bird ready to fly," Dani said. She glanced over her shoulder when she reached the door. "Don't leave without talking to me first."

"I won't." Hawke smiled and crouched beside Sage. "He's lost a lot of blood. I didn't find him for hours after it initially happened. And the two were hurrying through the forest to get away from the killer."

"Have him drink water while I get the supplies I need." Sage stood and walked into her bedroom.

Hawke motioned to the kitchen area. "Seth, fill a cup with water and help me hold Alex up while he drinks."

Seth stepped into the kitchen and poured a glass of water from the pitcher sitting on the counter. He returned to the cot and helped Hawke brace Alex with their arms so the young man could drink. "You need to drink as much water as you can to help replenish your blood," Hawke told him.

"What are the chances I'll be playing football this season?" Alex asked.

"I'm not a doctor, but having seen how much you've endured since getting shot and seeing your younger brother's determination, I'd say you'll make a quick recovery." Hawke glanced at Seth and recognized pride in the young man's face.

Sage returned. She cleaned the wound better, added a salve, and bandaged it up. By then Kitree returned with the food. She handed the first plate and bowl to Hawke. He took it and sat at the table. She handed the next one to Seth. Hawke watched the young man stare at Kitree for a couple of blinks before he muttered "thank you," and sat at the table.

Kitree waited for Sage to get Alex sitting up before placing the last plate onto his lap.

"Thank you," he said, glancing around at all of them.

Tuck and Dani entered the bunkhouse.

"The copter is ready to go," Dani said, taking a seat next to Hawke. "You're lucky I don't have to fly anyone out tomorrow."

"I asked the Creator on the way here to make sure you weren't already down in the valley having delivered someone." Hawke shoved his empty bowl and plate to the middle of the table. "Delicious as usual, Sage," he said to the woman standing with her arm around Tuck's waist. She smiled.

Dani laughed. "He couldn't have changed things if I had been."

"I know but it eased my mind a bit." Hawke rose.

"Dot and Horse aren't going to be too happy with me for taking them back up the trail but I need to make sure the killer doesn't try to hide the body."

"Tyson could go with you. You could ride one of our horses and string the other two. Then he can bring the two back to us tomorrow," Tuck offered.

Hawke liked Dani's nephew, Tyson. In fact, because of their first meeting, Tyson had been working on a degree in criminal justice. "I'd appreciate giving my two a break and having Tyson along." He shifted his gaze to Dani. "Are you okay with me taking Tyson?"

"As long as he comes back tomorrow. We have a large group coming in over the weekend and we'll need all the wranglers."

"He can turn right around and head back when we get there," Hawke said.

"But then you'll be alone," Seth said.

Hawke studied the young man and smiled. "I won't be alone. I'll have Dog and my horse and mule. I'll also have a crime scene team by noon, two o'clock at the latest."

"I'll go drag Tyson away from the card game." Tuck headed to the door. He stopped. "Kitree, bring those dishes along, please."

That's when Hawke noticed she was staring at Seth as if she'd never seen a boy before.

"Kitree," Tuck said, a little louder.

She jumped up and grabbed the dishes, ducking out the door ahead of her father. Tuck shook his head and made eye contact with his wife.

Hawke glanced at Dani. She rolled her eyes. It appeared Kitree was starting to get an interest in boys. He bet that was making for some interesting discussions this summer.

When Tuck returned, he and Hawke carried Alex to the helicopter and settled him inside beside Seth.

Hawke put a hand on Seth's foot. "When you get Alex settled in at the hospital, call this number." He handed the young man his sergeant's business card. "You tell Sergeant Spruel what happened and what I'm doing. It will be a big help."

Seth nodded and shoved the card into his pant pocket.

"Thanks." Hawke shut the door and backed away as the rotors on the helicopter started up. He waved as Dani lifted off and disappeared into the star-dotted sky.

"You sure you and Tyson will be okay?" Tuck asked as they walked to the barn.

"Yeah. If the killer did go back and hide the body, he'll be on his way home by now. If he didn't, then he headed home to figure out what to do next. Best if no one knows the brothers were airlifted out tonight. From what I can tell, the killer doesn't know who they are and didn't get a good look at either of them. As long as their being up here and the bullet hole isn't publicized, they should be safe."

"I'll radio that to Dani before she gets out of range." Tuck jogged toward the lodge as Tyson stepped out of the barn.

Hawke shook hands with the young man. "How's classes going?"

"Good. Taking off in the middle of the night with you is the most excitement I've had all summer."

Hawke laughed. "I heard you've been chasing the young ladies up here."

Tyson snorted and said, "The young ladies up here

aren't my type." He led Hawke into the barn. A lantern lit up the inside showing Dot and Horse chomping on grain and two other horses tied up and saddled. One had Hawke's saddle on it.

"I'd thought about taking some of the weight off of Horse, but then I saw the packs aren't that heavy. He should be fine." Tyson patted the mule on the hip and Horse picked up a back hoof threatening to kick Tyson.

"He's good. Thank you for taking care of them. You ready to go?" Hawke walked between his two, tying Dot's lead rope to the D ring on Horse's pack.

"Yep, just lead them out and I'll turn off the lantern and follow."

Hawke grabbed the reins of the horse wearing his saddle and led the three out into the moonlight.

Tyson closed the barn doors and they mounted.

"Take the lead," Hawke said and fell in behind Tyson, wondering what he'd find when he arrived at the crime scene.

Chapter Five

Early morning sun bathed the canyon with ethereal light as Hawke took the lead to head off the trail to the crime scene. Moonlight had made traveling the trail easy. Other than spooking a pair of deer and an owl, the last six hours had been uneventful. Just the way he liked to ride. He'd even dozed off a time or two in the saddle.

Working his way toward the crime scene, he went slow and scanned the trees and bushes for any movement. Even though he'd told everyone he believed the killer would be gone, there was a slight possibility that if he returned and saw the tarp over the body, he'd wait to see who showed up.

"You look a little tense," Tyson said. "Something I need to know?"

"Just making sure the killer didn't come back," Hawke said softly and peered down at Dog. The poor guy had to be exhausted but his ears were forward and

Wolverine Instincts

he appeared as cautious as Hawke.

"You can sleep while I look around and wait for the crime team to show up," he said to Dog.

"What was that?" Tyson asked.

"Nothing. I was talking to Dog." He glanced over his shoulder and saw Tyson shaking his head. Yeah, most people thought he was crazy the way he talked to Dog and his horses, but he talked to all animals. They were his People's connection to the land. Animals were the first speakers. Once they had taught his People how to live, they became quiet.

He walked the horse into the area he'd come upon the day before. The tarp had been pulled off the body, but there wasn't any sign of the killer. He had a pretty good idea that a predator pulled the tarp off.

"Okay, we're here. I'll unsaddle this horse and you can head back." Hawke dismounted, keeping the horses away from the crime scene.

"I'll stay until you get backup. You said, noon, two at the latest. That will still get me back tonight and I'll be ready to go for the weekend." Tyson hopped off his horse and began unsaddling it.

Hawke could manage alone, but he'd enjoy Tyson's company while he tried to figure out how the wolverine fit into all of this.

They unsaddled the horses and took the pack off of Horse. Then Hawke pulled out some granola bars and bottles of water. They ate that while Dog ate dog food and the horses munched on grass. When they finished, Hawke told Dog to rest and he and Tyson approached the body with evidence bags and the camera Hawke carried in his pack.

"Let's cover the body back up and start with the

cage over there." Hawke pointed to the mess under a tamarack tree.

As he replaced the tarp, Hawke noticed teeth and claw marks on the body. His first impression that a predator had pulled the tarp off was confirmed.

He and Tyson walked over to the area where the cage had been shattered.

"What happened here?" Tyson asked.

"I think someone lured a wolverine up that limb and when he jumped down onto the rotten deer leg the rope snapped and he landed in a cage." Hawke peered up at the frayed end of the rope dangling in the tree. "See how frayed the end looks? I'd say it had help getting that way."

Tyson tilted his head back and snapped a photo.

Hawke returned his attention to the ground. "Wolverines are strong for their size. I bet he was pissed when he fell into the cage. From what the brothers told me, the killer could have been provoking the wolverine. Which wouldn't help his anger. I'm sure the gunshots scared the creature even more. I'd say, he fought like hell to get out of that trap." Hawke walked over to where he'd seen blood on the ground debris. There it was. Dried and harder to see but there. He knelt and scraped it into a small evidence vial. "He hurt himself getting out of the trap. But he got out." Hawke heard the satisfaction in his voice. He was happy the animal had gotten free. They didn't hurt humans and were on the threatened list. There was no reason for anyone to trap one other than Fish and Wildlife to tag and research.

He spotted a set of footprints that hadn't been there yesterday. The hair on the back of his neck tingled. The killer had come back looking for the wolverine. He'd ignored the tarped body but followed the tracks of the animal he'd trapped.

"Take photos of all of this. Maybe we can figure out who bought the mesh or even find a fingerprint or two from some of the pieces." Hawke wanted to follow the man's tracks, but keeping the crime scene safe was more important. The small amount of blood on the forest floor wasn't enough to slow the wolverine down. He could be miles from here by now. Hawke had read that they could lope for hours and cover lots of country until they became tired.

He crouched by a piece of wood that had the bent hinges screwed to it. He pulled a latex glove from his back pocket, tugged it on, and picked up the board with hinges, placing it in a large evidence bag.

"What's that smell?" Tyson asked as he leaned down to get a close-up photo of a small piece of mesh.

"A mixture of rotten deer leg and wolverine spray. They're both nasty. Looks like something made off with the deer leg. It was lying over there when I came across the torn-up cage." Hawke pointed to the spot where he'd seen the rotten haunch.

"Did you get photos of it?" Tyson asked, leaning back and drawing in air.

"One. That will have to do to prove the wolverine had been lured into the trap." Hawke wanted to get the killer not only for the murder but for trapping a threatened animal. He picked up a few more pieces of the cage that might have prints on it and bagged them.

Rising, he took the bags to the pack saddle and put them inside. He glanced over at the tarp covering the body. He should let the crime team deal with the evidence there. From what the brothers had said, he doubted the killer touched the body since it was lying pretty much as they'd both said it landed.

"Now what?" Tyson asked, breaking into his thoughts.

"I'm going to do a perimeter search, see where all the tracks come from and go to. You and Dog can just relax here in the shade." Hawke reached for the camera.

"I'll follow and take photos. This is a good learning exercise for me." Tyson smiled. "After all, you are my mentor."

Hawke felt a smile twitching his lips. He liked the sound of being called a mentor. It was as it should be. The elder showing the nephew how to track. "Come on. But don't step in front of me, you might cover up what I'm looking for."

Tyson nodded, and Hawke settled his gaze on the ground. He made slow back and forth swaths of twelve feet looking for boot impressions. He found them. Coming into the area from a direction he hadn't expected. He'd figured the poacher/killer had come from the west, Union County. But the direction the killer's boot print came from would indicate he came from Wallowa County. That would make him easier to find but also put him in the middle of where his eyewitnesses were.

《》《》《》

Seth sat in the waiting area at the Wallowa County Hospital. He'd called Sergeant Spruel of the Oregon State Police like Trooper Hawke asked him to do as soon as the doctor had said Alex would be fine once they took the bullet out of his leg. He was in surgery and Seth was waiting for his parents to arrive from

Ukiah and the sergeant who wanted to speak to him personally.

He'd found a quiet spot in the corner of the waiting area. Only one old man was sitting there. From what Seth gathered, he was waiting to hear news about his wife.

Seth pulled his recording device out of his pocket and walked outside. He found a concrete bench to sit on and started dictating what had transpired since Trooper Hawke found him.

A State Trooper walked into the hospital. Seth figured it was the sergeant looking for him. He stopped the recording and headed for the entrance. Just as he stepped through the doors, a white Dodge pickup pulled into the parking lot. He would have ignored it except the man who stepped out resembled the one that had shot at them, right down to the camouflage clothing and hat.

Seth hurried over to the reception desk to find the State Trooper. "Sir, a man just got out of a pickup in the parking lot." He glanced out the glass windows. "And he's coming in here. He looks like the person who shot my brother."

The State Trooper escorted him over to the woman in a small cubicle. "Maureen. Take this boy where he can't be seen and if anyone comes asking you about someone here who was shot, you tell them no one showed up with a bullet wound." He studied the woman. "Clear?"

"Yes, Sergeant Spruel," she said, ushering Seth through a door behind her cubicle.

Seth tried to see through the door before it closed to watch the trooper confront the man. But it closed before either of them came into view.

The woman settled him in what appeared to be the staff break room. "Help yourself to any of the drinks and here's some money to get something out of the vending machine. I have to get back to work."

He nodded and stared at the door she disappeared through. The drinks must have been in the refrigerator. Seth crossed the room and opened the door. He found a soda he liked, popped the top, and drank.

Leaving the money she'd dropped on the table where it was, he dug in his pocket and pulled out enough to buy his favorite corn chips. Back at the table, he sipped his drink, nibbled on the chips, and waited.

Fifteen minutes passed and the State Trooper entered the room.

"Sorry for that. I wanted to keep you safe if he turned out to be the suspect." Sergeant Spruel poured a cup of coffee and sat across the table from Seth. "I'm Sergeant Spruel." He reached a hand over the table.

Seth shook hands with the trooper and leaned back in his chair. "Was it the person who shot my brother?" He thought it would be weird if it was.

"From the way he pivoted and hurriedly walked back to his vehicle when he saw me, I think it might be. I managed to get the first three numbers of his license plate before he disappeared around the corner." The sergeant sipped his coffee and then pulled out a notebook. "Tell me everything that happened yesterday."

Seth was telling Sergeant Spruel about being brought to the hospital by helicopter when his parents were ushered into the room.

"Seth!" His mom scurried over, pulling him into

her soft warm embrace.

"Mom, the doctors say Alex will be okay." He wanted to reassure her. She tended to always think the worst.

She leaned back, tears trickled down her plump cheeks. "We know. We talked to the doctor before they said you were back here."

"What happened, Seth? Did Alex get that bullet saving you?"

Seth heard the disappointment in his father's tone when he asked Seth what happened and the pride when he mentioned Alex being a hero.

"No. He called out to a man we saw shoot a hiker. The guy turned and shot at us. We were both running when the bullet hit Alex. I helped him go as far as I could." His voice grew quieter as he saw his father's face turn to stone. The look he got when he thought Seth wasn't telling the truth.

Sergeant Spruel stood and held out his hand. "I'm Sergeant Spruel with the Oregon State Police. One of our Fish and Wildlife officers found Alex and Seth in the Eagle Cap Wilderness. He got them to a hunting camp where the owner flew them out last night." He put a hand on Seth's dad's shoulder. "Could I have a word with you?"

When the two men left the room, Seth's mom dropped onto the chair beside him. "Seth, I was so worried. You know I thought this trip was a bad idea."

"I know, Mom. It was going great until we decided to follow that hiker. He went off the trail and Alex thought maybe he knew of a tougher trail and wanted to see. That's when everything went wrong." He'd had a bad feeling when Alex said they should follow the hiker off the trail. From now on, he'd follow his gut and not his brother's ideas.

"We booked a room at a motel. We'll stay here until Alex can go home." She pulled out her phone.

"Mom, you can't tell anyone about what happened. The killer is looking for us." Seth grabbed her phone out of her hands and quickly went to her social media feed to see if she'd mentioned that her son had been shot. He was relieved to see she hadn't mentioned anything yet. He handed it back to her. "Don't mention Alex was shot to anyone. The State Police don't want him to come looking for us."

"You mean you're still in danger?"

"Yes. Until the police catch the killer, we are."

Chapter Six

Hawke had sent Tyson back to the lodge at eleven and was taking a nap when he heard the sound of horses approaching. Dog's tail tapped against Hawke's side. He must recognize someone. Hawke rose slowly, giving him time to see who approached while not being seen.

Bob Sullens, Hawke's counterpart in the Fish and Wildlife division of the OSP, was in the lead. Behind him was Sheriff Rafe Lindsey, followed by Dr. Gwendolyn Vance, the county Medical Examiner, and then several members of the OSP forensic team.

Hawke stood and waved a hand to bring the group on horseback over to where his animals were tied up. They didn't need half a dozen more horse hooves mucking up the scene.

"Hawke," Bob rode over and dismounted. "Good thing you gave us the GPS coordinates or we wouldn't have known when to leave the trail."

"There wasn't a trail through here before. But with all the activity lately, there will be." He watched as

Rafe held the head of the horse Dr. Vance was dismounting.

"Thank you, Sheriff," she said, once she stood on the trampled grass. "No matter how many times you haul me up here on a horse, I don't think I'll ever feel safe until my feet are on the ground."

"You didn't have to make the ride up here, Dr. Vance. The reason for his death is pretty clear. Not only from looking at him but from witness statements." Hawke led the way over to the still tarped body. "He was shot with a hunting rifle. According to witnesses, the victim dropped the instant the bullet hit." He pulled back the tarp.

"How long has the body been here?" Dr. Vance asked.

"It happened yesterday morning. While I was transporting an injured witness, a predator thought about having him for dinner." Hawke nodded toward what had caused the doctor to ask about the length of time the body had been exposed to nature.

The forensic team began taking photos and processing the evidence around the body.

"Tell me what happened," Rafe said, pulling out his notebook and pen. Hawke told him about coming upon the body after hearing the shots, finding the brothers, and taking them to the lodge where Dani transported them. He explained the return trip and discovering the killer most likely was a Wallowa County resident. He made eye contact with Bob and Rafe. "I'm sure from the footprints I saw that he came in the same way you did, from the Lostine."

"Bob, this is what we need to work on." Hawke led Bob and Rafe over to the shattered cage. "The killer set up a trap for a wolverine. I bagged evidence that might help us figure out who did it. What I want to know is how he knew there was a wolverine in this area. Fish and Wildlife and the biologists keep that information locked up to prevent this type of thing happening. I couldn't find any cameras around here, so I don't think this area was being monitored."

Bob wrote everything down in his notebook. "I'll check in with everyone at ODFW in the county and in Baker and Union Counties and see who knew about the wolverine in this area."

Dr. Vance walked over. "He died due to a bullet to the chest. From what I can see from my preliminary examination, it went straight into his heart. Your killer is an excellent shot."

Hawke mulled that over. If he was an excellent shot, why did he only get Alex's leg?

"Who is taking me back down to civilization?" Dr. Vance asked.

Hawke had picked up all he needed and had evidence he wanted to send to the OSP forensic lab in Pendleton. "I can take you down. I want to check in on the brothers and send what I found to forensics."

"We'll wait for these guys to finish gathering evidence and be behind you," Bob said.

"You sure you're ready for another long ride without walking a bit?" Hawke asked. He knew the only time the doctor rode a horse was when she was called to the mountains as her job as a medical examiner.

"If we can walk for a bit and lead the horses, that would be nice," she said.

He glanced down at her athletic shoes. "Since you

aren't wearing cowboy boots, we can walk a bit. You can sit while I gather my stuff and saddle my animals." He indicated a downed log about ten feet from where he'd be working.

"I think I'll stand. I sat for six hours on the way here." She walked over to Dot and ran her dark hand down his white face. "This guy is pretty. I don't think I've seen him before."

"That's Dot." Hawke settled the pack pads on Horse's back. "He's younger than Jack and does better up here."

She waved a hand at Horse. "What about him? Isn't he getting too old for this?"

"He's younger than Jack by seven years. He'll be good until I'm ready to retire." He cinched the pack saddle. Horse's ears went back and he bloated up. His usual display of annoyance at being cinched.

"And when will you be ready to retire?" she asked.

He grinned at her. "When I no longer want to get out of bed and go to work." He placed one of the pack bags on the saddle.

"Well, if you came out here every day for your work, I can see why you aren't ready to quit. But you spend most of your time in the county dealing with not as pleasant work conditions." She raised an eyebrow when he glanced her direction.

"As I said, when I no longer want to go to work, I'll retire." He finished putting the packs on Horse and picked up Dot's blanket.

"I'm just curious since you are older than I am and I've been thinking about retiring." She continued to stroke Dot's face.

Hawke stopped reaching for the saddle and studied

Wolverine Instincts

her. "You're too young to quit working. And this county needs good doctors like you."

"Maybe, but I feel like I'm missing out on things. My kids are heading off to college and I haven't spent enough time with them."

Hawke wasn't sure why she was unloading to him. They only knew each other through events such as this. "I guess we can discuss that as we ride off the mountain."

《》《》《》

Hawke arrived at the Two Pan Trailhead at 5 pm. He said goodbye to Dr. Vance as she slid into her car in the parking area. When the woman drove away, he drew a deep breath and let it out slowly. While he unsaddled the horse she rode and tied it to the sheriff's horse trailer with water and feed Hawke thought about their conversation. He wasn't one to tell someone how to live their life, but that was basically what the woman asked him. With her also being a person of color, she thought he would have some insight into dealing with issues her children had come up against. He'd told her to draw from her experiences and that took them off on how the world had changed from when they were young.

All the talking and listening had worn him out more than missing a night's sleep. He unsaddled Dot and Horse and led them into his horse trailer.

"Come on Dog, I'm ready for some dinner, a shower, and my bed." He opened the pickup door and Dog hopped in.

He turned on his cell phone and it started dinging. "Looks like I was missed." He recognized his superior's number and that of his neighbor, Darlene. She and her husband looked after the place he and Dani bought next to them. And there were three messages from a number he didn't know.

Before starting up the vehicle, he tapped the first message. "Trooper Hawke, this is Seth. You know, from the mountain. I think the killer started to come into the hospital and left when Sergeant Spruel arrived. What do I do?"

Hawke ground his teeth. He hoped that's what Spruel's call was about. But he tapped the second message from Seth. "Trooper Hawke, my parents arrived. They're taking us back to Pendleton when the doctors release Alex. I think my mom already told people we were in the mountains and Alex was shot."

"Shit!" Hawke knew if there was any chance the killer was half as smart as the wolverine he had tried to poach, he'd learn who the witnesses were sooner rather than later.

He pushed the third message too hard and lost the voicemail app. He scrambled and pulled it back up again. This time he didn't let his anger propel his finger and the message started.

"Trooper Hawke. Alex is doing well and the doctors say he can go home tomorrow. Are we safe?"

Hawke glanced at when the call was made. Two hours earlier. That meant he had to get to the hospital and talk to Seth, Alex, and their parents before he went home.

"Looks like it will be burgers from the Rusty Nail on our way to the hospital," Hawke said to Dog as he started up the vehicle. When he knew he could make a call without being dropped he called the Rusty Nail.

"Rusty Nail, Justine speaking," his friend answered.

"Hey Justine, it's Hawke, Dog and I would like our usual."

She chuckled and said, "Heard you were up on the mountain and brought a—"

"Stop. That isn't news that should be going around," he interrupted her.

"What's up?" she asked in a whisper.

"I'll tell you when I pick up my dinner. Just don't talk about it to anyone." He ended the call and grumbled, "I should have known there would be rumors about Dani landing in the middle of the night and the ambulance being called to the airport."

He pressed Sergeant Spruel's name and tapped the phone icon as a white early 2000s Dodge pickup rattled by him on the gravel road. The man driving didn't even look at him. He had a beard and a camouflage ball cap. Hawke didn't believe in coincidences, however, many men in the county wore similar caps and drove early 2000s model white pickups. Following his instinct, he tried to see the license plate number but the vehicle's exhaust and the dusty road made it impossible for him to pick out any number or letter.

"Hawke, you there?" Spruel's voice boomed through the cab.

"Yeah, I'm here. I'm coming down the Lostine. I'll grab dinner at the Rusty Nail and head to the hospital. Seth Finlay called me several times. He said he thinks our suspect was headed into the hospital when you arrived. Do you know who he's talking about?"

"Yeah, I got a look at him and the first three numbers of his license. I've had Ivy checking through DMV records to see what we can come up with as a match. So far nothing. The plate may be from some other vehicle. It will take a lot of phone calls to every person with those three letters on their plate." Spruel heaved a sigh.

"Yeah, I think he just headed up the Lostine. It was an early 2000 white Dodge pickup. The guy driving had a beard and a camo hat." Hawke had a feeling it was the man. He hoped Bob, Rafe, and the forensic crew stayed wary. "Can you get ahold of Bob and let him know the killer may be coming his way?"

"I'll contact him by radio. What do you plan to learn from the brothers? From what Seth told me it sounds like we'll need them to I.D. the guy but they can't do much else."

"They need to stay low and their parents need to know that they must keep quiet if they want their kids not to be targets." Hawke liked the brothers. He wanted them to be safe.

"I talked to them. The mom is weepy and the dad is old school. Treats the oldest boy like a hero and Seth like he's a wimp." Disapproval rang loud and clear in Spruel's voice.

"Well, Seth is the hero. He got his brother to a safe place and tried to lure the killer away. I'm going to talk with him and his parents. I'll be in tomorrow morning to write up my report. I'll either take the evidence I collected to Pendleton or catch up to someone headed that way."

"Sounds good. Enjoy your dinner."

Chapter Seven

Hawke drove into Winslow from the Lostine River Road and parked in front of the Rusty Nail. He barely cleared the door and Justine was backing him out with a bag that smelled like his dinner in her hands.

"What's going on? Is Dani in danger?" Justine asked when they stood on the sidewalk in front of the café.

"No. She isn't in danger, it's the boys she brought out. What is the gossip going around?" He took the bag from her hands, opened it, and ate a fry waiting for her to tell him.

"First person in the café this morning said that Dani had airlifted two boys out of the wilderness and an ambulance picked them up at the airstrip." She cocked her hip and studied him, crossing her arms. "Then the next person who came in said that Dani was airlifted out of the mountains." Her brows furrowed. "Then Bud, his wife works at the hospital, said that one of the boys had a gunshot wound and they thought the brother shot him."

"The only true thing is that Dani did bring two brothers out of the mountains at my request. But they didn't shoot each other. They came across someone shooting a hiker and then shooting at them." He held up his hand. "You didn't hear any of this from me or anywhere. Got it? But keep your ears open. The suspect was poaching a wolverine."

"I didn't even know they lived around here," she said.

"There are less than five that I've heard of in the Wallowas and Eagle Cap. They stay to themselves. Again, you didn't hear that. All we need is this crazy person trying to trap them all." He pulled a couple more fries out of the bag and shoved them in his mouth. After he chewed, he said, "If you hear anyone mentioning wolverines or the shooting, find out who they are and let me know."

"I will, and you know, I can keep secrets." She pivoted and entered the café.

He knew how well she kept secrets. She'd helped him put her sister and father in jail by not telling her family he was on to them.

In his vehicle, he gave Dog the cheeseburger with pickles and pulled out his burger with cheese, no pickles. Driving to Alder, he wondered how they would catch someone who could be any number of people who lived in the county. And with only half the license plate number.

He parked in the hospital parking lot so that the pickup and trailer wouldn't get boxed in by anyone visiting that evening. He walked through the door and up to the information desk.

Wolverine Instincts

"Trooper Hawke, it's been a while since you've been in here," the woman, working the desk, said.

"I've been lucky and haven't been in any domestic disputes." He leaned in closer and said quietly, "Could you tell me which room the boy is in who was brought in last night?"

She glanced around the waiting area and whispered back, "Twenty-four."

"Thanks." He headed to the double doors and heard the door buzz just before he reached it. He raised a hand thanking her for buzzing him through.

He waved at the nurse in the nurse's station. He'd known her for a long time.

"Here to check up on Alex?" she asked.

"Yeah. Is the family with him?" Hawke hoped they were and he wouldn't have to look for them.

"Yes, they showed up about an hour ago. But I think the brother went down to the cafeteria. He doesn't stay in the room very long when his father is here." She gave him a knowing look.

"I heard there is something between him and his father. Think I'll talk to him first." Hawke changed direction and headed down the hall to the door that would take him to the cafeteria.

He spotted Seth sitting in a corner, staring out a window that looked into the parking lot.

"How's it going?" Hawke asked, taking a seat where he could stare into the parking lot as well.

The boy shrugged. "Okay, I guess. They said the bullet didn't do damage to anything that would keep Alex from playing football. That's good. But he'll have to sit out the first half of the season."

"That's good news. What about you? How are you

doing? Did you get any sleep last night? Seeing someone shot isn't an easy thing to get over." Hawke studied the boy's profile. He was definitely in turmoil. His cheek twitched like he was grinding his teeth and his eyes never stopped scanning the parking lot.

"We're doing all we can to try and figure out who the guy was that shot at you and Alex." Hawke knew the boy wanted to know he was safe. But there wasn't any way to guarantee that until they had the suspect in custody.

"I thought of a way to get him to show himself," Seth said.

"We are not putting you or your family at risk. We'll use our police methods to find him." Hawke turned in his chair to face Seth. "Don't go trying to be the hero. You did that already by saving your brother."

Seth slowly shifted his gaze from the window to Hawke. "I do a podcast. It's mostly about the nerdy things I do and how people react to them, but I've been keeping an audio journal of what has happened. I could put it out on my podcast and I'm sure word would get to the person who shot my brother. When he comes looking for me, you could get him."

The earnestness in the boy's eyes reminded him of the times he'd felt certain if he took the garbage out or did a chore his stepfather wouldn't come home and beat up his mom. It never worked. And this wouldn't work either. Hawke shook his head. "A guy who goes out into the wilderness to poach a wolverine won't be listening to your podcast. And knowing about it, means I have to tell you that if you do try to do that you would be obstructing this case and you could be fined."

Tears glittered in Seth's eyes. "There has to be

more I can do than sit here and stare at everyone who enters the hospital."

"When we find the suspect, we'll bring photos of him mixed in with others to your house and you and Alex can pick out the killer. Until then, it is best you both keep low and don't talk to anyone about what happened. I'm going up to tell that to your parents."

"Good luck with that! Mom put it on social media that she was going to the hospital to see if her poor boy was still alive after being shot, and Dad has been calling all his friends and telling them his son was shot but he was a Finlay after all and would pull through just fine." Seth stared into his eyes. "This is why we have to make him come to us. My parents don't give a crap about our safety, only that they are being hailed for having such a stoic son." He ducked his head and then said, "I don't think I can take waiting for you to find him. I'll be jumping at every person who walks by or says anything to me."

Hawke put a hand on the boy's shoulder. "You are stronger than you think. Don't let your father's words dictate how you behave."

He stood. "Do you want to come with me to talk to your parents? It beats sitting here staring out the window. I'd also like to talk to you and Alex alone. I need a few more details about what you remember."

Seth peered up at him and slowly rose. "I'm only coming along because you need to talk to me and Alex. I don't think I can take any more of my father's puffed-up pride over his son being shot."

Hawke put an arm around the young man's shoulders. "Some fathers don't realize the harm they do by their actions and words. Believe me, I know all too well. Only mine was a stepfather."

Seth studied him. "You're not just saying that?"

"Nope. Just feel lucky you don't have physical scars. I decided I wasn't going to be like him. I wanted to be the opposite. After joining the Marines, I came back and went through the State Police Academy. I wanted to be the complete opposite of my stepfather. And I am. You can be the opposite of your father. Just follow his rules and orders, and in a year, you'll be out of his house and can make your own life."

They walked out of the cafeteria and back to the ward where Alex was a patient. Hawke stopped outside the door. "You go in first and let them know I'm right behind you."

Seth nodded and walked into the room. "Mom, Dad, Trooper Hawke is here."

Hawke stepped into the room. Mrs. Finlay sat in the chair next to Alex's bed. She had a hand on his arm. Alex had a smile on his face and from how goofy it looked, Hawke figured he was on some pain meds.

Mr. Finlay stood up and held out his hand. "Thank you for getting our boys off that mountain and to safety."

"All I did was find them and give them a faster way to get off the mountain." Hawke put a hand on Seth's shoulder. "This one hid his injured brother and had the foresight to lure the killer away from the hiding place. That gave me more time to catch up and help."

Mr. Finlay studied Seth with a critical eye. "You didn't say you did any of that."

"You never asked me what I did. You just assumed that Alex had kept us from the killer." Seth shrugged.

Hawke motioned for Mr. Finlay to sit. "I'm here

first to speak to you two." He glanced at the husband and wife. "The killer is still out there. He knows two male hikers saw him kill the other hiker. He will want to keep them quiet." He studied the pair to see if what he said sunk in.

Mrs. Finlay gasped. "You mean, they aren't safe?"

"They will only be safe if no one knows they were in the mountains and that one of them was shot. The killer knows he shot one of them. He was following the blood trail from Alex's leg."

"How do you know he was?" Mr. Finlay asked.

"Because I was following him. When I came across the body of the hiker he shot, I followed his tracks over to where I saw someone else had been shot. Then I followed your son's tracks and that of the killer. When I came upon him, he shot at me and fled."

"Then you can identify him," Mr. Finlay said.

"No, I can't. He was hidden when he shot at me. I don't have any idea what he looks like." Hawke could see the man was skeptical. "I can tell you he wore a size twelve boot with an aggressive sole, and I would put him at about two-twenty in weight, but that's all I know about him. What his tracks told me. He also has an anger issue. That was apparent by the way he crashed through the brush to get to Seth and Alex."

"How can we keep them safe?" Mrs. Finlay asked.

"By not telling anyone where they've been and saying Alex's accident happened at home. Not that it's a bullet wound." Hawke saw Mr. Finlay flinch. "The only way to keep these two safe is to not tell anyone about what happened. If you have a relative that lives in Washington or Idaho, it would be a good idea to send them there until Alex starts school or we get this guy caught."

"My sister lives in Yakima. We could take them up there," Mrs. Finlay said.

"That would be a good idea. Just make sure I get information on how to contact them." Hawke motioned to Seth, "I'll talk to you and Alex now." He turned his attention to the parents. "Would you two go get a cup of coffee or something so I can talk to the boys alone? It's about details that they might remember now that they have settled down a bit."

"Sure." Mr. Finlay took hold of his wife's arm and led her out of the room.

Hawke motioned for Seth to take the chair his mom vacated. He sat and waited.

"Hey Alex, do you feel awake enough to join the conversation?" Hawke asked the young man in the bed.

"Yeah, but my mouth's dry," he said, reaching for the plastic cup of water with a straw on the stand beside his bed.

"Here, I'll set you up." Seth grabbed the bed control and raised his brother's torso to a sitting position.

"Thanks." Alex sipped on the water and asked, "What did you want to ask us?"

"Can you remember anything specific about the shooter? Did you see him before he shot the hiker or after you heard the shot? If before, what was he doing?" Hawke pulled out his notebook. "We might be able to figure out a little more about him if we have more information."

Seth leaned forward. "Alex was ahead of me. He saw what was happening first. I didn't really see anything until I heard the guy laugh. It was creepy.

Something like you'd hear in a horror movie."

Hawke studied the young man. "What do you mean by that? Did it really sound creepy or are you just saying that now that you know he shot someone?"

"No, it was creepy," Alex said. "Real deep and kind of crazy. His voice carried. He'd been talking to something. He was facing away from us. It took a minute for me to see him because he blended in with the surroundings when his back was to us. The hiker yelled at him and he swung around. That's when I saw the face and beard."

"Could you describe his face to a sketch artist?" Hawke asked, thinking this might be the break they needed.

Alex moved his head back and forth slowly. "I'm not sure. I wasn't close enough to see anything that would help. Just his beard and the red of his face."

"He had a temper," Seth said. "I could tell by the way he acted when he raised his rifle and fired and when Alex yelled at him, he shook and then aimed at us. I took off and heard the boom. I glanced back and saw Alex go down. Beyond him, I could see the man moving toward the hiker. I got Alex up and we took off as fast as he could move."

"Does any of this help?" Alex asked.

"Yes, a little. We have the first three numbers of his license plate if he was the man Seth saw in the hospital parking lot. Putting all this together we should be able to find him." Hawke studied the brothers. "Go to your aunt in Washington and don't speak of this to anyone. If you think of something or want to know what is going on, Seth has my number. Call me. We'll do our best to catch him as soon as we can. It's just going to take some leg work." Hawke stood.

Seth did too. "Thank you for coming to see us. I wish we'd been more help."

"Every bit you can think of helps." Hawke walked out of the room, down the hall, and out to the reception area. Mr. Finlay stood and walked over to him.

"Thank you again for getting my boys out safe."

"They're good boys. Both of them. Don't tell anyone what has happened if you want them to stay safe." Hawke stared at the man.

Finlay squirmed. "About that. We, the wife and I, may have mentioned the gunshot and such to some friends."

"You need to tell them not to mention it to anyone to keep your boys safe. We don't know who this guy knows and if he will discover who he shot. He might think they can identify him as the man who shot a hiker. Don't tell anyone else." He nodded to the wife and walked out the door.

Hawke hadn't had the good fortune to have children of his own. But these brothers had become special to him, just as Kitree had after he saved her in the mountains. He'd keep an eye on them to make sure their father didn't screw them up.

In his vehicle, he started it up and headed for home. Dog peered at him from the passenger seat.

"Don't worry, we're going home now. We need a good night's sleep before we head back up to the crime scene tomorrow."

At the barn, he unloaded Dot and Horse, brushed them down, and put them in the pasture with Jack. The three hung their heads over the gate and he gave them an alfalfa cube treat.

"Let's go get cleaned up."

He stepped on the back porch step and heard a four-wheeler approaching. "I think Herb is coming over to see how long we'll be home for this time," Hawke said to Dog.

The four-wheeler's engine died and Herb walked around the corner of the house. "Good to see you two back. Heard Dani made an emergency flight last night."

Hawke rolled his eyes. "Come on in. I'd like to hear the version you heard." He opened the door, allowing Dog to trot in, then flicked on the kitchen light and walked in, leaving Herb to close the back door.

The house was stuffy from being closed up while he and Dani were away. He went through the house opening all the windows. Then turned on the fan in the bedroom. When he returned to the kitchen, Herb had the coffee pot gurgling.

Hawke hadn't planned on that long of a stay for Herb, but he pulled out two mugs and sat them by the pot. "So, what did you hear about Dani's flight last night?"

Chapter Eight

"I heard she brought down two young men who got in a fight and one shot the other." Herb poured the coffee into the cups and set them on the table. "You don't happen to have any cookies, do you?"

Hawke grinned. He stood up, walked over to the refrigerator, and opened the side freezer door. He grabbed a tin that Darlene, Herb's wife, had given him the day before he left on his shift in the Eagle Caps. "They're frozen but your wife's cookies taste good cold, hot, or in between."

"That's for sure," Herb said, taking two chocolate chip cookies out of the tin when Hawke set it on the table.

Hawke grabbed two cookies and set them on a napkin by his cup of coffee. "I can't tell you everything about the rumor. Just, please, don't spread what you heard around because it isn't true." Hawke picked up a cookie, dunked it in his coffee, and took a bite. After he swallowed the bite and some coffee he asked, "You wouldn't know of anyone in the county who has bragged about getting themselves a wolverine, have you?"

Herb was hunched over his coffee dunking a cookie. He straightened and swallowed the bite in his mouth quickly. "Wolverines are a threatened species. And last I heard there were only a couple in the mountains around here."

"When was that and who told you?" Hawke asked, interested that it hadn't surprised Herb to know the creatures were in the mountains.

"When I was a kid, one of my pack trips up in the mountains I saw one. He'd climbed the tree I had my pack hanging from. I heard him and flashed a light on him. They are beautiful creatures. Once he caught the beam in the eyes, he skedaddled down the tree and I lost sight of him on the ground." He sipped his coffee and cleared his throat. "Before logging was shut down a couple of the loggers talked about seeing a pair of them where they were cutting down trees." He shook his head. "Haven't heard any talk of them since then. I figured the pair probably moved on with all the logging happening in their territory."

"A hiker was shot by a guy poaching a wolverine." Hawke went on to tell Herb about coming across the shattered cage and body. "You keep an ear out when you're visiting with your friends in cafés and see if you can't hear about someone seeing or wanting a wolverine."

"I can do that. Can't believe someone would be fool enough to try and catch one with a cage."

"I agree. Fish and Wildlife has learned you can't keep a wolverine in a cage long enough for someone to get there to see it. That's why they use hair snares to gather information." Which gave him an idea. When the biologists set up hair snares, they usually set up cameras. This time of year they didn't try to monitor the animals because it was too hard to discover their tracks without snow. But if he could learn where the cameras and snare were set up, he might be able to figure out where the wolverine's den or dens were. Then he could set up his own wildlife cameras to monitor who was looking for them.

Could the killer have learned where the wolverines had been sighted? If so, how did he find out? All questions, he'd be asking tomorrow. "When you finish your cookie, turn off the coffee pot. I'm going to take a shower. I may be headed back up into the mountains late tomorrow afternoon. I'll let you know if I am, so you can keep an eye on Jack while I'm gone." Hawke dumped the rest of his coffee in the sink and headed down the hall to take a shower and go to bed.

"Guess that means you get a cookie," he heard Herb tell Dog, before the back door closed.

«»«»«»

The next morning, Hawke stopped at the Winslow OSP office and wrote up his report on the incident with the wolverine and the body. He asked the Fish and Wildlife biologists if anyone from the Winslow office had set up a hair snare for wolverines or cameras near the GPS location where he'd found the cage. They said they didn't, but to check with the La Grande biologists. Since La Gande was on his way to Pendleton, he decided to stop in and ask rather than call.

Wolverine Instincts

An hour after leaving Winslow, Hawke pulled into the Fish and Wildlife office in La Grande.

"Hey, Hawke. Heard you were mixed up in poaching this week," biologist Irvin Murray said when Hawke walked through the door.

"Yeah, that's why I'm here." Hawke leaned on the counter. "Did you or one of the other biologists set up a hair snare near this GPS location?" He showed the coordinates to the biologist.

"What type of a hair snare?" he asked, jotting the numbers down. "That will make it quicker for me to look up."

"Wolverine." Hawke studied the man as he raised his gaze from Hawke's notebook to his eyes.

"Was the poacher after a wolverine?"

Hawke nodded.

"Shit. Did he get it? We don't have that many in the Eagle Caps."

"No. The poacher got distracted shooting a hiker and going after some other people who witnessed the shooting. While he was chasing them, the wolverine tore up the cage and got away. But I think this poacher is angry enough that he's going to keep trying to get a wolverine."

Irvin shook his head. "Damn, I hate poachers. They tend to think the threatened and endangered animals are more sport." He held up the paper he'd written the coordinates on. "Give me a minute and I'll see what I can find out." He disappeared down the hall to the cubicles the biologists used for their offices.

Hawke turned his attention to the receptionist. He'd watched her in his peripheral vision. She'd been hanging on every word. "How are you today?"

"Horrible. I can't believe there is someone out there hurting a threatened species." From her green hair that looked like she'd used a razor to cut it, the three studs in her ears and large hoops dangling from the last hole in her lobes, to the 'Animals are God's creatures' T-shirt, baggy pants, sandals, and the young woman's attitude, Hawke wondered how she was working out with the Fish and Wildlife department. She probably became upset when the biologists darted an animal so they could tag it.

"How long have you been working here?" he asked.

"About three months. I needed a job, and my uncle, he cleans the building, said they were looking for a receptionist. But you know, there are days, I go home and cry when I hear what is done to some of the animals. I took this job thinking we were saving them but most days I wonder."

Irvin returned. He glanced at the back of the young woman's head and then said to Hawke, "There was a hair snare about a hundred yards up the mountain from this point. It was set up by Joe Berry to get information on wolverines."

"Do you know if he set up cameras or may still have a camera working in that area?"

"You'll have to ask Joe. His records only say what cameras he checked out and what came in. The numbers don't match but that could be because he set up a camera somewhere else."

Hawke asked for Joe's phone number and thanked Irvin. Out in his vehicle, he tried calling the biologist. No answer. He left a message for the ODFW biologist to give him a call about the wolverine near Glacier

Mountain.

Once the call was made, he started his vehicle and headed to Pendleton. He'd get the evidence to the OSP Forensic Lab and head home to grab Horse, Dot, and Dog. He wanted to get back up on the mountain before dark. Catching the poacher after the wolverine would bag him a killer. The man had committed murder and attempted murder. He deserved to be behind bars, not the wolverine.

《》《》《》

It was dark by the time Hawke reined Dot off the trail and through the trees toward the crime scene. He'd discussed the case with Spruel and Bob. They both felt the same as him that the poacher would try again. Hawke was back on the mountain to catch him when he tried. This was the area where the killer knew to find a wolverine, if his last attempt hadn't sent the animal looking for new territory. It was a sure thing he wouldn't be able to catch the wolverine in the same type of trap again. They were too smart for that. That was why biologists had gone to using hair snares. Less stress on the animals and they weren't hurt so they didn't avoid a hair snare or the area where they were set up, like they did anything that had trapped them.

Hawke decided to camp in the trees near the crime scene. He'd work his way up to the hair snare on foot in the morning after he found a good place to hide Dot and Horse and make a camp that, hopefully, the killer wouldn't find.

As he unsaddled, he thought about Seth and wondered how the boy was doing. If this trip didn't get him the killer or information about him, he'd have to go off the mountain and try to find the man through the three numbers on a license plate and asking around about someone interested in wolverines. Having Justine and Herb keeping an ear out was better than him asking questions. They were always talking to or listening in on conversations. Justine when she waitressed at the Rusty Nail, and Herb having coffee several days a week at different cafés and going to local meetings.

He settled Dot and Horse on a picket line with their grain bags and fed Dog his food. Hawke rolled out his sleeping bag and grabbed a handful of jerky before settling on his bed. He'd had a late lunch early dinner on his way back from Pendleton. Dried meat and water were all he needed to keep his belly happy until morning.

Dog finished his food and lay down beside Hawke. He sniffed and licked his lips, staring at the jerky.

"This is my dinner. You had yours," Hawke said, before handing Dog a piece of jerky. Dani told him all the time he was a softy and it was a wonder Dog didn't weigh a hundred pounds.

Finishing the dried meat, Hawke pet Dog and said, "Tomorrow we'll find a spot for a good base camp and then do a walk around and see if we can find tracks."

Dog smiled and lowered his head onto his paws.

Hawke tipped his hat over his face and closed his eyes.

Chapter Nine

The following morning, Hawke found a ravine on the opposite side of the river that would hide his animals and camp from the view of anyone checking out the area around the crime scene and where the hair snare had been during the winter.

Once the camp was set up and the animals were staked out to eat grass, Hawke and Dog set off back across the river in a direct line toward the location where he hoped to find a trace of the killer. As he hiked, Hawke kept an eye on the ground, looking for boot tracks. He had a feeling the killer backpacked in, it was easier for him to move about without being seen or heard.

The only tracks were ones that should be found in a forest. Wildlife. As they drew closer to the area where the snare had been, Hawke slowed his pace, listening and watching the trees and brush. If he came upon the killer, he wanted the upper hand, not to be caught by surprise like the first time.

Approaching the area, he heard a snuffling sound. Crouching, he motioned for Dog to sit while Hawke peered through the branches of a huckleberry plant. Parting the limbs, he came face to face with a yearling black bear. The creature sniffed at him, berry juice dribbling over his bottom lip, and then backed up.

Dog quivered next to Hawke. He put a hand on Dog's collar to keep him from going for the bear. Slowly, Hawke released the branches and stood, still gripping the collar. He backed up, making Dog do the same. Once they were out of sight of the bear, Hawke drew in a breath and let it out slowly. "Let's not do that again," he whispered to Dog as they started around the north side of where the snare had been located. Now he could see down onto the area from his uphill advantage.

The black bear still slurped berries off the bushes. Hawke wanted to check the area for cameras and wildlife activity. He found a rock and sat, pulling out his canteen and drinking. Dog sat beside him and lapped a drink from Hawke's hand when he offered.

"We'll wait until that yearling gets his fill and moves on." Hawke pulled out his binoculars and studied the thicket of fir trees below them for any wildlife cameras. Shifting his gaze to the barren mountain descending behind him, he studied the rocky surface. Several dark holes in the side of the mountain could be dens for all sorts of creatures. He knew that wolverines preferred to hide their den openings under boulders and downed trees. They also preferred sub-alpine and alpine elevations. He honed in on dark spots at the base of boulders. If he knew this about wolverines, he imagined the killer did too. He hoped he could arrest the killer before he harmed a wolverine.

Wolverine Instincts

Dog whined and Hawke trained his attention on the bear. The yearling was waddling off down the mountainside his furry flanks jiggling. Now was their chance to check out the area. As they walked down to the thicket of trees, Hawke scanned the ground for tracks. He spotted the bear's prints. He'd wandered down the mountain to get the huckleberries.

Several hooved animals had passed through the area. From the direction they were heading, they were on their way to the river to get water. Those tracks didn't interest him. It was the side of a boot print that caught Hawke's attention. He stopped Dog and crouched to study the half-inch wide and two-inch long print.

It was evident by the pattern of the ground and debris beside the indention that the person who made the track was wearing something over their soles to keep from leaving book tracks. He could think of only one person who wouldn't want his presence known at this spot.

The killer.

Hawke scanned the area around him before dropping his gaze back to the impression in the dirt. He pulled out his phone and took a picture. Then he studied the ground and found the other footprint. This one had the boot sole completely covered, but he could make out the impression of the masked print.

He stood and peered down at the two marks. He wanted to be able to see them when he came across them again. When he was confident the size, shape, and depth were imprinted in his mind, he moved forward, staring at the ground.

Moving slowly, he followed the tracks to a point

where the person had remained in one place long enough to make several impressions one over the other. The killer was either antsy or excited, hard to tell from the indentions.

Hawke followed the veiled tracks along the side of the mountain a quarter of a mile before he returned to the snare area and looked around for wolverine footprints. He thought he saw a couple of toes that might be from a wolverine, but they'd been walked over by the killer. Hawke believed he'd covered the animal's tracks on purpose. The killer didn't want anyone else to know a wolverine had been through here. The best Hawke could judge from the tracks, they were several days old. Possibly before the animal had been trapped or it could be a different animal. This was the time of year that the pairs mated.

After learning all he could from the ground, he scanned the trees. It was an excellent place to set up a hair snare or trap. The trees were easy for a creature like a wolverine to climb. The nylon belt with the metal gun brushes that captured the hair would easily strap around the trunks.

It would also make a good spot for the killer to try and set up another trap to capture the wolverine.

A breeze caused the branches to sway and whisper. Hawke turned his face into the breeze and caught a glint of something in one of the larger pine trees on the edges of the younger firs. He walked over and looked up the trunk of the tree.

There was a game camera.

He set his backpack and shotgun on the ground at the base of the tree and pulled out his parachute cord. Using the cord, he ran it around the tree trunk and then through and around his upper legs. With intention in every step, he used the cord to climb up the trunk like a lineman for a power company until he reached the first limb. He rested on the limb a minute before unwinding the rope from his legs. Now there were enough limbs to use to climb up to the camera.

He read the inscription on the camera. It belonged to ODFW- Oregon Department of Fish and Wildlife. He wrote down the serial number and then slipped the SD card out. He wished he had another one to put back in so he didn't miss anything. Or that he'd brought a laptop with him to see what was on the card and then put it back. But he hadn't had the foresight to do that so the camera would sit here without capturing anything until he could return and put this one or a new one back in.

He shoved the SD card in his pocket and climbed down to the bottom limb. There he put the cord on and walked down the tree.

With the SD card in his pocket, he was torn between getting down to civilization and looking to see what was on the card and following the tracks of the killer. There was a chance there could be a photo of the man's face on the SD card which would hasten their knowledge of the man.

However, he was sure that the tracks he saw weren't that old and the man was on the mountain looking for the wolverine or a new place to set up a trap.

《》《》《》

Seth leaned back in his desk chair and reread the message.

"young skunk bear when i catch the ghost skunk bear well have to meet up"

"I found you," Seth said under his breath. He'd been searching various trapping and hunting message boards using all the names used for a wolverine with young in the front of it, skunk bear, woods devil, carcajou, to see if the killer was on one of the boards. He'd come across Skunk Bear King the day before and wondered if he was the man trying to trap wolverines. From the things the man had posted, it sounded as if he was indeed the man who wanted a wolverine. When he'd responded that was a cool idea, he'd heard how much the animal was revered, the King had responded enthusiastically to his comment.

He wanted to tell Trooper Hawke he thought he'd found the killer, but when he tried to call the phone went to voicemail. He'd thought about calling Sergeant Spruel, but the man wasn't the same as Trooper Hawke. Instead, he took screenshots of the conversation and then began to dig into the I.P. address and see if he could come up with a real name or address for Skunk Bear King.

His eyes were tired and his back and neck were sore when his aunt called him to dinner. He'd learned a great deal about the man he believed killed the hiker and injured Alex. He'd sleep on the information tonight and if he couldn't get ahold of Trooper Hawke tomorrow, he'd find a way to get back to Wallowa County and give the information to him.

《》《》《》

Hawke and Dog followed the tracks until the killer walked across a shale slide. From the way the shale from above had slid down and covered the little bit he could discern of a trail from moved rocks, he knew the slide had been created by the killer to hide his tracks.

"Come on, let's go back to the valley and see what's on this SD card." Hawke turned around and headed back down the mountain toward his horse and mule. They'd been climbing for several hours following the tracks. They'd reach camp as the sun went down. It wouldn't be the first time he and the animals had gone down the trail in the dark. They all knew it well.

Now that he had a plan to get back to the valley and see what was on the SD card, that's what he wanted to do, not spend another night on the mountain and return in the morning.

When they arrived at the camp, everything looked untouched by critters or man. He saddled up Dot and Horse and they were on the trail in thirty minutes. Hawke chewed on jerky and drank water as they passed Minam Lake and headed down the trail to Two Pan where he'd parked the truck and trailer.

Chapter Ten

Hawke's phone started dinging as he drove down the Lostine River Road. It was the spot where he always picked up cell phone service. He pulled over in a wide spot on the road and read through all the calls. Forensics in Pendleton, ODFW biologist Berry, Spruel, and Seth had tried to call him three times.

He called back Seth.

"Hello, Trooper Hawke?" the young man asked.

"Yes, I see you tried to call me. I was up on the mountain looking for information about the killer." Hawke knew the boy was anxious to see the man who shot his brother was caught.

"I think I found him."

Hawke stared at the road in his headlights. "Found who?"

"The guy you're looking for."

"Where are you?"

"In Washington with my aunt."

"How did you find the man?" Hawke was curious

how this boy could have found a man that was so elusive.

"I went on some sites about trapping and read a bunch of conversations and I think the killer is Skunk Bear King on the Trapping Outlaws site."

"What makes you think that?" Hawke asked.

"Because I went on there as Young Skunk Bear wanting to get an up-close look at a wolverine and Skunk Bear King said he'd have one for a mascot soon." There was a pause. "I searched to see if I could figure out his I.P. address and I think I found him."

Hawke was impressed but also worried. "You didn't try to contact him, did you?" Even as he asked, he knew the man was on the mountain hunting for the wolverine which led him to wonder who Seth had been talking to and whose address he'd dug up.

"Only on the website. I was hoping you'd be back to give you the name and address."

Hawke was pleased the young man had the sense not to try and meet up with the person himself. "Can you text that information to me?"

"Sure. Have you learned anything?" Seth asked.

"I don't think you were talking to the person who did the shooting. He's up on the mountain. I saw his tracks and they were fresh. But it might be someone close to him that you found." Hawke heard his phone ding from the text message. "I did find an ODFW wildlife camera and pulled the SD card. I'm hoping there will be a good photo of him. Did you give your description to a police sketch artist yet?"

"Yeah, a person came yesterday. Between Alex and I, we gave her the best description we could."

"Good. That will also help us find him. Thank you

for contacting me. I have more phone calls to make and Dog and I are hungry," Hawke said as Dog licked his lips.

"Okay, I'll let you go. But you'll let me know if you learn anything?" Seth asked.

"I will. Thanks." Hawke ended the call and looked at the name and address that Seth had dug up. The last name sounded familiar but he didn't know why. He forwarded the information to Spruel. Hawke told him he was back and had an SD card he would look at. He'd let him know if it was of any significance to the case.

After that, he called the Pendleton Forensic lab and started driving. He had the call going through his vehicle's system. After being passed through two receptionists, he was told to hold for the forensic pathologist working on his case.

"Trooper Hawke, this is Abigail DeWitt the acting pathologist tonight. How can I help you?"

"Abigail, I received a phone call from Cassie Warren about the evidence I brought in from Wallowa County." He waited while keyboard keys tapped on the other end of the line.

"Here it is. It says she sent you the report via email."

"Her message said that but it also said she wanted to tell me something she noticed after sending the report. Can you see if there is a notation somewhere on the report? Something she would have added after she sent the report."

The woman heaved a sigh and the clicking sound came through the phone and then silence. He hoped that meant she was scrolling through the report for the information.

"There's a notation that says she thinks that the partial prints are from two different people."

"Does it say how she came to that conclusion if there are only partial prints?" Hawke knew if you had full prints you could tell the difference but on partials? He'd never heard of that before.

"There is a notation in red at the bottom. It says one print had whorls and the other loops, meaning they came from two different people."

"But it will take longer to discover who because they are only partials, correct?" Hawke asked.

"Yes. But you know that two people touched the pieces."

"Thank you." Hawke ended the call wondering if the person on the mountain and the one Seth had contacted via the internet were the two who belonged to the fingerprints.

He'd worry about calling Spruel in the morning. Right now, his stomach was talking to him and it said, feed me. "Looks like you'll get a burger again. I'm going to go in and sit down and see if I can learn anything from whoever is at the Rusty Nail."

Hawke pulled into the Rusty Nail parking lot and discovered it was nearly empty. That was good for him since he was pulling a horse trailer. He had plenty of choices where to park. He stepped out of his vehicle, dusted off his pants, and headed to the front of the building. That's when he spotted Herb's pickup parked at the corner.

He entered and stood a minute scanning the room. He spotted Herb at a table with Solomon Hendrix. He was about ninety and had worked with the fish and game department for thirty years before retiring at the age of 62. Hawke joined them.

"Hawke, do you remember Solomon Hendrix?" Herb asked.

"I do." Hawke held out his hand and shook with the older man. "It's good to see you, Solomon."

"Hawke, I believe you are hanging on as long on this job as I did," Solomon said.

A smile twitched Hawke's lips. "I'm trying to stay on longer than you."

The old man laughed and then coughed. When he had his breathing under control, he said, "I knew the first time I met you that you were going to do this job until you couldn't sit a horse anymore."

"That's probably the way it will be," Hawke agreed.

Justine arrived at his side, placing a glass of iced tea in front of him. "Are you here to eat?"

"Yes, I'll have a Reuben sandwich with salad and I need a cheeseburger with pickles to go."

"Dog must be out in your truck," Herb said.

Hawke nodded. "He's been all over the mountain just like I have."

"I'll get that going for you," Justine said and walked away.

He peered after her. It wasn't like her to not be talkative.

"What mountain were you on?" Solomon asked.

Hawke pulled his attention back to the two men. Herb gave him an inquisitive look. He ignored his neighbor and said, "Glacier Mountain. I'm trying to catch a poacher." He thought it best to not link the poaching with the killing. And Solomon might have a few ideas about the poacher.

Wolverine Instincts

"Herb said you were looking for some guy trying to catch a wolverine," Solomon said, in a quieter tone.

Hawke glanced at Herb. That was why he was buying the old game warden dinner. He'd been asking questions. "Yes. His first attempt, well, I'm guessing it was his first attempt, the poor animal mangled the cage and harmed himself. There was blood around the shattered cage and footprints with blood marks heading away from the area."

Solomon nodded. "Those creatures are tough. I saw a three-legged one once fight off a wolf for a mountain goat carcass. I wasn't working at that time. I was on a winter hike with some friends. We watched the standoff through binoculars on a ridge below."

"Which mountain was it on?" Hawke asked.

"Matterhorn. It was a sight. I never saw one while I was on patrol up in the high lakes." Solomon picked up his cup of coffee and sipped.

"Did you ever come across any trappers who were illegal?" Hawke asked as Justine placed his dinner and a paper bag in front of him. His eyes dropped to the writing on the bag. *Talk to me before you leave*. He wondered why she hadn't just said that to him instead of being so secretive.

Solomon was watching him. "Something wrong?"

"No, sorry. I didn't think I was that hungry but when Justine put the food down and I smelled it, my stomach grumbled." He picked up his fork to dive into the salad and repeated his question.

"They are either all dead or can't get around well enough to be trapping," Solomon said, taking another sip of his coffee.

Justine returned with a coffee pot and refilled

Solomon and Herb's mugs. Hawke gave her a slight nod, so she'd know he got the message.

Herb was studying him. Hawke shrugged and asked Solomon, "Any of them have kids that might be carrying on the business?"

Solomon shook his head then stopped. "Only one I can think of is Jasper Baxley. His boys were trapping when they were in high school to make extra money. You could have a talk with them."

"Thanks, I'll do that."

"You want some pie, Solomon, or are you ready to go?" Herb asked.

"I'm stuffed. Thanks for buying me dinner. With my wife gone and my son spending weeks at a time in the mountains since that bomb went off under his Humvee, I have to fend for myself." Solomon stood and shook Hawke's hand. "It was good seeing you again. Don't be a stranger."

"I'll try to come by now and then," Hawke said as Herb and Solomon walked out of the café. When Justine walked by to lock the door since it was closing time, he said, "I'm ready to talk and it looks like it's just us and the cook."

She nodded, locked the door, and took a seat across the table from him. "Even though you were talking about the wolverine, I didn't want to bring it up with Solomon here."

Hawke studied her. "Why not?"

"He gets all wound up if he hears about anyone disrespecting the wildlife. I think that's why you and him are good game wardens. You care about the animals."

"What would have riled him up?"

"There was a man came in here the other day reeking of something like skunk. When I mentioned it, his eyes got wide and he said, he didn't smell bad." She nodded to the door. "After he left, I said something to Delwin and he said it smelled like skunk, maybe the guy had been smoking pot."

She shook her head. "It didn't smell like skunk or pot. I've come out of the restaurant a time or two and had to walk through pot smoke from someone sitting in their car smoking."

"You don't know this guy's name? Did you see what he was driving?"

"I don't think I've ever seen him before. He was anxious, a brown beard, wild eyes, and he drove off in a white dodge pickup."

Hawke had a feeling she'd just described the killer. He wiped his mouth with the napkin and placed it on his empty plate. He'd eaten while Justine talked. "Dog's probably pacing the seat waiting for his dinner." He stood and put more than enough for his dinner and a good tip on the table. "If that guy comes in again, call me or Sergeant Spruel."

She studied him. "Do you think he's the poacher?"

"Your description is close to what the witnesses said."

"I'll watch for him. You've been spending a lot of time up in the mountains on this case. Have you had time to visit the lodge?" Justine asked.

"No, only to get the brothers to Dani so she could bring them out." Hawke studied Justine. "Is there something going on you haven't told me about?"

"I wondered if you knew when Dani might be coming out to the valley. I'd like to visit with her."

Paty Jager

Justine didn't meet his gaze.

"I see. When I talk to her again, I'll let her know."

"Thank you." Justine picked up the dishes and headed to the kitchen.

Hawke let himself out, wondering what Justine would want to talk to Dani about.

Dog enjoyed the burger as they drove from Winslow to the house. To his surprise, Herb was sitting in his pickup in front of Hawke's house.

Exiting his vehicle, Hawke walked over to Herb, who now stood beside his pickup. "What are you doing here?"

"What's going on between you and Justine?" Herb asked, his face set in a scowl.

Hawke shook his head. "She wanted to know when Dani would be back in the valley. Said she needed to talk to her. Must be women stuff because she was acting weird." He shrugged.

"You think Darlene could help her?" Herb asked.

"I don't know. She seemed pretty set on talking to Dani." Hawke pulled his Stetson off his head and scratched. "She also said that a guy came into the Rusty Nail a while back and smelled like skunk but she didn't think that's what it was."

Herb's eyebrows rose. "You think he's the one after the wolverine?"

"He's a possibility. I know that Justine thinks he might be. Her description matches that of the boys who saw him shoot the hiker."

"Did you tell her not to say anything?"

"Yeah, I told her to call me or Spruel if he comes in again."

Herb slid back into this vehicle. "You sticking

around for a while?"

"I'll be here tomorrow but can't tell you what the next day will bring until I talk to people." That reminded him. "Do you know who Colby Durn is? The name sounds familiar but I can't place it."

"Durns are a family that lives out Promise. One of the grandsons went to Juvey for hurting a girl. Ever since he came back he's rarely seen and stays out at the old homestead. His father died when the kids were young and the mom left the boys with her father-in-law." Herb asked, "Is Colby mixed up in this?"

"I'll know soon enough. There were two sets of prints on the pieces of the cage I took to forensics. Seth and Alex described the poacher to a sketch artist so we have that to compare the prints and photos to Colby Durn and his grandson. Have a good night," Hawke said to send Herb on his way so he could put Dot and Horse out in the pasture, get a shower, and take a look at the SD card in his pocket.

Chapter Eleven

After a shower, Hawke grabbed a handful of cookies, a glass of milk, and his laptop. He sat on the couch and inserted the SD card. There were video clips of wild animals, including a wolverine twice, as he clicked through the disk. The camera appeared motion-activated and started running when something came into the motion detector's range.

A video of a person walking by showed a side view and then his back. Nothing to get a good look at him. He had his head down as if looking at tracks.

There were more videos of animals and then the man returned. Was his showing up there twice coincidence or did this spot have significance to him? He wouldn't know why the person found this spot fascinating until he caught the man.

He continued watching the videos. The wolverine wandered through and then there was a view of the wolverine loping and favoring a foot. That had to be after the animal tore its way out of the cage.

Wolverine Instincts

Hawke watched to the end of the videos and didn't see the man again. He yawned and stretched. He'd have the SD card sent to forensics and see if they could get a still photo of the face of the man that could be used to determine who he was.

《》《》《》

The next morning Hawke dressed in his uniform, checked on the animals, and climbed into his work vehicle. His first stop would be the office in Winslow. The report on the case needed to be updated and he wanted to read the forensic report from beginning to end as well as look up addresses for the persons of interest he had acquired yesterday.

Parking in the lot behind the OSP office, he was surprised to find ODFW biologist Joe Berry getting out of his vehicle.

"Hawke, I heard you were looking for me and I had some research to check in the Eagle Caps and thought I'd drop by on the off chance I could catch you." Joe held out his hand and they shook.

"I planned to give you a call when I got in the office. Come in, this time of the morning the coffee shouldn't be too bad." Hawke led the way into the back of the building avoiding the ODFW personnel in the front of the building. They climbed the stairs and went up to the State Police office.

Sergeant Spruel stepped out of his office as they topped the stairs. "Hawke, good to see you're back. Howdy, Joe. You here about Hawke's case?"

"I am. How's life treating you, Nathan?" Joe asked.

"Good. The oldest is getting ready to pick a college. Doesn't want to be a policeman, he'd rather be in the medical field," Spruel said.

"I thought Jenny would follow in my footsteps; she likes animals so much. Instead, she wants to be a vet tech." Joe shrugged.

Hawke filled three cups with coffee while the men caught up. He offered them to the other men and then packed his into the conference room. The two followed.

Once they were seated, Hawke said, "There is a poacher trying to catch the wolverine on Glacier Mountain."

"At last count, there were three on that mountain. A grown male and female and one of their offspring. The rest of her last litter took off except for the one. He has a deformed foot and the parents help him hunt." Joe leaned back and sipped the coffee. "Not bad."

"Can you tell which animal is which by looking at them?" Hawke asked.

"Yeah. Each one has distinct markings."

Hawke pulled the SD card out of his pocket. "I took this from the wildlife camera in the area where the poacher set up a trap to catch a wolverine. He succeeded until a hiker came upon him and the poacher shot him and wounded another hiker. While the poacher hunted down the person he wounded, the wolverine tore up the cage and got away." Hawke took the laptop Spruel brought into the room. He'd left when Hawke pulled the SD card out of his pocket.

"Thanks, Nathan." Hawke slipped the card into the slot on the computer and then clicked on the icon for the card. The video came up. He fast-forwarded through the animals until the wolverine appeared. Pausing the video so Joe could study it, Hawke also made note of the markings on the animal.

"That's the young male. See how he throws that front foot out to the side when he walks? Not sure if he was born that way or an accident broke it and it grew back crooked." Joe pointed to the photo. "You can also tell because his lighter-colored hair is more white. As they age, they get more cream-colored."

"Okay. What about this guy?" Hawke fast-forwarded to the video of the man scanning the ground. "Have you seen him before?" He paused the video so both Spruel and Joe could get a good look at the man.

"He's wearing what most hunters wear," Joe said. "But there's something about his walk… it looks familiar." He made a circle motion with his finger. "Roll it again."

Hawke reversed and then went forward. The man did have a different walk. A bit of a limp. That could be why the fabric he'd put on his soles had worn off to one side leaving the partial of a sole print.

"I can't place who it is, but I'm sure I've seen him walk before." Joe shook his head. "Sorry I'm not much help."

"That's okay, you've given me more to add to the description of the man." Hawke fast forwarded to the loping wolverine. "Which animal is this?"

"Play it again and pause it," Joe said.

Hawke did as he was asked and paused the video with the animal stretched out in a lope.

"That's the young male. Damnit! If it were the male or female, we could check their dens. I don't know where the young male has been denning up."

"How far from this area do you think he'd travel, given his parents have been helping him find food?" Hawke asked.

"If being in a trap scared him enough, he could be clear on another mountain by now. Where exactly was that camera?" Joe asked.

Hawke told him the coordinates.

He shook his head. "That doesn't sound right."

"It was about thirty yards to the east of your hair snare." Hawke said, pulling out his notebook and showing Joe the information he'd received from Irvin at the La Grande office.

"I took all my cameras down from there when I pulled the hair snare."

"It was marked ODFW and here's the serial number." Hawke showed him the number in the book.

Joe pulled out his phone. "I'll call the office and see who was assigned that camera." He stood, taking Hawke's book and walking out into the hallway.

This was a new development if no one with ODFW put that camera up.

"Are you getting any closer to finding the suspect?" Spruel asked.

"I'm slowly building a description of him. The Finlay boys described him to a sketch artist. I need to see if I can connect the sketch to some names I've come up with." He pondered whether or not to tell Spruel that Seth had come up with a name and address for a possibility. Best he knew it all. Hawke told his superior about his call with Seth.

"I thought that boy seemed like a go-getter. He just doesn't do it on an athletic field." Pride was sprinkled in Spruel's voice.

"We also need to show the sketch to Joe if the person in the video looks familiar." Hawke used the laptop to pull up the sketch the artist had sent to him.

He studied the face and then spun the laptop toward Spruel.

"He looks like the outdoorsy type," Spruel said.

Joe entered the room. "According to the records, that camera hasn't left the building. Irvin is going to go through the ones in the building and look for it." He frowned. "If that's an ODFW camera then someone stole it from the office."

Hawke didn't say anything but they'd had a wolf collar go missing several years earlier from that same office. Only the person who stole it then was in prison for murder.

"I'll need to look into your employees," Hawke said.

Joe glared at him. "No one in our office would set out to harm an animal."

"Joe, we're not saying it's one of the biologists. But it could be one of the employees that aren't engaged in what you do. A cleaner, receptionist, a construction worker who might have been in the office in the last year?" Spruel said to cool the biologist down.

The biologist nodded. "You're right. There have been several workers doing remodel work on the supply room and back parking area. They use the restroom in the building. I'll have Shelly pull those names together."

Hawke thanked him and spun the laptop so Joe could see the sketch. "Does this man look familiar?"

Joe studied the sketch. "The eyes do but the rest of him I'm not sure who it is. All that hair on his face hides a lot."

"You've never run into him up in the mountains?" Hawke asked, hoping to jog Joe's memory.

The biologist stared at the sketch and slowly shook his head. "No, not that I recall."

"Ok. Thanks. I have a report to write and some people to talk to. Thanks for stopping by and clearing up some things," Hawke said, standing and handing the laptop to Spruel.

"Sorry I'm not more help," Joe said.

"Where are you going today?" Spruel asked.

"Ironically, I'm headed up to the area around Glacier Mountain. I'll be taking samples in the Minam River."

Hawke spun around. "Be careful. I think the killer is still on the mountain. And he's disguising his footprints."

Joe nodded. "I'll be on the trail except when I'm down by the river collecting samples."

"Just be careful. He seems to not like people to see what he's doing." Hawke hoped the biologist was careful. There was no telling what the killer would do if he thought Joe or anyone else was following him.

At his computer, Hawke entered the recent information such as the names he'd collected, and then began looking them up in the database. The person Seth came up with was a good candidate. He'd been caught poaching a couple of times but he was in his 80s. Too old to be the person on the camera or who moved so quickly through the forest. However, he did have a son who could have used his father's computer. Hawke circled the name and made sure he had a current address.

His curiosity made him wonder why Solomon's son preferred the mountain life over being with his father. He put in Solomon's son's name and saw he had been brought in for a couple of disturbance complaints since he'd returned from military service. But there wasn't anything else.

Having been in the military and seen things no one should see and felt the anger at having little control over events that happen around you, Hawke could understand the man's outbursts. With reluctance, he circled the name and made sure he had a current address. He couldn't overlook any lead, even if he liked the father and had compassion for the son.

Hawke then sent an email to the OSP Lieutenant in La Grande to have an officer go to ODFW and get a list of anyone who worked there and follow up on where they were the day the hiker was killed and Alex was shot. Including the biologists. While he told Joe he didn't believe one of them would try to capture an animal for anything other than studies, he had seen people snap and do what they normally wouldn't do.

Once that was sent, he opened up the email from the forensic lab. The evidence gathered between him and the lab told him nothing more than he already knew other than the added note about two different prints on the cage materials.

Hawke leaned back in his chair and thought about the materials that were collected. He hadn't noticed anything that couldn't be purchased at a hardware store. Could it be the print of someone who sold the materials to the poacher? Or did two people put the cage together? Or one made the cage and another person carried it to the mountain and set it up?

This case had too many questions and not enough answers.

Chapter Twelve

Hawke stepped out of his vehicle and three large dogs charged around the side of the house, barking and baring their teeth. He stood still to show he wasn't there as a threat. The three remained back ten feet and continued snarling and barking.

"Willy, Waylon, Johnny, get your asses back here!" yelled an elderly man from the open door.

The dogs tucked their tails and slinked under the porch where the man used a cane to walk to the top of the porch stairs.

"Can I help you, officer?" the man asked in a raspy smoker's voice.

"I'm Trooper Hawke. I was wondering if I could speak with your son."

"My son's dead. Is this some joke?" The man said, his eyes narrowing.

"Is there someone living with you?" Hawke asked, wondering how the information he came up with about a son had still been in the system.

"My grandson."

"Could I speak to him?" Hawke asked, searching his mind for any mention of a grandson.

"He's not here. He went up into the mountains to fish about a couple of days ago. I don't expect him back until next week. Whatcha want to speak to him about?" The man's watery eyes studied him from behind thick lenses.

"I wanted to see if he was up in the mountains last Wednesday. We're looking for witnesses to a shooting and your grandson might have been one of the witnesses."

At the word 'shooting,' Hawke noticed the man's eyes widen before his lids quickly lowered.

"If you didn't know I had a grandson then how the hell do you know he might have seen something?" The man glared at him. His knuckles on the head of the cane were white he gripped it so tight.

"Does he look like your deceased son? Because someone had noticed him in the area earlier and mentioned the name." Hawke hadn't a clue if the grandson had been on the mountain, or not, but it was a good hunch since that's where he was now.

"You're full of shit! Get off my property or I'll sic my dogs on you." The old man thumped his cane on the porch floor three times, and the dogs barreled out from under the structure, snarling.

Hawke stood his ground and held a business card out to the man. "When you see your grandson, have him give me a call, please."

The man didn't make a move to grasp the card. Hawke tucked it in the crack on the end of the handrail and slowly turned to walk back to his vehicle. He knew showing that the dogs scared him would only make the man's day. He continued to the pickup at a leisurely pace even though he felt sweat beading on his forehead and trickling down his back.

He slid into his vehicle, waved to the man, and started the engine. Backing out of the driveway, he surveyed the house, outbuildings, and anything else that might be used to hide poached animals.

He parked beside Al's Café in Eagle and pulled up Colby Durn on his computer. Searching through the records he discovered the man's son had died, leaving behind a wife and sons. The wife no longer had an Oregon Driver's license which led him to believe she no longer lived in Oregon. He couldn't find any record of her death.

A rap on the window drew his attention from the computer as he was about to type in the grandson's name. Closing the computer, he spun his gaze to the window and smiled. Ivy Bisset, the youngest recruit on the Wallowa County OSP team, stood on the sidewalk beside his vehicle.

Hawke turned off his vehicle and stepped out into the warm afternoon air. It was a bit of a shock from sitting in the A/C of his vehicle. "What's up?"

"I was stopping in for lunch and wondered if you had the same idea." She waved a hand at his vehicle.

"That was my plan once I'd checked out something." He stood with his thumbs tucked into his utility belt.

"Oh, sorry I disturbed you. I just thought maybe you might have a few minutes to visit."

This was a different Ivy than he'd seen before. She seemed anxious, uncertain.

"I can finish what I was doing later. Let's grab a table before everyone thinks we're getting ready to do a raid on the place." He grinned and she smiled.

They entered the establishment and Lacie, the co-owner, offered them a table in the back of the eating area with a view of everyone who entered. She'd seated him many times since she and her husband purchased the café.

"What would you like to drink?" she asked, glancing at Ivy first.

"Diet Pepsi, please," she said.

"My usual," Hawke said with a smile.

"Iced tea no lemon it is," Lacie said. "I'll be back and get your order when I bring the drinks."

Hawke nodded and set his ball cap on the chair next to him. Ivy did the same and then sat at the table tapping with one fingernail.

"Hey, what has you so upset?" Hawke asked.

She glanced around and then leaned over the table toward him. "I heard you were going to speak to Colby Durn today."

Hawke nodded. "I just came from there. What do you know about him?"

"Not much. I mean, I've only met him once." Her cheeks deepened in color. "I've been seeing his grandson, Zach, off and on for about four months."

Hawke could see she wondered what that would mean for her job with him looking into the family. "I see. Then maybe you could tell me if he looks like this." Hawke pulled out his phone and scrolled to the sketch made from Alex and Seth's descriptions.

She studied the photo. "No, he only has the popular five o'clock shadow, not a full beard and his eyes are wider apart and normal looking. That guy looks like he's high." She studied the photo a little longer. "But he does look like a guy Zach was talking to outside the Blue Elk about three weeks ago. We'd gone there for dinner and this guy walked in. Zach hustled him outside and they talked before the guy got back in a white Dodge and drove off."

She drew in a deep breath and let it out. "What have these two done? Does it have something to do with the poaching and—" she stopped as Lacie approached with their drinks.

"What would you like to eat?" she asked.

"I'll have the grilled cheese and seasoned fries," Ivy said.

Hawke ordered a hamburger with a salad. When Lacie walked away, Hawke leaned forward and said quietly, "He may be caught up in the poaching. If he wasn't on the mountain at the time the hiker was shot, then he may not be an accessory to the murder." He studied the young officer.

She nodded. "Want me to pretend I don't know anything and see if he's up to having dinner with me? I could ask him questions."

Hawke shook his head. "Wait and see if he asks you out and then starts asking you questions." He glanced around. "If he learns you were seen talking with me, he may think you know something. Once he learns I've been out asking his grandfather questions he might just stay away from you." He watched her. "You did tell him you're with the State Police?"

"Yeah, I tell anyone I date that right up front." She picked up her drink. "It makes me feel safer going out with someone I don't know that well if they think I'll

Wolverine Instincts

have State Police looking for me if I don't show up."

Hawke grinned at her. "That's a good plan. Do you date many people you've never met before?" He was concerned for her safety if that were the case.

She shrugged. "There aren't that many eligible men in this county. I sometimes date people from the Lewiston, Tri-cities, and Pendleton areas. We meet online. But I do a full background check on them before I agree to meet them anywhere."

"That's a good plan."

Lacie returned with their food. "Enjoy!"

"Thanks," Ivy said before she picked up half of her sandwich.

Hawke ate in silence, allowing his mind to wander over Ivy's relationship with Zach and how it might help his investigation.

"You're quiet," she said after she'd finished half of her sandwich and picked up a fry.

"Just wondering how deep Zach is caught up in the poaching. Could just be a coincidence that he spoke to the man we're looking for."

Ivy shook her head. "No, it looked like the man was looking for Zach when he came into the tavern. And Zach didn't want anyone to hear what they talked about."

"But that was before someone was killed. They must have been talking about poaching the wolverine. Did Zach ever mention wolverines to you?" Hawke finished off his salad and picked up a half of his burger.

"No, I don't remember him ever mentioning them. He talked a lot about cougars and bears, but not wolverines." She set her glass down. "He did talk a lot about live trapping. But I thought it was because he's studying to be a biologist."

Hawke leaned forward. "Has he ever been out to the La Grande ODFW building?"

Ivy shrugged. "I don't know. We haven't been together that long and only had about half a dozen dates."

Hawke nodded, though he felt frustrated that Ivy had a connection to their possible poachers, but had a slim hold on being kept in the loop of what Zach was doing. "Don't push him for any information or even to go on a date. That might get him suspicious. Best to play low-key and see if he contacts you to learn anything. And if he does, let me know."

"I will," Ivy said, though her mind looked like it was buzzing behind her green eyes.

"I need to get going. This is on me," he said, motioning to her food.

"Thanks!"

He walked up to the counter and paid Lacie.

"Sounded like you two were talking about work," Lacie said, taking his money.

"A little bit," Hawke said. He rarely gave away what he was doing to anyone other than Herb, Darlene, or Justine. They were his eyes and ears around the county.

She leaned slightly over the counters and whispered, "I can tell you the guy she's been seeing was in here not two weeks ago with a girl the complete opposite of Ivy."

"Did they seem like friends or more than friends?" Hawke asked in a quiet voice.

"More than friends. I saw them hugging and kissing when she drove up and got out of her car."

"Can you describe her?" Hawke asked, pulling out his notebook.

"To start with she had green hair."

Hawke stopped his hand mid-air. Could it be possible that was the connection to the missing ODFW camera? "Sorry, go on."

"She had lots of earrings. Big hoops dangling from her lobes. And her green hair looked like someone had used a weedwhacker on it." Lacie nodded as if that was the truth.

"Thank you. This is very helpful. Could you call me if either the man or the woman shows up here again?" he asked.

"Sure. If they're in trouble with the law, I don't want them hanging around."

Hawke nodded and headed out to his vehicle. Knowing Joe was up in the mountains, he called the ODFW office and asked Shelly to put him through to Irvin. As he waited, he wondered what the woman thought she was doing getting a camera for her boyfriend and why the boyfriend was dating a state police officer.

"Hey, Hawke. I didn't expect to hear from you since your guys were here not that long ago," Irvin said, out of breath.

"Yeah, I hadn't expected to call but I was talking to someone and I need some information."

"Sure thing."

"Are you in your office or out in the lobby?" Hawke asked, not wanting to let on to Shelly that they knew her connection to what was going down.

"Lobby." He heard the confusion in the man's voice.

"Okay, say something like I'll have to go look that up and then go to your office and call me back."

The man did as he was asked and Hawke waited for his phone to ring. When it did, he answered, "You're in your office now?"

"Yeah, what is this about?"

"What is Shelly, your receptionist's, last name?"

"Smith. Why?" Irvin's tone held suspicion.

"She's been linked with someone of interest in my case."

"You're kidding me!" It sounded like a door slammed. "I just kicked my door closed. How the heck did you put her in on this?" He sucked in air and then said, "Did she have something to do with the murder?"

"Calm down and don't talk so loud," Hawke said, trying to calm the man down. "She may not know that someone was killed from her boyfriend's actions. I'm pretty sure when we dust the camera, her prints will be on it."

"You believe she took the camera from our storage area? She would have had access and there are some days she is the only person in the office. But why?"

"I'm pretty sure she was bragging to her boyfriend about the stuff you have stored and he asked her to get him a camera. Whether she knows about anything else I won't know until I question her. If you can, act like you don't know anything and keep on looking for the camera. I can't pull her in until I retrieve the camera and have it checked for prints. Until then it's all speculation and I can't hold her on anything." Hawke could bluff and say her prints were on the camera, but he would only do that if the camera didn't reveal her prints.

"I have more digging to do. Don't tell anyone else what I told you, and please, try not to act strange around her. She's probably already wondering about the call I made. Just tell her I asked you for more coordinates." Hawke hoped Irvin could keep it all together and not jeopardize the case.

"I'll do my best."

"That's all you can do. Thanks." Hawke ended the call and immediately pulled out his laptop and typed Zachary Durn.

Chapter Thirteen

After gathering all the information he could on Zachary Durn, Hawke pulled up Bryce Hendrix. There wasn't a driver's license for him. Hawke checked the Department of Motor Vehicles records for the vehicles owned by Solomon. The only pickup that came up was the one Solomon drove around and a car.

He put in a request for Bryce's military records. Maybe that would shine a light on whether or not he was the person on the mountain.

As much as he hated questioning Solomon about his son, he needed a photo and to learn if he drove around in a white Dodge pickup.

Driving through Winslow, Hawke glanced at the Rusty Nail parking lot. He didn't see any vehicles that were part of this investigation. He wanted to get up on the mountain and see if he could find the shooter. His gut was telling him that the man was still after the wolverine.

But he had to clear up all his leads here first. He

had already asked the Troopers local to La Grande to keep an eye on Shelly.

Halfway between Winslow and Alder, he turned right onto Holman Lane. Solomon and his wife had a few acres at the base of the mountains.

The long driveway into the Hendrix property was lined with fir trees. The house sat in a small opening at the base of Ruby Peak. He imagined getting in and out of here in the winter would take a lot of snow plowing.

As Hawke parked, he wondered how Herb had made it back to his place so quickly the other night when he'd had dinner at the Rusty Nail with Solomon. This place was a good thirty minutes from Winslow. Herb would have had to drive back home which was at least another fifteen minutes. Hawke knew he hadn't talked that long to Justine. He'd have to ask Herb when he saw him.

The door to the small log home opened and Solomon stood in the doorway. He squinted in the sunshine. When he recognized Hawke, he smiled and waved. "Come on in. I just put on another pot of coffee."

Hawke exited his vehicle and strolled to the door, letting himself in. The house was still tastefully furnished. Piles of magazines and newspapers next to a recliner with wear spots on the arms and headrest showed this had become the home of a widower. The wife's touches were everywhere beyond the clutter of a man who didn't know what to do with the things he used every day.

"Want some cookies with your coffee?" Solomon asked, placing a mug of steaming coffee on the table.

"I never turn down cookies," Hawke said, sitting

and raising the mug to his lips. The robust aroma told him the drink would be strong. He sipped and felt his hair straightening.

"I don't bake, but I can buy from the bakery. Try those jumble ones. They taste even better with coffee." Solomon placed a box of cookies from Sunshine Bakery, a business run out of Patrice Bunton's home in Prairie Creek.

Hawke plucked one of the cookies out of the box, dunked it in his coffee, and took a bite. The cookie cut down the bitterness of the strong coffee. "Those are good together," he said, smiling.

"You didn't come out here to have coffee and cookies with me. Not after Herb bought me dinner the other night to ask me about poaching." Solomon dunked his cookie.

"No. I need to ask you questions about your son, Bryce." Hawke dipped the cookie in his coffee but kept an eye on the man across from him. "Does he drive an early two thousand white pickup?"

"No. He can't drive." Solomon sat back in his chair. "After Arlene died and I heard Bryce was coming home, I thought I'd have someone to help me with things. I didn't learn until about a month before he came home that he'd been in a vehicle that was hit by a bomb. When he came home from Afghanistan, he could barely walk and couldn't talk. It was hard trying to care for him while I was grieving Arlene. He did most of his recovery on his own. I took him to his medical appointments in the Tri-cities and then Walla Walla. He can walk now and spends most of the year up in the mountains. He only comes down here in the winter for supplies because it's harder for him to forage then."

"You must miss him if he doesn't stay with you for very long." Hawke could see the man seemed to be grieving for his son as much as his wife.

"Yeah, I'd hoped he and his family would be my comfort as I aged. But with him hiding out in the mountains all the time, I don't see as how I'll have any grandchildren." The man sounded angry rather than sad.

"Do you have a photo of Bryce I could look at?" Hawke waited while Solomon went into the other room. He returned with a photo of Bryce in his early twenties in his military photo. He saw a young man full of eagerness, looking forward to a life of excitement. It sounded as if he found too much excitement.

"Do you have anything more current?" Hawke asked, not seeing any resemblance to the man in the sketch.

"No. He couldn't talk when he came back, but he made sure we understood he didn't want any photos." Solomon swallowed. "You see, he came home with some of his skull missing and a disfigured face."

Hawke thought about the sketch. A guy in a ball cap and beard. "Can he grow a beard that would cover his scars?"

"No. The skin grafts don't grow hair. When he's up in the woods, he usually wears one of those ski masks that cover the face. I bought him some that are lighter weight. I've been putting his disability check in the bank for him every month and only using money out of it for his clothing and supplies." Solomon's eyes swam in tears. "I would love to have him here with me, but he feels freer up in the mountains."

"I'm surprised I haven't come across him sooner,"

Hawke said, thinking of all the territory he covered in a summer.

"He stays up high and away from all the trails."

Hawke thought about that. If the poacher was following the wolverine, he could end up coming in contact with Bryce. "Is Bryce armed?"

"A shotgun and a knife. He mostly snares small animals or fishes to eat. He also forages and eats the plants, berries, and roots." Solomon's voice held pride.

"Could he defend himself if he comes in contact with a violent person?" Hawke asked, wondering if he needed to find Bryce before the shooter.

"He was skilled in combat and has gained his strength. He still walks with a bit of a limp, but he would be tough to take down." Again, pride laced Solomon's words.

"Which leg does he limp on? He may have been caught on an ODFW camera." Hawke wondered what Bryce had been doing down that far. His father said the man stayed away from trails.

"It's his right foot. You say he was caught on camera by ODFW? Where?"

"Near the case I'm investigating."

"The poaching? Then he probably knows who the poacher is." Solomon sat up in his chair. "Are you going back up there?"

"Tomorrow. I have to find the poacher. We haven't made this public but he also killed a hiker and wounded another one. I need to find him and bring him in." Hawke could see the old man was eager to see his son.

"I could go along. Maybe talk to Bryce," Solomon said.

Hawke shook his head. "I understand why you

want to go, but I can move about quieter on foot with just my dog." He'd already planned to go up the Minam and have someone from the hunting lodge ride to the crime scene with him. He'd have them take his horse back to the lodge while he and Dog went after the shooter on foot. "I'll keep an eye out for Bryce and if I make contact, I'll let him know you'd like to see him."

"I guess it was foolish to think I could sit a horse for that many hours. I would appreciate you giving him that message."

"Thanks for the coffee, cookies, and information. I'll keep you updated on what I learn. And don't spread around the fact there is a killer in the mountains. We don't need a panic or a vigilante looking for him."

"I understand. Thanks for stopping by." Solomon walked him to the door and waved.

Hawke drove straight back to the office in Winslow. He had more to add to the report and to fill Spruel in on his next move.

«»«»«»

"You're saying Solomon's boy has been living in the mountains most of the time he's been back from Afghanistan?" Spruel asked.

"That's what he said. And the person we saw on the video may have been him. He has a limp. I'm wondering if he is following the poacher having seen that he killed a hiker, or if he feels a need to help the wolverine since he has a limp as well. I'm asking forensics to see if Bryce's prints match that on the cage. He might have helped the animal get loose." Hawke had thought about it all the way back to Winslow. If the person on the video was Bryce and he saw the hiker shot and the wolverine in the cage, he could have helped the creature and then hid to wait and follow the killer.

However, he hadn't seen any tracks other than the murderer's. He'd have to call Solomon and see what his son wore on his feet while traipsing around the mountains.

"That is plausible."

"Once I add to the report, I'm going home and riding into Charlie's Lodge. I'll spend the night, then have someone ride with me to the crime scene. I'll have them bring my horse back to the lodge and Dog and I will go on foot from there."

"What about what you told me about the woman at ODFW and Ivy's friend?" Spruel asked.

"I told Ivy to let me know if he contacted her. But you'll need to have her call you and then debrief her after she meets up with him. I'm going to dig into Shelly Smith's background and see if I can connect her with anyone who might go too far to collect an animal. If I come up with anything, I'll let you know."

"You better get busy or you won't get to the lodge until after dark." Spruel turned his attention back to the papers on his desk.

Hawke took that as his cue to leave. At his desk, he pulled up the information on Shelly Smith. She had been arrested for some sit-ins over ecology arguments but nothing as serious as someone being killed. She may have thought she was doing a favor for an animal and not realizing it was being caught illegally. He'd give her the benefit of the doubt, but he also remembered her eagerness to listen in on his conversation with Irvin.

He typed up the information he'd found out and

logged out of his computer. Now to head home and fill his backpack with enough food and water tablets to get him and Dog through at least a week in the mountains.

Chapter Fourteen

Hawke rode Dot up to the barn at Charlie's Lodge as the moon shone down on the corral and milling horses. "Let's be quiet and not wake anyone up," Hawke whispered to Dog who kept whining and looking toward the bunkhouse where he knew Kitree slept.

"We aren't bothering them tonight. Or anyone. We'll sleep in the barn." Hawke slid the wooden bar up out of the metal brace and opened the right side of the double barn doors to lead Dot inside.

"Hey, who's there?" a familiar voice asked.

"Tyson, it's Hawke, Dog, and Dot."

A lantern light flickered on. Tyson stood beside the light, an air mattress with a sleeping bag at his feet, scrubbing at one eye with a fist. "What are you doing here at this time of night?"

"It's only eleven. Took me longer to get on the trail than I'd anticipated." He led Dot over to a wall lined with saddles and untacked him while the animal

Wolverine Instincts

munched on grain. Once Dot was down to his halter, Hawke led him out to the corral and let him loose with the other horses. They'd been together before. After a bit of prancing about and snorts, they settled down.

Back in the barn, he noticed Tyson had pulled out another air mattress.

"Why are you sleeping out here?" Hawke asked.

"We had a couple want to stay another week and my room was the only one 'not occupied' as Dani said." He scoffed and added, "I don't mind sleeping out here. It's actually quieter than in the lodge with all the people milling about, coughing, sneezing, and talking."

"Thanks for the mattress. I'll need someone to ride with me to the crime scene and bring my horse back here. Dog and I will go by foot after that."

"You still looking for the killer? Don't you think he'd be hiding out down in the valley?" Tyson lay on his bed with one arm behind his head as he studied Hawke.

"He's after the wolverine. We still don't know who he is, but I plan to catch up to him before he hurts someone else."

Tyson narrowed his eyes. "You know something. I can tell."

"I learned there's been a man living up here in the mountains for nearly eight years. He has a slight limp and a disfigured face. I believe he saw the shooting and is following the killer. I need to keep him safe." The urgency to catch the killer now had Hawke wishing he'd stayed on the trail rather than heading to the valley to ask questions.

"Does this guy wear a mask?" Tyson asked.

Hawke studied him. "Why do you ask?"

"I saw a guy three years ago when I was hiking around on Glacier Mountain. There were some snow packs but I thought it odd he was wearing a ski mask. When I called out to him, he disappeared."

"Did you notice what he was wearing on his feet?"

"That was the cool thing. I thought maybe he might be Native. He was wearing knee-high moccasins." Tyson's face lit up. He was proud of his heritage.

"That would explain why I didn't find any boot marks besides the killer's. Good to know. Let's get some sleep. I want to get out of here as early as I can so that Dani has someone available to go with me. If I'd brought Jack, I could just let him wander back to the lodge but I'm not sure Dot would know to do that yet."

"I think Kitree will be available the earliest in the morning. I have a group of eight to take on a trail ride." Tyson turned off the lantern.

Hawke settled back onto the air mattress. He'd enjoy visiting with Kitree on the ride up but worried about her coming back down by herself.

«»«»«»

"Why didn't you wake me up last night?" Dani asked as she walked into the lodge kitchen and her gaze landed on Hawke having coffee and talking to Sage. Dog rose from his spot at Hawke's feet and walked across the room to nudge her hand with his nose.

Hawke smiled. "It was late and I didn't want to rouse the whole lodge." He pointed with his thumb in the direction of the barn. "Tyson gave me an air mattress and I slept fine."

"You would have been more comfortable in my bed," Dani said.

Sage giggled and turned her attention back to the

breakfast she was cooking. The aromas were what brought Hawke into the kitchen after talking to Tuck.

"I agree. But again, I didn't want to cause an uproar." He walked over and kissed Dani.

"How long are you staying?" she asked, leaving her arms wrapped around his neck.

"About an hour."

She dropped her arms and studied him. "Are you still after the person who shot that boy in the leg?"

"Yes. I believe he's still up here chasing after the wolverine." Hawke motioned for her to sit at the kitchen table where the staff ate. "I'd like someone to ride up to the crime scene with me this morning and bring Dot back down here. Dog and I are going to see if we can locate the killer and arrest him."

Dani peered into his eyes. "I'll ride with you. The only other person I'd have available is Kitree and I don't want her riding around alone if there is a killer loose."

"I know you are capable, but I'm just as nervous about you being alone as I am Kitree," Hawke said.

Dani smiled the wicked smile that showed she hoped someone would tangle with her. "Kitree doesn't know how to use my Beretta M9 or a rifle. I'll be just fine."

"Then let's eat and get on the trail," Hawke said.

As they ate, Dani instructed Sage on what she would need to do in Dani's absence that day.

"I can handle it. You enjoy a ride. You've been working too hard," Sage said as she handed them a basket with lunch provisions.

Out in the barn, Hawke saddled Dot and Dani saddled her favorite Appaloosa horse, Chief. They were headed up the trail by 8 a.m. When the trail allowed, they rode side by side visiting about the lodge, Herb and Darlene, and the case.

"You think there is someone else already following the killer?" Dani asked after he'd explained about Bryce Hendrix.

"That's my thought. We saw him walk by the wildlife camera that showed the wounded wolverine running for his life. I think he saw what the killer did and is following him. What he plans to do, I don't know. But I hope to catch up to them before one of them kills the other." He didn't want Bryce taking things into his own hands. Then he would have to go to jail and living on the mountains seemed to be what made him happy.

"I don't like you going after those two alone." Dani stopped Chief and stared into his eyes.

"I'm not alone. I'll have Dog. He's better than a human. He can hear and see things they can't. We'll be fine." Even as he said it, an icy chill fluttered up his spine. It was a feeling he'd had several times while in the military and a couple of times in these mountains. He would be extremely careful, knowing he'd had a premonition that something would go wrong.

«»«»«»

At the crime scene, Dani and Hawke ate the lunch Sage had prepared.

"I don't like the idea of you going after two men alone. I could come with you," she said.

"You don't have provisions or a backpack," Hawke said, taking her hand. "Don't worry about us. Dog and I can handle ourselves. You get the horses back to the lodge and forget I'm out here."

She snorted. "Like I can do that when I brought you here. Those men have a day or two head start, how do you plan to catch up to them without using horses to move faster?"

He saw what she was trying to do. Get herself on the trail with him. Shaking his head, he said, "You aren't coming with me with or without a horse." He shoved all the picnic stuff back in the basket and strapped it onto the back of Dot. "Get going so I can get on the trail faster." He kissed her and turned her toward her horse.

"You know this is a bad idea. You going up there alone," she said as she walked to the horse and mounted.

He smiled. "It's my job. I found the body and I need to bring the killer in. It's as simple as that."

She shook her head, looking down at him. "No, it's not that simple. You could have come up here with a group and searched the area. But you chose to tackle it alone. Just like you always do. You aren't saving other people, you're sacrificing yourself." She gave him one last look as her words sank in.

She was right. He would rather sacrifice himself than let someone else get hurt. It stemmed from stepping in as a child and taking blows from his stepfather that were meant for his mom.

"It's who I am." There wasn't anything else to say. "Take care of Dot. I'll be back as soon as I can to get him."

"Be careful."

"We always are." Hawke put his hand on Dog's head to let her know he wasn't alone.

She faced forward and headed the horses back to

the trail.

Hawke shouldered his pack and headed up the side of the mountain. Keeping his gaze on the faint tracks of the man wearing a cloth over his soles, he pondered what Dani said. She hadn't told him anything he hadn't already been telling himself. But he refused to send others up here to tackle a person who sounded as if he wasn't right in the head.

Bending to get a better look at the track, he saw the faint indention of the heel of a foot. The indention looked as if the heel spun just a little. Bryce Hendrix was following the shooter.

Hawke's heart raced hoping he could get between the two or at least catch up to Bryce and talk sense into him. With this new information spinning in his head Hawke climbed faster, barely raising his gaze from the tracks. Dog would tell him if there was anything amiss around them.

They climbed the mountain up to a shale slide. On the slide, he couldn't see the shooter's prints but he could see where the rocks had been spun from the heel of Bryce's foot.

Their momentum slowed as he carefully scanned the shale to discover which direction the two were going. Finally, they exited the slide and continued traveling toward the highest point of Glacier Mountain.

The tracks led him to, and across, a small ice field. The tracks were easy to follow. This was the first time he recognized a wolverine print. The shooter was following the animal. Hawke didn't see any trace of blood. He hoped that meant the animal had a superficial wound that had already begun to heal.

As they traveled higher in elevation, the warmth of

the sun helped to keep his muscles from stiffening since the air was colder and made breathing harder.

Gazing up at the sun, Hawke figured they'd been climbing for four hours. He stopped, facing the sun, and drank from his canteen. Dog chomped on snow from a small bank in the shadow of a boulder.

"How far ahead do you think they are?" he asked the animal.

Dog tilted his head, listening.

"Do you think they went all the way over the top and are going down the other side?" Hawke always found talking things out with Dog worked well.

Dog walked over and put his head on Hawke's knee. "We'll keep going till dark. No sense in doing anything different." He shoved the canteen back into a side pocket of his pack, shouldered it, and they set off following the tracks.

Chapter Fifteen

The sun had slipped away and the moon looked so close, Hawke imagined reaching up and touching it as he lay in his sleeping bag staring up at the stars. He was tired. So was Dog. The animal was already asleep next to him. His foot twitched and his eyes moved under his eyelids.

It had been a while since Hawke had hiked this much in one day. From what he could tell of the tracks he'd followed, they were at least a day old. That meant he had to either move faster or hope they slowed down. The way the wolverine kept moving, he wondered if the animal was looking for a new territory. If he was, they could end up in Idaho.

Hawke didn't like the idea of following the animal and the shooter that far, but he would. The man needed to be held accountable for his actions. Just as his eyes drifted closed, he heard the call of a Great Horned owl. It reminded him of the picture they had hanging in their house that Dani had been given from her uncle Charlie.

Wolverine Instincts

And how a Great Horned owl had helped him stay alive in these mountains before. Charlie was looking out for him.

《》《》《》

The glow of sunshine chased away the gray of dawn when Hawke shouldered his pack and he and Dog set off to follow the tracks. He'd dreamed of coming upon the shooter high on the mountain where the man didn't have anywhere to hide. He'd also dreamed the man had crept up during the night and stolen Dog. That's what exhaustion did to him. Gave him nightmares. He'd learned that about himself in the Marines.

Putting one foot in front of the other, he continued the upward climb. It wouldn't do for him to be too tired to raise a weapon when he caught up to the shooter. He stopped, sipped water, and studied the scene in front of him. There was only a scattering of scraggly bushes in the alpine ecosystem near the top of the mountain. Boulders, crags, small glacier areas of years of snow piled in crags and dips. It was a white and gray landscape.

He was visible to anyone who might be hiding in a crag or behind a boulder. There was nothing he could do about it. The only way to know the direction the shooter traveled was to follow his tracks.

"Let's keep going," he said to Dog and shifted the weight of his pack before resuming the ascent of the mountain. It was clear the shooter was following the wolverine's tracks. There were easier ways to get to the top of the mountain than going straight up the front.

Another two hours and he was almost to the top. But the tracks had veered to the northeast. They were headed to a lower notch along the top of the mountain. "At least we aren't going straight up anymore," Hawke said to Dog as they walked toward the notch.

The tracks went over the ridge. He hunkered down and slowly raised his head to scan the north side of the mountain. This would be a nice place for the wolverine to find a den. There were larger pockets of granular snow that hadn't melted.

He used his binoculars to see if there was any sign of the shooter or Bryce. When Hawke didn't see any movement, he and Dog dropped over the edge. They stayed in the shadow of the mountain as they slid on loose rock and worked their way over to better footing.

He came across a bit of snow and found tracks. They were pointing toward a larger patch of snow. It was evident the tracks had been made at least twenty-four hours earlier. The presence of dirt blown in the tracks and crumbling edges gave him that information.

Every ten yards, Hawke scanned the area. All the small pockets of snow were the perfect place for the animal to have denned up which meant the shooter could have him in his crosshairs.

Fifteen minutes later, Hawke stood where the shooter had stood, staring at a hole in the ground. It appeared this was where the wolverine had denned up. But where the hell was the shooter?

As the thought crossed his mind, the hairs on the back of his neck tingled and Dog growled.

Slowly, trying to appear casual, he raised his gaze from the hole and studied the area up the mountainside. He saw an outcropping of rock large enough to cover him and Dog in his peripheral vision to the left.

"Come," Hawke said low enough for only Dog to

Wolverine Instincts

hear. The animal had stopped growling but he had his head turned, peering at something up on the mountainside.

Hawke grabbed his canteen and took a sip to wash away the dryness that had appeared at the feeling he was being watched. Walking to the outcropping, he wondered why the killer hadn't shot them. He had to know they followed his tracks to the hole.

As soon as he was close to the cover, he ducked behind the rocks and commanded Dog to follow. When his heart stopped pounding in his ears, he pulled his binoculars out of his pack and slowly rose to look over the top of the rocks.

Someone was working his way down from a vantage point on the mountainside. Hawke zeroed in on the weapon in his hands. It appeared to be a shotgun. Raising his binoculars, he stared at a face covered in a ski mask. Bryce.

Hawke's mind eased a bit. If this man had been following the killer and was now walking toward him in the open, the killer must not be here. He stepped out from behind the rocks and waved a hand.

Bryce stopped, stared, and then continued down the mountainside. Twenty minutes later he stopped in front of where Hawke and Dog were eating lunch.

Hawke held out his hand, "Bryce Hendrix, I'm State Trooper Hawke. Your dad told me I might meet up with you."

The man shook hands and continued to stare at him.

Hawke pulled his badge out from under his shirt by the chain around his neck. "I took over your dad's job when he retired. I'm with Fish and Wildlife. I tracked the man who shot a hiker and wounded another to here. Can you tell me where he is now?"

Bryce pointed northeast.

"Did you follow him?"

The man nodded.

"Where was he headed?" Hawke knew the man could speak. His father said he could.

Dog walked over and sat at Bryce's feet, staring up at him.

"That's Dog. He's my partner when I'm in the mountains," Hawke said, to put the man at ease.

Bryce patted Dog on the head and staring at the animal said, "Lostine Trail. Headed out."

The words were a bit garbled but Hawke understood. "When did he leave?"

"Yesterday."

"He must be going to get another trap." Hawke glanced over at the hole in the snow. "Is that where the wolverine is denned up?"

The man nodded.

"Could you tell if he was healed from the first attempt at trapping him?" Hawke hoped the animal didn't go in the hole and die.

"He healed."

"Good." Hawke wondered what to do. How long would it take the killer to make a new cage? How long to pack it back up here and set it up? At this point the Lostine Trail was the quickest way to get out of the mountains, but did he dare take off?

"I'll watch," Bryce said, pointing to the wolverine's den.

"Don't confront the man. He's already killed once to keep anyone from knowing he's after this wolverine." Hawke held Bryce's gaze until he was sure the man would heed his warning.

Hawke shouldered his pack and picked up his shotgun.

"Be careful," Bryce said.

"And you too." Hawke placed a hand on the man's arm and felt the muscle bunch under his touch. "I'll get back here as soon as I can if I don't catch up to him in the valley. I'll send a helicopter up to keep an eye on things as well. I'll tell them you aren't the suspect. Will you be wearing that blue hat all the time?"

Bryce nodded.

"I'll tell them you are keeping tabs for us." Hawke whistled to Dog, and they headed down the mountain toward the Copper Creek Trail.

By mid-afternoon, Hawke and Dog were on the Copper Creek Trail walking toward the West Lostine River Trail. The foot traffic was more than Hawke had seen all summer. Everyone must be out getting in a final hike of the summer. When the trail connected with the Lostine River Trail, he spotted an outfitter he knew.

Hawke waved his arm and the man looked over.

"Hawke, what are you doing up here on foot?" Josh Beasley asked, reining his horse up at the intersection of trails.

"Do you have a horse I could ride? I need to get down to cell phone range to make a call."

"Something happening I need to know about?" Josh asked.

"I'll tell you on the way down the trail," Hawke said, as the outfitter dismounted.

"I have a sat radio. You can see if it will work here." Josh walked back to one of the pack mules and opened the canvas flap on the pannier, handing him the radio.

Hawke dialed in the frequency he used for contacting dispatch.

"Dispatch this is Hawke, come in." He released the button and listened. Nothing.

"Dispatch this is Trooper Hawke, come in." Scratching noises and a squawk brought the radio to life.

"Hawke, this is Hector at the airstrip, what's up? Over."

Getting hold of Hector was better than no one. He was a former ODFW pilot.

"Hector, let Sergeant Spruel of OSP in Winslow know that I found what I was looking for and am waiting for the suspect to return. Tell him the suspect is in the valley looking for supplies. Over."

"You're staying on the mountain, the suspect is in the valley getting supplies. Over."

"Copy. Hector, I'm going to send you coordinates through Josh Beasley. I want you to get a couple of helicopters to fly over the area several times a day to keep an eye on me and a guy in a blue cap. Over."

"Copy. I'll get someone rounded up for when Josh contacts me. Over."

"Thanks. Over." Hawke handed the radio to Josh. "You heard my conversation." He pulled out his notepad and then copied the coordinates from the GPS on his phone that he'd marked when he'd found the wolverine den. He wrote them down and handed the paper to Josh. "Get those to Hector at the airstrip as soon as you can."

"What's this about?" Josh asked as he put the radio

Wolverine Instincts

back in the pack.

"I found a poacher on Glacier Mountain. I believe he is in the valley making another trap. I'll take that ride back down to the trial head with you, but I'll stay there to try and catch the poacher when he returns."

"Hop on any of the mules, except the last one. He's back there because he likes to kick and not carry people." Josh hooked his thumb toward the line of four mules behind him.

"How come you don't have any people with you?" Hawke asked as he eyed the mules he could pick from.

"I took up the supplies for the coming week. Jan and Floyd are setting up the camp. I'll turn around tomorrow and take up the group that hired us for this week-long reunion."

Hawke nodded. He was glad to hear the animals had empty packs. He shoved his pack into the empty bag on the first mule and picked the next mule to ride. A rock stuck out enough for him to get a boost to get on the mule around the pack. Dog looked up at him expectantly. Hawke hopped down and put Dog on the mule in front of him.

Once Hawke was settled again on the second mule, Josh headed down the trail. An hour later they walked out into the parking area of Two Pan Trail Head.

"Thanks for the lift," Hawke said, helping Dog down and grabbing his pack.

"You're welcome, I'll get this information to Hector first thing. You be careful. Poachers are only one step away from someone who would kill a human." Josh walked away leading his string of mules as Hawke thought, *You don't know how true that is.*

Chapter Sixteen

Hawke made a small camp in an area where he could keep an eye on the trailhead. He wasn't sure how long they'd have to wait for the poacher to return and head up the trail with something that would look like a trap.

As he walked around picking up dry sticks, his phone dinged. Standing in one place he glanced to see who tried to call him. Seth. Now what had the young man found out? Hawke held his phone. One bar. All he could do would be to text.

I don't have good service. What did you want? Hawke texted.

You said not to make contact with Skunk Bear King, but he reached out to me.

"Shit!" Hawke glanced around. No one was paying attention to him and Dog. *What did he want? Did you tell Sergeant Spruel?*

I haven't told anyone. I kind of told him my dad is an ODFW trapper. He wants me to get him the plans to

Wolverine Instincts

one of their traps.

Hawke thought about this. If the person was Zach, he'd already have access to the plans through Shelly. Who the hell was this Skunk Bear King? *I'm on the mountain. Contact Sergeant Spruel and see if he can help set up a meeting.*

I'd rather work with you.

Sorry, I'm chasing down another lead.

Okay.

As soon as he read the one word, Hawke scrolled to Spruel's number and sent him the conversation he had with Seth. He added, *I'm at Two Pan waiting for the poacher to return with a trap. Found the wolverine den on the north side of Glacier Mountain. Also found Bryce Hendrix. He's watching the wolverine. Contacted Hector to do several flyovers.*

What do you expect to do if you see the poacher? Spruel texted.

Arrest him if I can. Or keep the casualties to a minimum. If the man showed up when there were a lot of people at the trailhead, he'd have to follow him until he could arrest him.

Do you want me to send backup?

Hawke thought about that. It would be good to have someone to help him out when the poacher arrived. But he could arrive before backup did. *If you can spare someone. Might make the arrest easier.*

Copy.

Hawke hoped Spruel came up with a way to keep Seth away from the poacher.

《》《》《》

Seth stared at the phone after talking to Sergeant Spruel. The policeman didn't even consider him as the one to meet up and give the plans to S.B.K. He'd made the contact, he'd come up with the plan, and now he was being shut out.

He didn't like it. He wanted to be there when the man who killed the hiker and shot his brother was arrested. The rest of the night was spent finding plans for a trap that no animal had ever broken out of. He added the ODFW type and logo to a corner and printed it. Then he contacted S.B.K. and told him he had the plans and would meet him tomorrow morning at Minam. All he had to do was sneak his aunt's car keys before she headed to work.

《》《》《》

Hawke and Dog spent a restless night, watching the trailhead and waiting. He finally dozed off about 4 a.m. and woke up at 6:30 when a group on horseback headed up the trail. Scanning the vehicles in the parking area, he didn't see any that hadn't been there the night before. The poacher must be having a hard time building or getting supplies to make his trap.

Or he stayed home in his bed and had a nice breakfast this morning. Deciding to see if anyone tried to contact him, he walked over to the area where his phone had a connection the night before.

Ivy left a message that Zach had contacted her and wanted to meet for breakfast. She'd fill him in later.

Hawke texted her back. *Tell Spruel. I have a bad connection.* Then he wondered where his backup was. Spruel had sounded like he was sending someone up.

He texted his sergeant. *Did you send backup?*

Needed an extra person to catch the guy wanting the trap instructions. If we can't catch him, Steve will show up.

Wolverine Instincts

Hawke sent him a thumbs up.

His phone dinged. Seth.

Don't be mad. I'm meeting the Skunk Bear King at Minam today.

"That dumb kid!" Hawke didn't bother to see who heard him this time. His anger, frustration, and worry were too high to care what others thought. "Shit!" He was stuck here without a way to get to Minam and all he could do was text first Seth, *Don't meet him. It could be a trap.*

Then Spruel. *Seth is meeting the Skunk Bear King at Minam this morning. Stop him.*

Copy was Spruel's reply.

Seth didn't text anything back. He wouldn't. He didn't want to be stopped. But what could he think to gain without police there to arrest the killer?

Hawke started pacing. What was the kid thinking? Why lure someone like that when the police were handling it?

Dog whined from their camp area. Hawke glanced over and noticed his friend had a paw on the pack. "Are you telling me to get back up to the mountain?" Hawke walked over and started picking up the few items he hadn't packed yet. "This is the quickest way for the poacher to go back up, but if he's meeting Seth at Minam and thinks it's a trap, he could head up into the mountains from there."

Shouldering his pack, he said, "Good idea. Let's go." If backup did show up, they'd have to get ahold of Hector to find out where Hawke was heading.

«»«»«»

Seth waited nervously at the picnic tables that sat in front of the Minam store. Every vehicle that drove up made his heart race. He'd received the text from Hawke telling him this was a bad idea, but he'd texted Hawke to make sure there were police here when he talked to S.B.K. He'd known if he'd contacted them too soon, they would have stopped him.

A white Dodge pickup like he'd seen at the hospital parked in front of the store. A man pulled a woman out behind him on the driver's side, heading into the store. The woman glanced around. Seth caught her gaze and wondered at the slight shake of her head. What was she trying to tell him?

He waited by the picnic table, trying to decide what to do. The two emerged from the store. The man stared at him and while he was dressed in jeans, a t-shirt, flannel shirt, and didn't have a beard, the eyes chilled Seth. They were the crazy eyes of the man who'd shot Alex.

His feet wanted to run but his mind said, *This is what you wanted.* He stepped forward. "Skunk Bear King?"

"Yeah." He glanced around. "How'd you get here?"

"My aunt's car." Seth pointed to the small SUV.

"Did you ask to take it and tell her where you were going?"

"No, I took her keys and she doesn't know where I went."

The man grinned. "Nice. We'll take your car." That's when the man revealed the gun that had been hidden behind the unbuttoned flannel shirt. It was pointed at the woman. "Now you go get the three packs that are in the back of my truck and bring them over to your aunt's car. If you do as I say, I won't hurt Ivy." He jerked on the woman's hair, making her head tip back and she squeaked.

It reminded Seth of when he'd accidentally stepped on a small dog's foot.

He ran over to the truck, used all his muscles to lift one pack out of the truck. He jogged the best he could with the weight of the pack and put it in the back of his aunt's car. He made the other two trips and the man opened the driver's door.

"You're driving."

After they were all in the vehicle with Ivy in the passenger seat and S.B.K. in the seat behind her with an arm around her neck, the shooter said, "Drive up Big Canyon Road."

Seth knew the road. It was the one he and Alex had gone in to get to the Minam trail for their last hike together. As he put the car in gear and headed away from the store, he hoped this wasn't the last time he entered the Eagle Caps.

He started out driving slow, until the shooter told him to speed up and Ivy groaned when the man tightened his arm on her neck. Seth had hoped the police would go by and he could stop them, but he didn't see a police car before he turned up Big Canyon Road.

The gravel road was used mostly by ranchers taking their cattle in and out of the backcountry. At least that's what his dad told him when he asked on one of their hunting trips. He could only go about 15 to 20 miles per hour over the ruts and potholes.

"Step on it. I want to be on Glacier Mountain by dark."

Ivy groaned and Seth could see the color draining

out of her face.

"Okay but hang on and let go of her neck."

He slammed his foot down on the accelerator and the car bounced from hole to hole and rut to rut as he wrestled with the steering wheel.

"You can slow down so you don't put us in the trees," Skunk Bear King snarled.

Seth slowed to 40 miles per hour and they arrived at Bear Wallow Springs an hour and a half after leaving Minam.

"Stop here. We'll hike from here."

Seth stopped the car and drew in a deep breath. This was exactly what he and Alex had done the day before Alex had been shot and they'd witnessed this man kill a hiker. His hands shook as he grasped the door handle. *Toughen up. You started this, you have to see it through*, he told himself. *And there's another person involved*. He slid a glance toward the woman being pulled out of the car.

He slid out of the car and walked to the back, opening the hatch.

"You seem wimpy, you take the lightest pack," S.B.K. told him.

"Ivy can carry the light one," Seth said, knowing his mom would be proud he was being a gentleman.

"How do you know her name?" The shooter shouted, spittle flying from his mouth.

Seth wondered if the man had rabies and answered, "You called her that at the store."

He grasped Ivy's arm, shook her, and asked, "Do you know this kid?"

"I've never met him before," she said, through chattering teeth.

S.B.K. shoved her away from him. "Let the big man take the heavier pack, but I'll kill either one of you if you try anything stupid." He glared into Ivy's eyes.

Seth shuddered but the woman didn't flinch. He grabbed the pack he'd thought was not the lightest nor the heaviest and set it on the back of the car to hoist the shoulder straps into place. When he was all buckled in, Ivy did similar since she was shorter than him. The shooter held the pistol in one hand and shoved his arms through the straps of the heavy pack with a rifle sheathed on the side of it.

"You, start up the trail first," Skunk Bear King pointed the pistol at Seth.

He obediently headed up the trail, watching his step as he got used to the weight of the pack. What was in the pack that made it so heavy and why were they going into the wilderness? The man never once asked for the trap plans.

Chapter Seventeen

Hawke and Dog made it back to the area of the Wolverine's den by early afternoon. As soon as he emerged from the trees, he spotted the snow bank. He studied the mountainside and didn't see any sign of Bryce. A glint of light off something caught his attention. Then he realized, it was Morse code. It had been a while since he'd used that manner of communication.

He set his pack down and pulled out a pen and notepad to see if he could figure out what Bryce was saying.

After jotting down the sequence of dots and dashes, he read: message copter

He flashed back: go ahead

Luckily Bryce must have realized Hawke hadn't worked with the code for a while. He repeated the message several times until Hawke sent him an O.K. Then Hawke stretched his brain to decipher what he'd put on the notepad: boy missing.

Wolverine Instincts

It had to be Seth. That was the only boy who Spruel would be contacting him about. Hawke wanted to find Seth and ask him what he was thinking.

more: Bryce flashed.

go ahead: Hawke replied.

This time it didn't take as many tries for the message to become clear: white Dodge at Minam.

Damn! That meant there was a good chance the killer had Seth.

more: Bryce flashed again.

go ahead: Hawke flashed back as his mind wandered to where the boy and the killer could be.

Hawke had to write the first part of the message several times before he realized it was numbers: 1500 drop sat radio.

That was the best news. If he had a radio, he could learn more and he could talk to the pilot who makes the drop.

o.k.: he flashed back. Then added: wait there.

copy: was the reply and the flashing stopped.

"Seth got himself into trouble," Hawke told Dog. "We'll wait here until we hear a helicopter then see if we can learn anything new." He dug into the pack and pulled out a sandwich that was several days old. Luckily, he was less likely to get food poisoning from a peanut butter and honey sandwich than any other kind. He put a handful of dog food on a flat rock for Dog.

They napped until Hawke heard the whop-whop of helicopter rotors. He stood out in the open looking up. The copter came into view with two people in the cockpit. The pilot was Hector and it looked like Steve Shoberg, another trooper, in the passenger seat. The copter landed and Steve ran out from under the rotor blades.

"Nathan said you wanted backup," Steve said, holding out a radio.

"What's going on?" Hawke glanced at the copter sitting on the ground. It would be a giveaway to the killer if he topped the mountain or came up the way Hawke had and saw the bird. "We should send Hector away."

"He needs to know how long to keep flying over," Steve said.

"Tell me quickly what happened to Seth?"

"We'd set up a sting to get Skunk Bear King but he didn't show and then Nathan got the text from you about the meet in Minam. By the time we got there, they were gone. We talked to the store owner. He said the man showed up with a small dark-haired woman. They came into the store and he could tell the woman didn't want to be there. Then they went out and talked to a teenager standing near the picnic table. The teenager put backpacks from the white Dodge truck into a small SUV that he arrived in and the three of them drove off. We showed up a good half hour after the owner said they left."

Hawke had a bad feeling. "Did anyone flash the photo of the killer at the owner?"

"Yeah, he said it wasn't that man. The guy had dark hair, a five o'clock shadow, and crazy eyes."

"Shit!" Hawke walked a small circle. "You need to get up in the copter and first, see if anyone has seen Ivy. She'd been dating one of our suspects and she texted me that he had contacted her. Then you need Hector to fly down the Minam and Bear Wallow trails and see if the three of them are coming on one of those trails. I'd venture to guess they are on Bear Wallow. It has the least amount of traffic. Then come back and let me know which way they are coming and where they're at.

"As for backup, I have Bryce Hendrix. He's up the side of the mountain watching. He saw the shootings and has been following the killer to make sure he doesn't harm the wolverine."

"What kind of backup is that? I heard he came back from Afghanistan a cripple." Steve said, his eyes narrowing.

"He isn't a cripple anymore. He's stronger than me and has tactical training. You go see if you can find where the three are."

Steve turned to head to the copter.

Hawke shouted, "What time were you at the Minam Store?"

"Nine."

Hawke waved and Steve ran under the moving rotors and climbed into the helicopter. The rotors spun faster and the bird rose into the air. The aircraft just topped Glacier Mountain and Hawke felt a presence behind him.

"I hope you don't mind. I told my colleague that you were my backup." He turned slowly and peered into Bryce's eyes. "I figure you and I know this mountain better than most people. And you have tactical training from the military. I do too but it was years ago."

Hawke moved to a spot inside the trees where he'd left his pack. He sat on a downed log and motioned for Bryce to do the same. "The killer is possibly headed this way up the Minam or Bear Wallow Trail with two hostages. The brother of the boy he shot the day he killed the hiker, and I believe a female state trooper the man had dated a few times. He may have thought she knew what we had planned and lured her to meet with him. The boy tried to do a sting on the guy and it backfired."

Hawke picked up his canteen and drank before saying, "The main thing we know is he left Minam store at eight-thirty this morning. I figure two to two and a half hours to get to Bear Wallow and then if they are all in good shape, they should arrive here around dark tomorrow night. If they stop and rest tonight. Otherwise, they could be here in the morning." Hawke glanced up at the sky. "Steve and Hector should be coming back soon and letting us know if the trio is coming up the trail and about where they might be." He held up the sat radio.

Bryce nodded. "Know which direction," he swallowed and continued, "make a trap."

Hawke grinned. "I was thinking the same thing. Let's get some rest while we wait to hear from Steve."

《》《》《》

Seth's shoulders ached from the weight of the pack. His legs felt like noodles, and his mind spun like the merry-go-round he and Alex played on in the park before the city took it out and put in a safer version.

"Pick up the pace. At this rate we'll be lucky to get to the wolverine by Thursday morning," S.B.K. said, as Seth felt a push from behind and a drag on his pack.

He stopped and Ivy pulled him to the ground.

"What the hell are you doing? Get up!" shouted the shooter.

Seth tried to push the woman off him and she whispered, "I'm a trooper."

She pushed off him and offered a hand to help him up.

He stared up at her and the next second S.B.K. dragged him to his feet by his pack. "Stop trying to grope my girl and get those awkward feet of yours facing forward and move 'em faster."

Seth's mind raced as he tried to walk faster. Has the woman been the one the State Police sent to do the sting on the shooter? But the guy called her his girl? Was she State Police or just mad at the man and said that to confuse him? How did she become his hostage? Should he trust her? He'd have to watch her and see what she was capable of. But it gave him hope that there might be a way out of this mess alive.

The beat of a helicopter's rotors echoed in the canyon.

S.B.K. cursed and told them to get in the trees.

Ivy tripped. The shooter grabbed her by the pack. Her body went limp as he tried to haul her into the trees as the helicopter went by.

Seth stepped out into the trail and waved his arms, before stepping back in the trees. He didn't want S.B.K. to see what he'd done.

The helicopter came back by and then headed east.

"One more stunt like that and you'll remain in the wilderness," Skunk Bear King said to Ivy.

"Like I'm expecting you to just let us go free after you catch the wolverine, Zach," Ivy said, thrusting her hands on her hips. "You should just shoot me now. I won't make getting to that poor defenseless creature easy."

Seth couldn't believe the woman was taunting the guy with the gun. She was either braver than him or a lot stupider.

"You aren't going to shoot me until we get to the top of the mountain. You need me to be your mule and get your pieces of trap up there." She smiled at him and motioned to Seth to start walking.

He glanced at Skunk-Zach. The man glared at her, then motioned with the pistol for him to start walking. This was something he hadn't thought about. Zach couldn't kill them until they reached his destination. That meant they had a chance to get away without him shooting at them.

《》《》《》

The helicopter hovered overhead. Hawke turned the radio on.

"Hawke, do you copy?" Steve asked.

"Copy."

"Looks like you were right. He has Ivy. She was giving him fits and keeping him in the trail while we flew by and the boy stepped out and waved at us while the killer was dealing with Ivy. Over."

"Copy. Where were they on the trail? Over."

"They're coming up Bear Wallow and should be to Miner Basin Creek by dark or earlier. If they stop there for the night, I'd say they'll be to you by tomorrow night. Over."

Hawke thought about that. They were hiking the longest way possible, but that trail had the least traffic. The radio crackled and he said, "Thanks. The helicopters can stay away until late tomorrow. Then we could use a few more bodies up here to help. Over."

"Copy. I'll bring a posse. Over."

"Copy."

Hawke turned the radio off and the helicopter flew

away. He turned to Bryce. "Know of a good place to spend the night?" They'd have tonight and tomorrow to figure out how to catch the killer without putting his hostages in danger.

Chapter Eighteen

Darkness made staying on the trail difficult. The new moon gave off faint light from the thin crescent that illuminated the sky. Seth finally stopped after almost tripping for a third time.

Ivy ran into the back of him, and the second jolt must have been Zach running into her.

"I can't see. Can we stop and rest? And I'm hungry." Seth didn't care if he whined. The more he irritated the man the more chance there was the man would leave him alone and he could get away. He'd studied a map of the trails in this area before he and Alex headed out on their trip. And he'd reviewed it again after they were flown out from the Hunting Lodge. If he was correct, the sign they'd passed that said 'Miner Basin' put them about five miles from the hunting lodge. If he could get away from Zach, he could get to the lodge and they could send in help for Ivy.

"Quit whining. All I have are granola bars." Zach

grabbed a hold of each of their packs and pulled them under a tree. "Sit here and take off your packs."

A flashlight blinded Seth as he unbuckled the strap across his belly. He groaned, easing the pack straps off his shoulders. It would have been nice to have had a flashlight after the moon had come up. Why had the man kept it to himself and not used it?

"What's the matter, tough guy? That pack heavier than you're used to?" Zach taunted, setting the flashlight on end giving light to all of them. He handed Seth a granola bar.

"What about water?" Seth asked.

"I only have one jug, no cup. You'll have to drink out of it or go without." Zach opened his pack and pulled out a gallon jug of water.

Seth didn't care if the man had a disease, he was thirsty. He grabbed the jug and drank until it was jerked away.

"You aren't drinking all of it." Zach glared at him.

Seth had forgotten about Ivy until Zach reached out and snatched her before she disappeared into the dark.

"Where are you going?"

"I have to pee," she said.

Seth squirmed feeling uncomfortable for the woman. If Zach made her pee here where they were, he'd never be able to look the woman in the eye again.

Zach pulled a thin cord from his pack and tied it around Ivy's neck. "You got as far as this cord lets you go and don't even try to get out of the knot, I'll know."

The vicious glare she shot at the man, made Seth shiver. She walked to the other side of a pine tree and he heard the zipper of her jeans go down.

His face heated and he looked in the opposite

direction. He'd been embarrassed more today than he ever had in his life. He hadn't thought himself naïve but now he wondered. Would Alex have let this man take him? Would he have stood up for the woman more than Seth had?

The zipper sounded loud as she secured her pants and stepped back into the light of the upturned flashlight.

"Take this string off my neck and I'll take that granola bar and water now," Ivy said, not looking at anyone.

Zach smirked. "The cord stays on. That way I know you won't make a run for it during the night." He handed her a granola bar and the jug of water.

She sat close enough to Seth, their feet touched. As she opened the granola wrapper, her foot tapped his.

He glanced over at her.

She glanced at Zach. When he stepped over to a tree and zipped his pants down, she mouthed, "Run!"

Seth didn't need to be told twice. He knew where he was headed. He grabbed the flashlight and with one move of his thumb, darkness enveloped them.

Seth ran deep into the forest. A rifle shot echoed through the trees. He didn't flinch, just kept his legs moving and his arms up trying to ward off the swats in the face from limbs and bushes.

His legs were still moving but he couldn't breathe anymore. Slowing, he glanced behind to see if the man followed. All he saw was darkness.

He stood doubled over, catching his breath, and listened. He didn't hear anyone crashing through the trees behind him. He found a spot with less trees and looked up at the sky. Studying the stars, Seth used the

Wolverine Instincts

Big Dipper to find the North Star. From there he knew which direction to take to find the Hunting Lodge. With the flashlight trained to the ground to help him wind his way through the underbrush, he headed in a southeast direction away from the star.

《》《》《》

Seth's legs were about to buckle when he saw a light through the trees. At first, he worried he'd gone in a circle and had walked back into the Skunk Bear King's clutches. Then he glanced up at the stars and knew he'd been heading in the correct direction. What he saw had to be a light from the hunting lodge.

He rested a few minutes, knowing he would be safe soon. He hoped his leaving didn't put Ivy in more danger. If she was really with the State Police, hopefully, she'd be able to fight her way against their kidnapper.

It had been cowardly of him to run and leave her behind. But she had told him to run. She was counting on him to get help. He pushed to his feet and continued toward the light.

A lantern shone in the barn. He glanced at his phone. It was midnight. He wondered who would be up at midnight in the barn. But since it was the only light, other than a faint one in the lodge, he wandered to the barn and walked through the open barn doors.

"It's okay, Buttons. Every mom goes through this," said a female voice he recognized.

"Who's Buttons?" he asked, moving into the lantern light.

The girl he'd met on his last visit here, Kitree, sprang to her feet and turned, her stance one he'd seen in fight movies.

"Hey, I'm not going to hurt you. I need to get help."

She studied him a moment and then said, "What are you doing back up here? And Buttons is a cat."

"It's a long story. I need to talk to your dad and the lady who flew us out." As he'd walked to the lodge, he'd wondered who to tell and decided the father and the pilot should be told.

"They're both sleeping." She stood now with her arms crossed.

"It's important. I was kidnapped along with a woman. The man who killed the hiker and shot my brother was taking us up the mountain to the wolverine. He had us carrying packs. Even though the woman told me to run, I think he may take it out on her. We need to help her." The urgency he'd felt when he'd run away now powered him into motion. "Should we get your dad first or the pilot?"

"The pilot is Dani and she owns the lodge. I'll wake her first. Come on. We'll go in the back door and only wake her, not the guests." She blew out the lantern and walked to the entrance.

He followed the girl out of the barn, waited while she closed the doors, and then followed her between the barn and a cabin. They walked on what felt like a bark path to the back of another building and then the lodge.

"There's three steps," she whispered and he saw her walk up the steps and open the door. He followed, closing the door behind him.

She knocked on the first door on the right. "Dani, it's Kitree. There's a problem."

A light filtered under the door and the woman who'd piloted the helicopter appeared. "Who's that with you?" she asked, curiosity rang in her voice.

"Seth, the brother of the boy you flew out of here last week. You need to hear him out." Kitree pushed by the woman.

Seth waited until the woman invited him into her room. It didn't look like his mom and dad's bedroom. This one had very few feminine touches.

"What are you doing up here—" She stopped and said to Kitree, "Go in the kitchen and get the medical box, a cloth, and a bowl of water."

Seth was surprised when the girl did what she was asked. "Ma'am—"

She stopped him with a raised hand. "Dani, call me Dani."

He nodded. "Dani, I did something dumb." He went on to tell her how he'd lured the killer out only to become his hostage. "He's on the trail from Bear Wallow with a woman. Her name is Ivy."

Dani rattled off a description.

"Yeah, that's her. How did you know?"

"She works with Hawke as a State Trooper."

"That makes me feel better. She said she was a trooper but the way the killer talked to her, I thought she was lying about that." A huge weight, heavier than that pack he'd been hauling, lifted from his conscience.

"Whereabouts on the trail?" Dani asked as Kitree returned with the things Dani asked for.

"We'd passed Miner Basin about twenty minutes before Ivy told me to run. We'd just sat down, had a granola bar and water. We hadn't put the packs back on and I'd hoped we were spending the night. I knew…ouch!"

Dani had begun washing at the cuts and scrapes on

his face. "Keep talking, it will hurt less."

"Anyway, Zach, he was going pee and she tapped my foot and mouthed, 'Run', so I grabbed the flashlight and ran. He shot once, but he wouldn't know where I was in the dark. But I'm worried about Ivy. He had a cord around her neck to make her obey."

Dani's lips formed a thin line as they pressed together. "Kitree, wake up your dad. If we're going to catch up to them, we need to get going."

"I can take you to them," Seth offered.

Dani studied him. "We can't ride right up to them if they recognize you. We'll have the benefit of surprise on our side by going up there just the two of us. Ivy will recognize me and she'll know what to do."

Seth shook his head. "I caused all of this. I want to help."

"You did your bit by getting away and contacting us. You stay here and help Kitree and Tyson run things while Tuck and I are gone. If they haven't gone off trail, we'll catch up to them…" she glanced at her watch, "today and be back here by evening."

He still wasn't happy about not being able to help, but he knew she was right. Without him along the Skunk Bear King wouldn't know they were there to thwart him.

In less than an hour from the time Kitree woke her dad, he and Dani were headed through the trees toward the trail from Bear Wallow.

Seth stood at the end of the bunkhouse with Kitree and her mom watching them disappear into the night. He sighed and asked, "Now what?"

"I'll take you over to bunk with Tyson in his room. He'll instruct you in the morning about what to do to help take up the slack of Tuck and Dani being gone." Kitree's mom nodded her head toward the lodge.

He glanced over at Kitree. She smiled and nodded. At least he'd get to spend time with her. Though his mind wouldn't be settled until he knew Ivy was okay.

Chapter Nineteen

Hawke was glad to have Bryce on his side. The man had good ideas and knew the mountains better than he did. They rose early and set up two traps on well-used wildlife trails that Bryce had seen the killer use before to enter this area. Their only problem with the traps would be the person leading would be the one caught in the trap. The good thing, if it was Seth or Ivy, he and Bryce didn't think the man would take the time to get them down, which would keep them safe. But it would also let the killer know they knew where he was going.

"We'll have to set up two different vantage points to keep an eye on the area," Hawke said, handing Bryce a piece of jerky.

The man nodded and took a bite. He chewed and chewed before he finally swallowed, drank, swallowed, and drank. It appeared the reason the man spoke garbled and very little was that his throat was messed up from his injuries.

Bryce pointed to a spot that Hawke had thought would be good. "There. No one will see, but I'll see everything."

Hawke nodded. "I thought of that spot too. And I'll be down the side of the mountain." He pointed to an outcropping of rock that would be shaded all day, so no one would see him sitting under it.

The sound of a helicopter brought them both to their feet. "I wonder what news they have for us." Hawke turned the satellite radio on and waited to be contacted.

"Hawke, this is Steve, can you hear me? Over."

"I hear you. Over."

"The boy got away last night. He ended up at the hunting lodge. From what Sage told Nathan this morning, Dani and Tuck took off around one a.m. to try to catch up to them. Over."

"Shit!" Hawke said and stomped around in a circle. Dani and Tuck had no reason to go after the killer. They weren't trained to deal with the likes of the people he dealt with.

Bryce put a hand on his arm and pointed up to the helicopter.

Hawke nodded. "Do you have a location on any of them? Over."

"The kid said they were on Bear Wallow trail past Miner Basin when Ivy told him to run. She must have known they were close to the lodge as did the kid. Over."

"Fly that trail and find them. Then let me know if Dani and Tuck have caught up to Ivy and Zach. Over."

"Copy." The helicopter lifted and Hawke stared at it not seeing the aircraft as his mind sped through the last time he saw Dani. She'd been upset with him for not spending the night. Damn, he hoped he had another night to hold her.

He turned the radio off, shoved it into his pack, and shouldered the backpack.

"Where are you going?" Bryce asked, stepping in front of him.

"I can't sit here and wait. My partner is going after that killer with her wrangler. They're no match for that lunatic." He whistled for Dog and started to walk away.

Bryce grabbed his arm, stopping his forward motion. "You'll make danger for her. Stay. He'll come here." He shrugged. "If she follows. You'll keep her safe." Then he swallowed and took a drink of water.

Those were the most words he'd said at once since Hawke met the man. And damn it! He was right. The killer was set on getting the wolverine. He would get here. Hopefully, Dani and Tuck would be safe following him.

《》《》《》

Hawke and Bryce waited until noon for the helicopter to return to learn what they could before climbing up to their lookouts. When it finally hovered, Steve contacted him.

"Hawke, we spotted Dani and Tuck. They were riding up the trail toward Steamboat Lake. We traveled up and down the trail a couple of times and didn't see any sign of Ivy and Zach. Over."

"He went off trail after Seth got away. Over," Hawke replied.

"Backup is coming up from Copper Creek right now. Over."

"What is their frequency? They need to head more

Wolverine Instincts

east to keep from running into Zach and Ivy. He could bolt if he sees that many law enforcement officers together. Over." Hawke wanted this guy bad. He was too cunning and needed to be put behind bars before he killed more innocent people.

Steve told him the frequency. "Want me to watch from up here or come down there? Over."

"It's good to have eyes up above. Stay in the copter, but don't hang around here too much. That will spook him too. Over."

"Copy." The helicopter rose and drifted over the top of the mountain.

Hawke dialed in the frequency Steve gave him. "This is Hawke do you copy? Over."

"Hawke, it's Rafe. We're just heading off the Copper Creek trail using the coordinates Steve gave us. Over."

"Rafe, go more east. I want you to come up east of the coordinates. That's the only direction I'm sure the suspect won't be coming from. Over."

"Any idea what time he'll arrive? Over."

"None. He's gone off trail according to Steve. Over."

"I'll keep this frequency open. I'll let you know when we're ready to come over the top. Over."

"Copy. I'll keep you updated. Over." Hawke glanced over at Bryce. "If he's going off trail, has lost one of his pack mules, and I'm sure Ivy is being a pain, how long do you think it will take him to get here?"

"Tomorrow." Bryce set down his pack and rifle and pulled out a handful of pine nuts.

Hawke sighed. That was his thoughts as well. Luckily, Dani didn't know this was where the man was headed. She would go to the crime scene, find no one, and hopefully return to the hunting lodge. That helped him relax, knowing she wouldn't catch up to the man.

But what did he tell the officers hiking in to capture the killer when they arrived this evening and no one was here? He hoped they brought overnight provisions.

《》《》《》

Seth didn't mind doing the chores and helping with the guests, but his mind kept going to what would happen if Dani and Tuck said the wrong thing. Would they end up dead? Or would they be able to overtake him before he hurt anyone else? And what was Trooper Hawke doing all this time? He'd said he was in the wilderness. Did he find the wolverine den and was waiting for S.B.K. to return to trap it? Man, he wished he was there.

"Hey, I've told you twice not to do that," Kitree reprimanded him.

He looked down at the uncoiled rope at his feet. "Sorry. I keep wondering what is going to happen when Dani and your dad catch up to S.B.K."

She laughed. "What does S.B.K. mean?"

"Stands for Skunk Bear King. It's what he calls himself online. That's how I set up the meeting with him. I chatted online with a bunch of people who are obsessed with wolverines. He was the one who responded to my questions with the right answers. It's how I knew he was the one who shot my brother and killed the other guy." He peered into Kitree's eyes. "He's dangerous. I don't want your dad to get hurt."

"He'll be fine. He and Dani have helped Hawke with a couple of his investigations up here. They know how to handle themselves."

"How can you be so calm?" he asked, knowing if it were his family chasing down a killer he'd be beside himself.

"I know what they are capable of and they both have a lot to live for. They won't do anything stupid. Dad loves me and Mom. He wouldn't want to do anything that would make our life harder. And Dani loves Hawke. She wants to grow old with him. And we're all like a family. We depend on each other and care about each other. They won't do anything to jeopardize the family." She bent down and picked up the rope. "We have to get this coiled back up before Tyson sees this. He is OCD when it comes to the tack and barn."

Seth smiled and helped her get the rope coiled back up on the hook.

Tyson walked in and grinned. "What are you two love birds doing in here? Hiding from Sage or just from work?"

"We're not—" Seth stopped, seeing how red Kitree's cheeks were. "We were tiding up your rope. What do you want me to do now?" he asked, taking the conversation away from him and Kitree. But his face grew warm thinking Kitree was a pretty girl and she was smart.

《》《》《》

Hawke glanced up at the sky. It would be dark soon. Rafe had radioed an hour earlier that they were just over the rim on the east side. Hawke had suggested they bed down for the night. He didn't think anything would happen until morning, if Zach could keep Ivy moving without sleep.

He was sitting halfway up the side of the mountain

where he could keep an eye on the wolverine den and see the spot where Bryce was waiting. Dog lay beside him, his head on his paws, his eyes closed. But his ears twitched as he picked up different sounds.

Steve had swung by on the helicopter. They hadn't seen anything to help with whether or not the killer and Ivy were getting close or even headed this way.

Was Zach headed here? Would he want a wolverine that wasn't perfect? Hawke thought about that, and wondered if the killer wasn't coming here but rather to where he knew there was a pair staying. If he had information about the wolverines from Shelly, she would have been able to pull the files up and give him the coordinates of the male and female dens.

This was becoming too complicated. Had he brought in too many officers to take down this man who most likely wouldn't even show back up here.

He pulled the radio out of the side pocket of his pack. "Rafe, do you copy? Over."

"Hawke, I copy. Do you see him? Over."

"No. I was thinking that he may not be coming back here. We'll give him until the morning to show, and if he doesn't, we'll bag it. Over." Hawke hated to have wasted so much money the last two days but the more he thought about it, the man had a plan and he was sticking to it. He wanted the big male, not the one with the deformed foot. Which he would have figured out from following the tracks that the one here wasn't the one he wanted. Unless he thought it was the big male and he'd been hurt from getting out of the trap and after he followed it here and watched it, he realized it wasn't the one he wanted after all.

"Copy." Rafe ended the conversation.

Hawke glanced up at the spot where Bryce was settling in. "Come on," he said to Dog. "Let's go have another conversation with Bryce."

Hawke made it halfway up to where Bryce was waiting and the man walked up to him.

"I think Zach is headed back to where he set up the first trap. He wouldn't settle for the younger one with a deformed foot. He'd want the big male. This guy calls himself Skunk Bear King." Hawke watched the other man as he stated his reasoning.

Bryce nodded. "Makes sense. You want to go?"

Hawke glanced over where his backup was sleeping and then down at the snow bank where the young male wolverine had his den. "I think that's where he's headed. We could be there by morning."

Bryce nodded toward the top of the mountain where the others waited. "What about them?"

"I told Sheriff Lindsey if the killer didn't show in the morning we'd bag it." Hawke didn't want to call Rafe back and tell him he was on his own in the morning and that he and Bryce were headed to the crime scene. But he needed to let the man know they wouldn't be on this side of the mountain to tell him anything.

"You say you were leaving?"

Hawke shook his head. "I need to radio and let him know." He pulled the radio out of his pack and contacted Rafe again.

"Did he surprise you? Over." Rafe asked.

"No. Bryce and I talked it over. We're going to the crime scene tonight. We have a feeling that's where he's headed. Over."

"What about tomorrow? Here? Over."

Hawke sighed and pressed the button on the radio. "I'll keep the radio and you can send some guys over the top at dawn and they can keep an eye on things. If you don't see him by noon, I say bag it, unless you get a call from me for help. Over."

"You're sure? He has one of your people hostage. We could come help. Over."

"I think the fewer the people the better. We'll get Ivy away safely and we'll get the killer. Over." He had confidence in his skills and Bryce's. He just hoped the young trooper would keep a clear head.

"Copy."

Hawke turned the radio off, shoved it in his pack, and tipped his head to the top of the mountain. "Let's get going if we want to be there by daylight."

Chapter Twenty

Zach was sick of Ivy. If she wasn't a State Trooper, he would have shot her right after the boy ran away. She'd had such a smug look on her face, he'd slapped her instead. He'd tried to split what was in the boy's pack between their two packs. The one Ivy carried weighed as much or more than she did. It made him happy thinking of how she struggled to carry it. The only downside, she was slowing down more and more each hour. At this rate he'd be lucky to get to the site to set up the trap by noon tomorrow.

He couldn't push her any harder, he knew her legs had to be giving out and he couldn't carry all of it.

After the boy took off, Zach left the trail. They walked for two hours and he stopped to let Ivy rest. They'd hiked through the wilderness all day, staying fifty yards up in the trees from the Minam Trail. It was the fastest and easiest route to where he wanted to go.

He'd hiked until he could tell the woman's legs wouldn't hold her up much longer. He tied Ivy to the tree and gagged her so she couldn't call out or go anywhere while he slept. Before turning in, he walked downhill from the camp to pee. He heard the sound of horses coming down the trail. A horse or two would help his problem immensely. He zipped up, grabbed his rifle and a flashlight, and worked his way down to the trail ahead of the sound of horses.

The moonlight wasn't any better than it had been the night before. He waited until they came around a bend in the trail and turned his flashlight in their faces.

"Hey!" shouted an angry female voice. "Get that damn light out of my face."

He laughed and said, "Get off your horses and walk toward me." He held the barrel of the rifle in the beam of the light. "Or you'll have spent your last day right here."

The woman and man dismounted and walked forward.

"That's close enough. Tie the horses to a tree and bring a rope over here with the two of you." He had this figured out. Yes, he was as smart and cunning as a skunk bear.

"We don't have any rope," the woman said.

"You've been up here in the mountains. You have a cord or a rope. You don't look like some sissy city person. Dig in that saddle bag and pull out something that will tie you up." He pointed the rifle at the man. "Or I'll put a bullet through your man."

The woman cursed better than most men he'd been around and opened the flap of the saddlebag. Out of the corner of his eye, he saw the man move toward his horse.

Without thinking, he pulled the trigger. The man

dropped and the woman threw something at him.

"You better take care of him or I'll put a bullet in you."

When she dropped to her knees by the man, he saw she'd thrown parachute cord at him. He chuckled, walked up behind her, and grasped her hands, tying them behind her back. She cursed and fought him the whole time but he finally got her tied and shoved her face down on the ground.

"You better hope someone comes along and helps you. If you follow me, I'll make sure you can't help him." He untied the horses and started through the trees to where he'd left his packs. Now he didn't need Ivy anymore. He'd leave her tied to the tree and keep on going. He'd be where he wanted to go by morning.

《》《》《》

Seth felt helpless. He'd expressed that when he'd been given a couple of hours to himself and he'd recorded a session for his podcast. He'd talked about how he'd tried to lure the killer and ended up a hostage, to running when Ivy told him to. He didn't like sitting at the lodge waiting for Tuck and Dani to return.

He could tell the others were starting to get worried. Sage kept glancing at the kitchen door every time there were footsteps or a door closed. Tyson had told him they'd saddle up horses if Dani and Tuck weren't back by morning. Kitree had stopped chattering. She sat at the table pushing her dinner around on her plate.

"How long does it take to get to where they were going by horse?" he asked, starting to feel the worry the other three were giving off.

"It should have been an easy ten hours there and

back if they didn't run into the guy who kidnapped you. Considering a struggle with the guy and then getting him and Ivy back, they still should be here by dark." Tyson picked up his glass of water and drank, not looking at Sage.

"And dark will be in about two hours," Seth said. "I think we should saddle up horses and go looking for them. They may need our help." He glanced at Sage, her eyes said yes, but her head shook.

"We don't need anyone else out there. They'll be here when they get here. Dani told us to keep things running as normal." Sage settled her gaze on her daughter. "Kitree, go get the kids playing games in the great room." Then her gaze landed on Tyson. "Light the fire ring outside and I'll get the ingredients together for the s'mores." She shifted her attention to Seth. "You can start on the dishes, while I get the s'mores tray ready."

He pushed away from the table and dumped the water Sage already had heating on the wood stove into the dishpan. He added soap and swished the water to make a few suds. While he was impressed with how well the lodge provided nearly 5-star accommodations when they did everything as it had been done a hundred years ago, he didn't like having to help with the household chores.

He poured the silverware that had been used by the guests into the pan and scrubbed it with a brush before putting them in a dishpan of lukewarm water and sanitizer to rinse. Then he set the silverware in an upright drying rack. He was halfway through the plates when Sage took over.

"Go get some sleep. If Dani and Tuck aren't back

Wolverine Instincts

by morning, you and Tyson need to go look for them."

Seth felt his chest constrict. These people had all been so nice to him. He hoped nothing had happened to the people they loved.

«»«»«»

Hawke and Bryce arrived at the crime scene just as a thin veil of sunlight broke on the top of the mountain to the west. He was tired but Bryce didn't seem to be lagging at all.

As they were hiking during the night he'd heard a far-off shot. He wondered if Ivy had dragged her feet one time too many and Zach shot her or if someone was taking advantage of his being preoccupied with finding the killer and was poaching.

"Now what?" Bryce asked.

"Do you know where the male wolverine's den is?" Hawke asked. He only knew it must be in this area for the man to have set up a trap and the biologists to have set up a hair snare.

Bryce shook his head.

Hawke ran a hand over his face and felt the beginning of a scruffy beard. How had Zach made it look like he had such a full beard when he was up here? And why a disguise if he didn't think he'd get caught? Another puzzle to find the answer to when he caught the man.

"Since we don't know where he might be headed other than this general direction, we should probably split up, maybe go up a bit higher. I don't see the animal having a den down at this elevation, do you?" Hawke pulled out a granola bar and offered it to Bryce.

"I'm good. And, no. He would be higher." He pulled out a pouch and poured pine nuts in his hand.

Hawke poured dog food on the ground for Dog. He ate his granola bar and sipped water, remembering what the ridge had looked like higher up. He swallowed his last bite and drank water before saying, "I think we should take up spots inside the tree line and watch the open area above."

Bryce nodded.

"He's not going to set up a trap right next to the den but he may visit the den to make sure the wolverine is still there."

"Makes sense." Bryce shifted the mask on his face with his hand and said, "What if he doesn't check the den?"

"I'm sure we'll know when he arrives. He thinks he's outsmarted the police. I doubt he'll be sneaking around." Hawke stuffed his canteen in his pack along with the granola wrapper. "I'll go north and you go south."

Bryce nodded, shouldered his pack, and headed south.

"Let's go," Hawke said to Dog and they started up the side of the ridge at an angle to the north. The sun was up and shining down on the white basalt of the ridge top when Hawke sat with his back against the trunk of a pine, with a view of anyone of anything coming up through the forest and a view of a long span of rocky ridge.

"Now we wait," Hawke said to Dog and settled back with his hat tipped slightly over his eyes to keep out the glare from the white rocks.

《》《》《》

Seth and Tyson headed up the trail as soon as it was light. Sage had put together a first aid kit, blankets, and food. They had those in their saddlebags.

"I didn't want to say anything in front of Sage…" or Kitree, Seth thought, "but since they haven't come back, do you think that means something happened to them?"

Tyson peered over his shoulder at Seth. "I'm pretty sure they must have run into the guy who shot your brother. Dani would have been home if there hadn't been trouble. Sage knows that too. Keep an eye out for anything that doesn't look right in the trees."

Seth's heart raced as fear and uncertainty kicked in. He swallowed and breathed in and out like Alex taught him to do when he was scared. I wish Alex was the one up here. He'd know what to do. But his brother wasn't here and Tyson would need his help with whatever they found.

He'd guess they'd traveled about three miles and Tyson pushed his horse into a trot. Seth followed his gaze on the trail ahead. That's when he spotted someone on the side of the trail. Then a person, Dani, stood up and waved her arms.

When they stopped and dismounted, Seth recognized Ivy sitting on the ground beside Tuck, who had blood on his shirt.

"What happened?" Tyson asked, getting the first aid kit out of his saddlebags.

"That son-of-a-bitch shot him. When I get my hands on him, I'll—"

Ivy stood up stopping Dani's rant. "We need to get back to the lodge and radio the state police. They have to let Hawke and whoever else is up here looking for Zach know he is loose and he has your horses." She glanced down at Tuck. "But first we need to get him bandaged up and out of here."

Seth dug in his saddlebag for the food and water, as Dani and Ivy used the first aid kit to clean and bandage the wound in Tuck's shoulder.

"Can you sit on the horse?" Tyson asked Tuck.

"I have to. I don't think I have the energy to walk." Tuck sat up and his face paled.

Seth stepped up. "We can get you on and walk beside the horse to make sure you don't fall."

Tuck glanced at him and gave a slight nod.

Tyson and Seth grasped him under the arm on his uninjured side and around his waist to get him to his feet. It took all four of them to get him in the saddle.

"I'll ride behind him and hold him up," Dani said, putting her foot in the stirrup and swinging up behind. "I'm glad you brought Snickers. He's used to all kinds of weight on him."

Tyson grinned and said, "I didn't know how well Seth could ride and didn't want him getting bucked off."

Seth glared at Tyson as Ivy pulled herself up into the saddle of the other horse. Dani led the way with Snickers, Tyson fell in behind leading the horse Ivy rode, and Seth took up the rear. He didn't mind following behind, though he had to jog every once in a while to catch up. The horses walked faster than he did.

When they arrived at the lodge, Dani took Tuck straight to the bunkhouse. She said to Seth, "Go get Sage."

He bounded into the lodge and burst into the kitchen. The woman wasn't there. He looked in each room after knocking and no one answered. Then he remembered the washroom out behind the lodge where a gas generator ran an industrial-sized washing machine. He found Sage there.

"You're back. What?"

"You need to come to the bunkhouse. Tuck was shot."

She dropped the sheet she'd been hanging and ran around the side of the building.

Knowing he wouldn't be much help with a wound, he picked up the sheet, hung it up, and continued hanging the rest of the laundry. When he finished, he wandered over to the bunkhouse. The horses were gone. He glanced to the barn, then walked up and knocked on the bunkhouse door.

Kitree answered the door. "It's you. Come in." She pulled him in and shut the door. "We don't want the guests to get worried if they know Dad's been shot."

"Does he need medical care?" Seth asked, watching Sage hover over her husband as Ivy wrapped a bandage around his shoulder. Dani and Tyson were gone.

"Dani is getting the helicopter ready to take him to the valley. She said a doctor needed to get the bullet out so it could be used as evidence against the man who shot him."

Ivy turned from helping Sage and smiled at Seth. "Good to see you knew where to run to." Her face was purple and scratched.

"Did he do that to you when I left?" Seth swallowed, fearing he had caused harm to the State Trooper.

"The bruise is from Zach. The peeled skin was me trying to get the gag out of my mouth while tied to a tree." She glanced at Tuck and back to Seth. "When I heard the gunshot, I knew he must have shot someone. I was trying like hell to get loose and finally managed to get the gag off and called out several times. Dani showed up. She said she was looking for us and that Zach shot Tuck. She got me loose and we did what we could to keep him from bleeding too much and keep him warm."

"Where do you think Zach's headed?" Seth asked. His anger was building at the man who killed a hiker and shot his brother and now Kitree's dad. Someone had to stop him.

"He is obsessed with getting a wolverine. He is wherever the wolverine is."

Tuck groaned and she went over to aid Sage.

Dani entered. "I radioed the State Police. They know that this guy shot another person and that he has two horses. If he harms them, I'll go after him myself." Her body vibrated with her anger and her eyes flashed.

"Hawke told me he was in the wilderness. Why hasn't he caught up to him yet?" Seth asked the question that had been banging around in his head.

"He has limited contact with the outside world when he's here. He may not know the guy kidnapped you and Ivy. He wasn't at the crime scene, we were there and waited around to see if Hawke or anyone else showed up. We would have been home shortly after dark if the killer hadn't blinded us with a flashlight and ordered us to give him the horses. Tuck went for his rifle and the guy shot him and tied my hands. I had my knife in my boot. I got to it and had my hands loose before he probably made it back to where Ivy was tied to a tree. But I didn't know she was up there until she called out later."

"It took me a while to get that damned gag out of my mouth after he left." Ivy glared at no one in particular. "I'd love to be the one to arrest him, but I don't have a clue where he was going. He never talked about where the wolverine was. He mumbled to himself more than he talked to me."

"I'd like you to stay here while I take Tuck and Sage to the valley and get him medical care. Kitree can take care of the meals. She's helped her mom enough and Sage has prepared several different easy meals for emergencies like this." Dani turned to Seth. "I told them to let your family know you will be here for a few more days. We could sure use your help and I don't have room in the helicopter to take you down along with Sage and Tuck."

"As long as my family knows I'm safe, I'm good with staying." He glanced at Tuck and asked, "Where's Tyson, I'll go see if he needs help."

Dani said he was in the barn preparing to take some guests on a ride.

Seth left the bunkhouse and hurried over to the barn.

Tyson glanced up from where he was tightening a cinch. "Hey, want to give me a hand saddling the horses. Those two over there need brushed and then put on the saddle blankets next to them."

"Sure. Where are you going with this group of riders?" Seth asked as he picked up a brush and quickly brushed the dirt off the animal's shiny red hair.

"Not toward Minam Lake, that's for sure. I have to keep these people safe. I'll take them up on Jim White Ridge. It's only a half-a-day trip." Tyson finished saddling that horse and put the bridle on.

Seth moved over to brush the next horse. "What do I need to do while you're gone?"

"Keep an eye on the horses, check on the guests hanging around the lodge, and make sure they are staying out of the off-limits areas." Tyson started saddling the next horse in line.

"What are the off-limits areas?" Seth asked.

"Dani's room and office, the laundry room, the bunkhouse, and the area where Dani's aircraft are tied down. Though it will only be her plane until she gets back with the copter." Tyson finished looping the cinch strap and turned to the horse Seth just set a saddle blanket on.

"If Kitree needs help, you can help her too. She's a pro at taking over for her mom when something comes up. But it's a lot of work to set out the dishes and cook the meal by herself."

Seth nodded. "I can manage all of that. You be careful." He helped lead the six horses out to the hitching post in front of the barn.

Two adults and three kids walked down from the lodge porch. City slickers, Seth thought and watched as Tyson took the time to explain to the family how to make the horse do what they wanted and reassured them that none of the horses bucked or bolted. That they were all gentle and had been taking people on rides for years.

When they were out of sight, Seth decided to walk around and see exactly where the off-limits areas were and then he'd see if Kitree needed help. Even though he had hoped to get on a horse and head toward Minam Lake and see if he could find a way to make S.B.K. pay for all the hurt he'd caused so many people.

Chapter Twenty-one

Dog's low growl woke Hawke. He put a hand on Dog to let him know he was awake and then eased his cowboy hat off his face.

He listened and scanned the forest that was within sight. Someone was coming with horses. The steady muffled thud of hooves and the cracking of small branches drew closer. Zach didn't have horses. Who else would be coming this way on horseback? It wasn't a designated trail. Not that trail usage was enforced.

The sounds stopped. A horse blew out air and the birds in the trees continued chirping. Hawke rose slowly and motioned for Dog to follow. He'd left his pack at the base of the tree but had his shotgun in his hands as he carefully made his way deeper into the trees and brush toward where he'd heard the horse snort.

Drawing closer he heard the creak of a saddle, an occasional thump of a hoof, and the swish of a tail catching on brush making twigs and leaves rattle.

Creeping closer, he stopped, seeing the dark shape of a horse beyond the brush in front of him. He moved to the edge of the brush and peeked around. His gut twisted and his heart hammered in his chest. The horses were the ones Tuck and Dani rode at the lodge. Two bulging packs were tied onto the saddle of Tuck's horse. They both had their heads down as if tired.

He scanned the area around the horses. He didn't see anyone. There was no guessing here. Zach had somehow taken the horses away from Dani and Tuck. He hoped like hell that he hadn't shot them both. Hawke's blood ran cold at the thought and then hot with revenge.

Dog whined and put his head against Hawke's fisted hand that ached as he clenched the shotgun.

He glanced down at the animal and relaxed his hand. He knelt beside Dog. "We need to get these horses away from here. You lead them downhill, while I cover their tracks."

Hawke walked out from behind the brush. Both horses glanced at him but didn't make a sound. He knew that Dani's horse was more likely to follow Dog. He took their bridles off as quietly as possible and then led Dani's horse by the lead rope with the second one tied to its saddle. They walked downhill about thirty feet, out of sight of where they had been tied and he handed the lead rope to Dog, who took it in his mouth. "Keep going. I'll be right behind you." He waved a hand motioning for the dog to continue downhill.

As the horse followed the dog, Hawke backtracked and using a limb from a tree, brushed back and forth across the trail disguising the horse's tracks. He followed Dog, brushing away the tracks, all the way down to the Minam Trail. Then he took the horses and led them to the spot where he'd hid his horse and mule earlier in the week. As he took off their tack, Hawke inspected it for any traces of blood. Finding none, he felt less anxious about what might have happened to Dani and Tuck. But the man could have caught them when they were on the ground and there was no telling what he would do to get hold of horses and get rid of Ivy. Shit! He hadn't thought about what the man might have done to her.

He grabbed the packs and stomped over to a large boulder. Anger had him throwing the packs behind the boulder out of sight. He walked back to the horses and staked them out so they could get water and eat. They both went straight to the trickling creek to get a drink.

"Come on. We're going to catch this guy once and for all." Hawke retraced their steps to the trail, once again covering their tracks. After they crossed the trail, he went straight up to where the horses had been left.

He wished he had a way of communicating with Bryce to see if Zach was checking out the wolverine's den. All he could do was wait here for the man to return. Waiting, especially when he was worried about someone he cared about, wasn't easy for him. His mom had always told him patience would gain more than boldness.

He and Dog didn't have long to wait. He heard someone coming through the forest from uphill and moved behind a tree with Dog at his back.

"I'll get you now skunk bear," the man mumbled as he came into sight.

Hawke peeked around the tree. The man walking toward him wasn't Zach. It was the man from the sketch made from Seth and Alex's description. Right down to the head-to-toe camouflage. How had he gotten hold of Dani and Tuck's horses? Hawke was confused. He knew that Zach had Ivy and Seth. No, he didn't know that. He only knew the man who called himself the Skunk Bear King had taken them. He assumed it was Zach because he had Ivy and the description he was given had matched the one he'd been given for Zach.

As he muddled this through his head, the man stepped in front of him and Dog lunged at the man's raised arm.

Hawke ducked and the blow struck him alongside the head. He rolled to the side and kicked out at the man's legs. The man went down. His leg landed across Dog, who yelped.

Hawke used all his strength to push to his feet. He had to save Dog and keep the man from getting away.

The man raised his leg, looked at Hawke, and slammed his leg down on Dog. The animal yelped again, and Hawke slammed his fist into the man's face before hopping on top of the man's chest and hitting him again. When the killer didn't move, Hawke, grabbed his leg and twisted it off Dog.

The man roared to life, coming up swinging. He landed a blow that knocked Hawke backward.

His head struck the tree making an awful sound, roiling his stomach, and causing stars before everything went dark.

《》《》《》

Water struck him in the face. Hawke sputtered and opened his eyes. The man standing over him swayed and had no face. "What the hell?" Hawke tried to talk

Wolverine Instincts

but it came out gibberish.

Whining filled his ears as a body pressed against his side. He moved the arm that was over the top of something furry. The body shook.

"I couldn't get here any faster," the faceless man said, his voice sounding as gibberish as Hawke's own words.

"What happened?" Hawke tried to sit up and his head whooshed and felt like someone stood over him pounding on his head with a pine tree.

"The wolverine poacher showed up. I watched him. I know where the dens are. When you didn't come out of the trees behind him, I just watched. Then he came back down here." The man swallowed, pulled out his canteen, and took a couple of drinks. "I heard Dog yelp and ran, but only saw you hit the tree with your head. The man ran that way." He pointed to the right of where he was standing.

Hawke thought hard remembering where he was. It slowly came back to him. "West? He's headed west?"

"More northwest, I'd say."

As the man talked and Hawke stared at him, he realized who the man was and why he had on a mask.

With this realization, he tried to look at Dog. The animal had been hurt to have cried out as he had. But lifting his head and trying to focus made his head throb more and his stomach heave.

He leaned away from the dog and vomited.

"You need medical help," Bryce said.

"How's Dog? What kind of damage did that son-of-a-bitch do to my dog?" Hawke wiped the back of his hand across his mouth and leaned back against the tree.

Bryce knelt beside him and checked out Dog. "He

may have a cracked rib. They're tender anyway." He shrugged.

Hawke tried to pull on his t-shirt under his flannel shirt and rip it up, but the movement made his stomach heave again. He rolled to his right and spilled what little was left in his stomach.

Re-centering himself, he said, "You need to try to wrap his ribs where you think they are cracked. He has to be able to walk without too much pain. The killer had Dani and Tuck's horses. I moved them down below the trail in a ravine. We'll need them to get me to the lodge."

Bryce stood and walked away.

"Where are you going?" Hawke asked, thinking the man had decided this was all more than he could handle.

"To get my pack. I dropped it back there when I heard Dog. I have a first aid kit in it." The man disappeared in the trees.

Hawke hoped the killer was far from here. He was in no shape to deal with him if the man returned to finish what he'd started. Dog wiggled beside him and Hawke closed his eyes. Damn, he'd made a mess of things.

《》《》《》

Hawke had barely dropped off and he felt someone shake him.

"Stay awake. I need you to help," a voice said.

Forcing his eyes open, Hawke once again stared at a faceless man. His memory kicked in faster this time and he remembered who the man was and why he needed help.

Dog whined as Hawke tried to turn toward the

animal against his left side. "It's okay boy. We have to fix you," Hawke said, putting his hand over Dog's muzzle. Not tight, just to be ready if Dog tried to take a bite out of Bryce.

"I'll be as gentle as I can, but it's going to be hard to try and put this around him and not pull it too tight." Bryce stared into Hawke's eyes.

"Go ahead. I'm ready."

"You don't look ready. Your skin is taking on a green tone and your eyes aren't exactly tracking."

"Go ahead, then go get the horses." Hawke didn't care about him. He had to get Dog fixed well enough to travel to the lodge and get him helicoptered out to the vet.

"Why don't we use your radio and see if I can get some help down here to help get you and Dog out of here?" Bryce asked.

"My pack is over by the tree where I was watching from. You can get the radio after you get Dog wrapped up." Hawke was beginning to drift off. He shook his head and made it start throbbing. He gritted his teeth and said, "Get this done."

Dog whined but he didn't try to bite Bryce or try to get loose. When they finished, he sat up and stared at them as if to say, 'Let's go get that asshole that did this to me.'

"I'll go get your pack. Then see if you can walk to the horses. I'm not very good with them." Bryce disappeared before Hawke could think of anything to say to that.

《》《》《》

Hawke wanted to scream at Bryce to leave him alone, but he knew that wasn't going to happen. The man had medals for bringing wounded out of enemy gunfire. He wouldn't leave Hawke behind even if he died. Finally, he stopped and they were in the area where he'd left the horses. The animals were still there, thankfully. Bryce had come back from getting his pack without it. He said there wasn't a pack there but he'd seen footprints around the tree.

Hawke knew who had it. The man they were after. That meant he had the radio on the frequency that he used to talk to Rafe. And he had Hawke's clothes, food, and dog food. Thankfully, Hawke had all his weapons and his badge hung around his neck. All the important things were still with him.

"Walk up to the red horse and grab the rope hanging from its halter, lead it over here, and tie it to a tree. Then go get the other one," Hawke said, lowering onto a downed tree. His head still felt like someone was beating on it with a pine tree.

He was nauseous but there wasn't anything left in his stomach to vomit. Dog was walking slow and sure-footed. Hawke didn't blame him. His ribs probably hurt and there was no telling what kind of bruising or possible internal injuries he could have sustained.

Every time he thought about the look on the man's face and how viciously he'd slammed his leg down on Dog, it made Hawke even more determined to bring him to justice.

Bryce led Dani's horse over and tied him to a tree. Hawke stood and using the horse to hold him up, walked over to where the blanket was draped over the saddle and picked it up. Bending to grab the blanket caused his vision to blur and he toppled over.

Chapter Twenty-two

Seth heard the helicopter returning before he saw it. The thump of the blades in the air was a clear sign Dani was about to arrive.

Tyson had returned from taking the family on a ride an hour earlier. They'd both unsaddled and put the horses in the corral. Then Seth went to see if he could help Kitree. She'd chased him out of the kitchen saying his talking distracted her.

Now he followed Tyson to the landing pad next to where the plane sat beside a grass runway.

The helicopter lowered down on the X made of dirt in the mowed circle that was the landing pad. Once the aircraft landed and the engine was turned off, Tyson began tying the helicopter down to the large concrete blocks with metal loops on top of them.

Seth didn't know how to make the knots so he met Dani when she walked out from under the rotors. "How's Tuck?"

"He'll live. He lost a lot of blood. They took the

bullet out and were pumping him full of fluids. The plan is to keep him in the hospital overnight and then he'll go to his family's ranch outside of Eagle and recuperate. Sage will stay with him, then when I fly guests to Alder in a couple of days, she'll come back with me."

Seth was relieved to hear Tuck would be fine. "That's real good news. Things here have been going fine. I think."

Tyson joined them. "Tuck?"

Dani repeated what she'd said and asked about the trail ride and if any of the guests had missed them.

"A few have asked. I just said there was an emergency and you had to fly Sage and Tuck out." Tyson glanced over at Seth. "Ivy's been giving people self-defense lessons and Seth's doing okay handling things. Just wish he could do some of the trail rides."

Dani shook her head as they entered the lodge. "He doesn't have enough horse sense or know his way around these mountains."

"I found my way here the other night," he said, thinking he'd been pretty lucky to have found the lodge but he wasn't going to tell anyone that.

"Dani, how are Tuck and Sage?" one of the guests asked.

"They're fine. Just had to take care of some family business down in the valley. How was your day?" Dani asked, moving the people away from the dining room.

Seth took that to mean he was to let Kitree know Dani was back and that Tuck was fine. He slipped through the swinging dining room door and into the kitchen.

Kitree had flour all down the front of her and long

noodles hanging over a rod that went the length of the table.

"Dani's back. She said your dad is doing well." He told her what Dani had told him.

A smile spread across Kitree's face. The first one since they'd brought her dad to the bunkhouse this morning. "That is good news!" she waved a hand at the table. "The noodles are done. As soon as the chicken and broth start boiling, I'll add them to the pot. Could you wash your hands and cut them into two-inch noodles?"

"Sure." He went to the sink and poured water over his hands, then scrubbed with a liquid soap, and rinsed. Grabbing a knife, he began cutting the noodles.

"What are you making besides the chicken and noodles?" he asked, used to having conversations when he helped his mom in the kitchen.

"I'm cooking potatoes to mash, and I made a large green salad from the greens Dani brought back from the last trip she made." Kitree stood by the wood stove stirring a large steaming pot.

He didn't see how she could cook on a wood stove this time of year. It was over 80° outside. He felt his t-shirt clinging to his perspiring skin as he cut the noodles. When he was finished, he put them in the bowl Kitree had provided while he worked.

"You can leave now, I can tell the heat is getting to you," Kitree said, picking up the bowl and moving back to the stove. "Just come back in to help set the table at five-thirty."

"I'll come back." He left the kitchen and dining room and used the back door at the end of the hallway that passed Dani's room. He was headed to the shower house to rinse off the sweat and wash out his t-shirt. He'd borrowed the shirt from Tyson this morning since all he had were the clothes he showed up in.

He stepped into the shower house and stopped. "What are you doing here?"

Zach's crazy eyes stared at him from the far side of the small building. His beard was no longer a five o'clock shadow. It now looked more like the beard he saw on him the first time they met. When he killed the hiker and shot Alex.

"This is where you ran to. I should have known. And you're the one who brought in all the cops, aren't you?" Zach lunged across the space toward him.

Seth stepped to the side and Zach hit the wall. He knew he was no match for the more muscled man who outweighed him by thirty pounds. But he had to keep him away from the guests and the rest of the staff at the lodge.

He dashed to the door, threw it open, and ran into the forest away from the buildings. He heard the muffled pounding of feet behind him as he ran for his life and to save all the innocent people at the lodge.

"I'll get you!" yelled Zach and then everything grew quiet except for his breathing, which sounded amplified. He stopped and looked over his shoulder. Nothing moved behind him. He spun around and searched the forest for any sign of Zach. It was as if he'd disappeared. How could that happen?

Seth's breathing slowed and he took one step and then another back toward the lodge. After about fifty feet, he started running. The crazy killer was going to the lodge. There were too many people who could get hurt there. He had to stop the man before he harmed anyone else.

He wasn't a hero but he couldn't let anyone else be hurt. Especially Kitree.

The door still stood open to the shower house. He stopped and surveyed the area behind the lodge and then around the barn and corrals to see if the man was hiding. When he didn't see anything out of the ordinary, he proceeded, straight to the back door. He had to radio the authorities and let them know the killer was here.

Once inside the lodge, he listened. Only the usual murmur of voices of guests visiting in the great room. He slipped into the office where the radio was set up and closed the door. On his twelfth Christmas, his parents gave him a ham radio. He knew all the rules and how to contact authorities.

He dialed in the emergency number and spoke, "This is Mini Nerd trying to contact any law enforcement agency. Over."

"Mini Nerd, this is Sheriff Lindsey of the Wallowa County Sheriff's Department. What do you need? Over."

"The man who kidnapped a State Trooper and a teenager is at Charlie's Lodge. Over."

"We're in the Eagle Caps looking for him. We'll be there soon. Over."

"Copy that. Hurry. Over."

"Roger that. Over."

He turned the radio off and leaned back in his chair. Now to keep people alive until the police arrived.

«»«»«»

The rocking motion of the horse didn't help Hawke's head or his stomach. He'd wanted to walk, but even though Bryce wasn't crazy about horses, he'd insisted they'd get to the lodge quicker if they rode. And Hawke had to agree, he didn't think he could walk the five miles to the lodge.

Several hikers and a string of horses passed them heading up into the mountains. They all stared at Bryce's covered face and then at him barely able to stay on the horse. And, of course, there was Dog with a dark blue wrap around his chest. They must have looked like something out of a horror movie. The victims that had gotten away from the zombies or some other creature reigning havoc on the world.

If they only knew there was a crazy man who wanted to poach a wolverine and had killed someone and wounded another. They would most likely all turn around and head home. Hawke leaned toward one of the hikers and said, "Be careful. There's a crazy poacher out there."

The group exchanged looks and continued.

By the time they arrived at the lodge, Hawke could barely keep his eyes open and make sense of anything thanks to the pain in his head.

Dog growled. Hawke saw the hair on his hackles raise. Using every ounce of energy he could muster, he called out to Bryce, "Something's wrong."

The man turned and that's when Hawke realized there wasn't a horse in the corral and the doors to all the buildings were open.

Bryce slid off his horse, landed on his feet, and disappeared into the trees.

If Hawke hadn't been with this guy the last few days, he would have thought he'd been abandoned, but he understood, Bryce was the only one of the two of them still healthy enough to possibly save anyone who

Wolverine Instincts

needed saved.

"Come on. We might as well see what's going on." Hawke urged his horse forward, walking by the one Bryce had been riding. He stopped in front of the lodge. Inside there were people sitting in chairs and a man walking back and forth.

Hawke slid off the horse and landed gently to not start up any new drums in his head. Dog started up the steps.

"Heel," Hawke whispered and moved around to the side of the building. Before he reached the back, Bryce and Ivy walked out of the trees and waved him over.

His balance was off and his eyesight still doubled now and then, but he made it to the two who then hauled him fifteen feet deeper into the trees. "What's going on?"

Ivy nodded toward the lodge. "Zach showed up. Seth found him and used the radio. He made contact with Sheriff Lindsey who said they'd get here soon because they were up here. Then Seth told us about Zach. We rounded up the guests and sent them down the trail with Kitree. She's to call family to come pick them all up when she gets to the trailhead." Ivy glanced at Bryce. "He said he's been helping you."

"He has. In case he didn't introduce himself, Bryce Hendrix meet Trooper Ivy Bisset."

Bryce's eyes widened and he shook hands with Ivy. Her cheeks darkened in color.

"Who's in the lodge?" Hawke asked.

"Dani, Tyson, Seth, and Zach. He's trying to persuade Dani to fly him out of here." Ivy glanced at Bryce and then peered into Hawke's eyes. "She dismantled something on both of the aircraft before he found her. They won't fly anywhere even if he tries."

"Does he know you're here?" Hawke asked.

She shook her head and then said, "I'm not sure. If he went by where he left me tied, he'd know that I got loose. And this would be the closest place to go for help. But he hasn't seen me, that I know of."

"I'm going to go in the front and pretend I'm worse off than I look. While I'm causing havoc, you two come in the back and apprehend him." Hawke leaned against a tree for a minute to stop the world from spinning.

"You don't have to pretend anything," Bryce said, steadying him.

"What happened?" Ivy asked.

"I'll tell you later. But I think Zach has an accomplice or vice versa." Hawke pushed away from the tree. "Come on, Dog."

"Want me to help you to the front?" Bryce asked.

Either Hawke's head was getting better or Bryce was talking better than when they'd met. "I'll be fine. Just wait until you hear a lot of noise and then come in."

Ivy and Bryce nodded all four of their heads and Hawke headed out of the trees trying to decide which trees to dodge and which to walk through. He and Dog made it to the corner of the building before he had to lean against the lodge and let his vision rest and his head simmer down.

He heaved a sigh, pushed away from the building, and walked to the front using one hand on the wall to keep him walking straight. At the front, he followed the raised porch to the steps and holding onto the railing, slowly ascended the steps.

The door flew open as he placed both feet on the

Wolverine Instincts

porch. "Who the hell are you?" A man who looked a lot like the killer asked him.

"Oregon State Trooper Hawke. I'm here to arrest you for the kidnapping of State Trooper Ivy Bisset and Seth." Hawke was lucid enough to know not to say Seth's last name. But he was seeing stars again.

"Hawke!" Dani yelled as the world went dark.

Seth watched as the state trooper collapsed on the porch. He sprung out of his chair at the same time as Dani and Tyson. He and Tyson tackled Zach while Dani dropped down beside Trooper Hawke.

They were still trying to get the gun out of Zach's hand when a booted foot came down on Zach's wrist and held it on the floor. Ivy swooped in and grabbed the weapon. The man connected to the boot had on a mask.

Seth sat back and watched as the masked man pulled Zach's arms behind his back and held him as Ivy tied Zach's wrists with plastic ties she must have taken from Dani's shop.

"Hawke, Hawke? Can you hear me?" Dani held Trooper Hawke's head on her lap and Dog had his head on Dani's lap, right next to the trooper's head.

"He's got a concussion," the masked man said. "The poacher gave it to him."

Dani peered up at the man. "Who are you and why are you wearing a ski mask in August?"

"Bryce Hendrix." He shrugged. "I always wear a mask since I lost half my face in Afghanistan."

"What do you mean the poacher gave it to him?" Seth asked. "The poacher is right here. Has been for the last two hours, that I know of."

The masked man, Bryce shook his head. "This man isn't the poacher. He looks like him but he's not the same man. I've watched the poacher. He has a beard, always wears camouflage, and laughs like a crazy person." Bryce pulled out his canteen and took a drink.

Seth studied Bryce. "That's the man we saw kill the hiker and who shot my brother."

Dani pointed to Zach. "He shot Tuck last night when he stole our horses."

Bryce tipped his head toward the horses. "We brought them back. He must have given them to the poacher at a determined spot. The poacher showed up at the wolverine dens with the horses. After he knocked Hawke around, I showed up and the poacher ran away. Hawke had taken the horses and hidden them. We used them to get here." Bryce pointed at Hawke and took another drink before adding, "He needs medical attention. So does Dog. The poacher hurt him too. I think his ribs."

Dani glanced around the porch. "If you can take care of things here, I'll fly Hawke and Dog to the valley and tell Kitree to bring back any of the guests who want to come back." Her gaze landed on Ivy. "Do you want to fly out with me?"

"No, I'll hang around for Sheriff Lindsey to show up to fill him in and hand over Zach."

Seth wondered at how the adults could so quickly start thinking ahead when the man who had kidnapped him and Ivy lay on the floor, his crazy eyes staring daggers at all of them as he listened.

"What about the killer who's still running loose up here?" He studied Ivy and then Dani. "I don't think the guests should come back until the other guy is caught too."

Tyson jumped in, "Yeah, what if he knows this guy

is here and comes to try and get him free?"

"I'll stay here until he is caught," Bryce said.

"I don't know who you are or what qualifies you for putting your life on the line to catch a killer," Ivy said.

"Special Forces in Afghanistan." Bryce stood like Seth had seen military men stand with their feet apart and their hands behind their backs. He could stand like that and it didn't mean he could take down a killer.

Ivy, however, seemed impressed. "That's good enough for me. We'll need all the help we can get if this guy's accomplice does come here looking for him." She and Bryce hauled Zach to his feet and took him to the barn.

Dani slid out from under Trooper Hawke and said, "Tyson, go get the stretcher. We'll carry Hawke to the plane. It will be easier to get him in and out of if he doesn't come to when I get to the airport."

Tyson ran into the lodge and returned with two long sticks with canvas in between. As they lifted Trooper Hawke onto the stretcher, his eyes fluttered and he muttered something Seth didn't understand. But Dani said something back to him that also didn't make sense.

He and Tyson picked up the sticks on each end of the stretcher and carried Trooper Hawke out to the plane. As they loaded him, Dani raised a flap on the side of the plane and clinked around, before closing the flap and climbing into the pilot's seat.

"I'll try to come straight back. I want to stay with Hawke but I also need to be here. I'll have a friend sit with him at the hospital." She started the plane and Seth hopped out of the cargo area.

"Safe flight," Tyson said and closed the door.

Seth and Tyson ran to the edge of the airstrip and watched her take off.

"Man, she's a good pilot," Seth said with admiration. He'd thought about becoming a pilot at one time and had taken lessons. But the first time they hit rough weather he couldn't keep from vomiting and his parents decided they were wasting money on his lessons.

"She should be. She spent twenty years in the Air Force flying wounded out and officials into secret rendezvous." Tyson's words were filled with pride.

"Let's go see what Ivy and the masked guy are up to," Seth said, wanting to learn more about the new guy.

They walked into the barn and found Zach tied tight to a post and a gag in his mouth. His eyes blazed with hatred. A shiver slid down Seth's spine and left him feeling cold.

"They must be in the lodge." Tyson spun away, but Seth studied the man. He could see a lot of resemblance to the killer. Were they brothers?

"Come on!" called Tyson.

Seth jogged out to where Tyson waited for him.

"Why did you stay in there?" Tyson asked as they climbed the steps to the lodge.

"He does look a lot like the killer. I think they might be related." Seth and Tyson didn't find Ivy and Bryce in the great room. They entered the dining room and then heard voices in the kitchen.

Ivy had dished up chicken and noodles for the two of them. She was sipping the broth from a spoon, while Bryce just stared down at the bowl.

"How come you didn't wait for us?" Tyson asked,

grabbing a bowl and filling it.

Seth followed, filling a bowl and sitting down on the same side of the table as Bryce. "How are you going to eat with that mask on?" he asked.

The man beside him swiveled his head and stared at him. He must have realized Seth was just curious and not being a smart-ass because a smile showed through the mouth opening.

"I only eat food that requires silverware when I'm alone and can take the mask off." He shifted his gaze to Ivy as if he thought she should know that.

"We're all friends here. There's no reason you can't take your mask off," she said with a smile.

He shook his head. "You will all lose your appetite if I remove the mask." He picked up the bowl and spoon. "I'll eat outside." He left the room taking long strides.

Ivy started to follow.

Tyson stopped her. "Leave him be. If he doesn't want people to see his face, let him have his privacy."

Seth was glad Tyson said something. It was obvious the woman's curiosity had taken over her good sense. "Yeah. I can understand. If he is missing part of his face that means he must have went through something traumatic. He's probably lucky just to be alive." Seth watched Ivy as what he said sunk in.

"You're right. I was just curious about why he would be hiding behind a mask. In my line of work, that means they don't want their identity to be known because they do illegal things."

"If Hawke trusts him, then I think we know he's a good guy," Tyson said.

Seth nodded. That was one thing he'd noticed

about Trooper Hawke; he was honest and he could tell when a person was holding back.

Chapter Twenty-three

The pounding wouldn't go away but neither would the beeping sound. He'd become accustomed to the pounding, where in the hell did the beeping come from? Raising his heavy eyelids, Hawke stared up at a white ceiling. He raised a hand to wipe his face and discovered it had something attached that wasn't his shirt.

"Hawke, rest. You're in the Hospital."

He recognized the voice. "Justine, why are you here?" He flashed through his mind trying to remember why he would be in the hospital. Then it became clear. "Is Dani okay?"

"She's fine. She flew you out to get you medical care—"

He remembered. "Dog? Where is he? How is he?"

"Dr. Ashley has him. She called me a while ago and said no internal injuries and no rib fractures. He's just badly bruised and crying for you."

"Go get him and bring him here. Or better yet, find

my clothes and take me to him," Hawke shoved to sit up and the world spun again.

"Dr. Cameron says you don't have any internal damage to your brain. You just have to rest until the headache goes away. I can take you to my place and keep an eye on you and Dog until Dani can get home."

"She can't come home until winter, you know that. But I'm worried about what could happen to her and the others if the killer shows up at the lodge." He eased his way into a sitting position. The pounding wasn't as powerful as earlier. "You can take Dog and me home. I'm sure Herb and Darlene will come by and check on us."

"Are you sure?" Justine didn't look like she was going to do it.

"But I will need you to stay and do some searching on a computer for me. Just looking at you is making my head hurt. Trying to read a screen would make me sick." He smiled. "Call the doctor and see when I can get out of here."

She studied him and asked, "You'll stay home and not go charging up into the mountains to save the world?"

Hawke crossed his toes and said, "I promise not to go into the mountains until I have recovered."

Justine smiled. "That will be in three weeks." The triumph in her eyes would have made him laugh if he thought it wouldn't rev up the pounding.

She left the room and he replayed what had happened since he found the horses and right before he'd blacked out at the lodge. There had to be two people working together. There was no other explanation. But who was the killer? He needed to get

Wolverine Instincts

on the computer and dive into the dynamics of the Durn family.

《》《》《》

As soon as they walked through the door of Hawke's place, he collapsed into a chair and Dog lay down beside him.

"What do you want to eat?" Justine asked him.

"There should be a can of soup in the pantry." He settled his head against the back of the chair and closed his eyes. His head settled down when his eyes were closed.

The sound of a four-wheeler grew closer. Herb. He wasn't in the mood to go over what all had happened but he could pick the man's brain about the Durn family.

There was a knock on the door, and before Justine could answer it, the door opened.

"Hey, Justine. We saw you bring Hawke home. Is he okay?"

Hawke opened his eyes and found both Justine and Herb staring at him. "I'll be fine after a quiet evening and a night's sleep in my own bed," he said sarcastically.

Herb grinned. "Charming as ever. What happened?"

"I hit my head and Dani flew me and Dog out." Hawke reached down and patted Dog's head. "We were both injured, but we'll both be fine with some rest."

"I need to check the soup," Justine excused herself and trotted into the kitchen.

"What do you know about the Colby Durn family? Particularly the grandsons?" Hawke didn't feel like writing any of what he said down, but figured it would be good to have it on record.

"They have been skating around the law for a long time," Herb started.

"Wait a minute. Could you get Justine back in here? It hurts my head to—"

"Justine! Hawke wants you!"

"yell," Hawke finished, flinching at the pain from the man's loud voice.

"Yeah? What do you need?" Justine asked, appearing in front of him.

"Could you dig out my phone and set it to record? I want what Herb tells me to be documented."

Justine picked up the bag from the hospital with all of his belongings. She set his sheath and knife on the table and then his ankle holster and backup pistol. "I'm surprised they let you in the hospital with all of this," she said.

"Dani forgot to take it off me before we entered."

She found his phone and handed it to him to unlock with facial recognition. Then her finger taped several times on the screen and she said, "You're good to go."

"Thanks."

She retreated to the kitchen and Hawke motioned for Herb to take a seat.

"Herb Trembley is telling me about the Durn family," Hawke said and then motioned for Herb to start talking.

"Colby has been an outlaw his whole life. His son turned out pretty good despite his father, but the grandsons, they are as bad as their grandfather, if not worse. When they were in school, they were caught hurting the pets in their classroom. Then they were caught snaring cats and leaving them to die or be torn up by their dog." He shook his head. "Then one of them was sent away to either a juvenile detention center, or something like that for hurting a girl who refused his advances."

"By them, how many do you mean?" Hawke asked.

"Two of them. The twins, Zach and Zeke. I think it was Zeke who was sent away. Colby never talked about him much after that. Zach has been living with his grandfather and working as an appliance repairman."

"Do you know if Colby had an infatuation with wolverines?" Hawke asked.

"Not that I know of. But he was a trapper and a poacher. The fur buyers could tell he'd acquired some of his pelts out of season. You can tell by their coats. But other than that, they couldn't prove it."

"Would he help his grandsons do something illegal?" Hawke asked.

"If it was physically possible, yes, he would. Like I said, he's been an outlaw, thriving on going against the law his whole life."

"Thanks." Hawke hit the off button on his phone. "I now know Seth and I aren't crazy. There had to be an explanation for two different people who looked similar to be in two different places."

Justine walked in with a bowl of soup and a grilled cheese sandwich on a tray. A steaming cup of coffee sat in the corner.

"Thank you. This looks great." Then it hit him. "When was I brought into the hospital?"

"About six hours ago," Justine said.

"Why haven't I heard from Spruel that they have Zach in custody and the lodge is secured?"

"Maybe he doesn't know you're down here. Want me to call him?" Herb offered.

"He knows. I had Dani call and tell him everything." Hawke's stomach grumbled but he wasn't hungry. Something must have gone wrong.

«()»«()»«()»

Seth pondered all that had happened to him in the last week as he washed the dishes after they had eaten. When he'd suggested someone might take something out to Zach, both Ivy and Tyson glared at him. He thought even prisoners deserved food, but then he thought about how the man had force-marched them, with barely anything to eat and little to drink, and shot Tuck. Maybe he didn't need any dinner.

After the dishes were done and he'd put the leftover chicken and noodles in jars and sealed them, he put the quart jars in a box to take out to the ice house where they kept things cold. He knew all the work both Sage and Kitree had put into making these and wanted to make sure it could still be eaten when they returned.

The box was heavy and he wondered why he hadn't put half of the jars in the box and made two trips. He set the box down next to the door in the side of a mound of dirt. Grasping the handle, he heaved it open. The dank darkness emitted a puff of cool air and an odor that he'd not encountered when he'd helped Kitree bring things from the ice house. It was a foul odor. Had something spoiled? He reached inside, grabbing the battery-fueled lantern that hung from a hook on the inside of the door jamb.

Flipping the switch, the area lit up. Someone had been in here. Empty food containers littered the floor and the stench. He quickly put the jars in a corner, box

Wolverine Instincts

and all, turned off the lantern, closed the door, and ran back to the house. He found Tyson, Ivy, and Bryce in the great room discussing when they thought Dani would return.

"Someone has been in the ice house eating the food," he said, then bent over to catch his breath.

"What do you mean?" Tyson asked, standing.

"There are empty food containers on the floor and it stinks." Seth noticed Bryce straighten in his chair.

"It wasn't just an animal?" he asked.

"No, an animal can't get in," Tyson said. "Dani had it built as a large metal cylinder that she flew up here with her helicopter. Then they put dirt inside and outside of the metal to make it more natural and to keep it cool. She planned it to keep animals out. Even the door, which looks like wood has a metal sheet in the middle of it."

"Could a bear unlatch the door?" Bryce asked.

"No, it takes a person with two hands to unlatch the door. And it was latched when I got there," Seth said.

Bryce stood up. "Let's go see this."

"And smell it," Seth added.

The masked man stared at him a moment and then followed him back to the ice house.

Ivy sniffed the air. "What is that?"

Bryce opened the latch and then the door.

Seth stepped back as the smell seeped out.

"Wolverine," Bryce said, closing the door and scanning the area. "The poacher is here. He's been in there eating."

"Zach!" Ivy took out at a run toward the barn.

Seth and the others followed, but Bryce was the first one to the door. He stopped and sniffed. "He's here or been here," he whispered and waved the boys to the side. Then he said to Ivy, "Cover me."

She pulled a revolver out of the back of her waistband and nodded.

Seth was in awe that he would see the two take down the killer. As soon as the two disappeared into the barn through the man door, Seth ran to look inside.

He found Bryce holding the rope that had tied Zach to the pole and Ivy cursing.

"Maybe we should have brought him some dinner," Seth said.

That caught him three glares.

They all walked out of the barn and found six law enforcement officers standing in front of the lodge looking around.

Ivy walked toward them followed by Seth and Tyson.

"Sheriff Lindsey, we had the person who shot Tuck Kimbal, but we just discovered his accomplice got him loose."

The sheriff's gaze peered at Ivy then slid to him and over to Tyson. "Where's Dani or Hawke?"

"Hawke and Bryce…" Tyson looked around and so did Seth. Bryce had disappeared. "Where did he go?" Tyson asked, shifting his gaze to Ivy.

"Who?" Sheriff Lindsey asked.

"A man, he said his name was Bryce Hendrix, brought Hawke and Dog here. They were both injured. Dani flew them to get medical attention. We had Zach Durn in custody, tied up in the barn, but sometime between tying him up and Seth discovering someone had been in the ice house, he was cut loose." Ivy had her hands on her hips. "Bryce said the smell in the ice house is wolverine and he thinks it was the poacher, who Seth says is the person who killed the hiker and shot his brother."

Sheriff Lindsey studied Ivy, then studied Seth. "You two were hostages the last I knew."

Ivy told him about Seth getting loose, hearing the gunshot and yelling for help, and having Dani get her. Then how they were found by Tyson and Seth, and Dani flew Tuck out for medical care.

"How did you get Zach?" the sheriff asked.

"I found him hiding in the shower house. I used the radio to call for help and got you. Then I told the others and we evacuated all the guests." Seth felt good knowing the guests were safe, as was Kitree.

"Then Hawke and Bryce showed up. Hawke was a distraction and Bryce and I apprehended Zach. And you know the rest." Ivy finished in a deflated tone.

Seth chimed in. "Shouldn't we be checking tracks or something to see where the two went?"

The group groaned.

Sheriff Lindsey quieted them. "We've been chasing all over these mountains on limited grub. Any chance you could feed us before we start tracking?"

"I'll go get the leftovers I put in the ice house." Seth took off at a jog to get four jars of the chicken and noodles.

Halfway to the building, he was grabbed from behind.

Chapter Twenty-four

Hawke called Sergeant Spruel as soon as he managed to get rid of Justine and Herb.

"Hawke, I heard you were in the hospital. You're getting too old to be chasing after killers," Spruel led with.

"I've figured out why we've been running in circles. The Durn brothers have been tag-teaming to get that wolverine. One, Zeke, shot the hiker and Alex Finlay. The other brother, Zach, they're twins by the way, kidnapped Ivy and Seth and shot Tuck Kimbal."

"How did you come to all of this now?"

Hawke told him about the similarities between the brothers and his talk with Herb. "If both of them are in the mountains, they will hurt anyone who gets in their way. I know where the dens are they've been watching to try to catch the wolverine. They are obsessed with getting that animal and I believe they will return there."

"Did the doctor say you could go back to work?" Spruel asked.

Wolverine Instincts

"He didn't say I couldn't," replied Hawke, knowing that the doctor had only mentioned resting and not doing anything strenuous for three weeks.

"Who was your doctor? I want to talk to him."

"Nathan, don't go over my head to stop me. Bryce Hendrix and I work well together. We know those mountains better than anyone else. We can get these two now that we know we are dealing with two. We've been one step behind them until the one took me by surprise."

"Rafe, two staters, and three deputies are already up there. Give me the coordinates and they can circle up and apprehend the brothers."

He could tell Spruel wasn't going to send him back into the mountains. It wouldn't be the first time he'd ignored what his superior told him. He had to get up there and help Bryce. Because he had no doubt the man was out to catch them.

He reluctantly gave Spruel the coordinates wondering if Rafe and his crew would get there before Bryce had the two caught or the two disappeared.

《》《》《》

Seth's heart pounded in his chest as the hand that had been over his mouth slowly drew away.

"It's Bryce, don't say anything, just follow."

Seth kept quiet and followed the masked man through the trees. When they were fifty feet away from the ice house, Bryce stopped.

Still whispering he said, "I found their tracks. I'm sure they are headed back to the wolverine dens. Tell the cops they are a hundred-thirty-seven yards northeast of the coordinates Hawke got for the hair snare."

"Are you going after them?" Seth asked.

"I'm just going to keep an eye on them. Make sure they don't hurt anyone. I don't have a badge and can't arrest them." Bryce stared into his eyes. "You, Tyson, and Ivy stay here. Dani will need to know what's going on when she gets back."

Seth knew the man was telling them to stay to keep them out of the way and out of harm. But he wanted to see the man who shot his brother arrested. "You won't have any way to tell us where they are going or what they are doing. I can go back to the lodge and find a radio so you can contact us."

"Tell the law not to use the frequency they were with Hawke. The poacher has his radio. Radio signals can be intercepted. I'll get word to you when I need to." Bryce turned and ran through the forest, disappearing among the trees like a wild animal.

"Seth! Seth, where are you?" called Tyson from over by the ice house.

He jogged back to the ice house and found Tyson with three jars of chicken and noodles in his arms. "I'll get the latch."

"What were you doing, taking a dump?" Tyson asked.

Seth took one of the jars. "No. Bryce drew me away from here and told me some things."

"Like why he took off when law enforcement arrived?"

"No. You'll hear when I tell the sheriff." Seth followed Tyson through the back door of the lodge and found the lawmen sitting around the dining room table eating bread. He carried the jar into the kitchen where Tyson started dumping them into a large pot.

Back in the dining room, Seth cleared his throat

Wolverine Instincts

and they all studied him. "When I went to get the food from the ice house, Bryce stopped me and said to tell you, the two men will be a hundred-thirty-seven yards northeast of the coordinates Trooper Hawke gave you for the hair snare. And that he'll be watching them and let you know if they leave."

Sheriff Lindsey stared at him. "How do we know this is true? We didn't even see the man."

Seth sighed. How did he make them believe? "He told me that Ivy, Tyson, and I were to stay here and explain everything to Dani."

"And how will he contact us?" another man asked.

Seth shrugged and told them what Bryce had said about the radio being compromised and the man said he would get word to them.

The sheriff shook his head. "We were at the hair snare coordinates and didn't see anything. We even spread out and looked around."

"But Bryce said they would be over a hundred yards from the snare coordinates. Did anyone go that far northeast?" Ivy asked, having entered from the kitchen a few minutes earlier.

They all exchanged looks and shook their heads.

"Then I'd follow what Bryce said. Hawke trusted Bryce to get him here for medical attention. You all know Hawke. Would he trust just anyone he came across?" She had her hands on her hips, flicking her gaze around the room at the men.

"No. He'd be suspicious until the person proved himself," Sheriff Lindsey said. "And he did mention a Bryce in one of the radio conversations. Steve also said Hawke had a man with him who wore a facemask."

"That's Bryce. He doesn't take it off. He said

because he is missing part of his face from fighting in Afghanistan." Seth added, "Special Forces."

The sheriff grinned and said, "No wonder he and Hawke hit it off."

Tyson entered from the kitchen with a tray of steaming bowls. He set them in front of the men and they dug in.

Seth motioned for Ivy and Tyson to return to the kitchen and he followed.

"What's up?" Ivy asked. "Did Bryce tell you something else?"

"Yeah, he wanted us to stay here and let Dani know what is happening when she returns. He said he would get word to us if Zach and the other guy leave the wolverine area."

"How's he going to do that without a radio?" Tyson asked.

"I don't know, he just said he would." Seth hadn't a clue what the man would use to get word to them. For all he knew the man had messenger pigeons.

The sound of a plane overhead took them out through the dining room and over to the airstrip.

The plane tipped a wing on a pass then centered, rolled down the airstrip, and to a stop, before taxiing over to where it was tied down. Dani opened the cockpit door and climbed out.

The three ran over to the plane and all started talking at once. Dani held up a hand and her gaze went over their heads.

Seth glanced over his shoulder and watched Sheriff Lindsey and two other men walk toward them.

"Sheriff Lindsey, are you here to help arrest the men terrorizing these mountains?" Dani asked.

Wolverine Instincts

"I was wondering how Hawke is," the man said.

"He has a concussion. The doctor said he needed to rest and not do anything stressful. I left him in the care of Justine. When can I get my guests back up here?"

Seth was glad to hear Trooper Hawke's injuries weren't more than a concussion. His brother suffered a couple from playing football.

The sheriff shook his head. "We're headed back up the Minam Trail to an area where Hawke and this Bryce guy think the two are looking for the wolverine."

"I hope you find them. We can't have them going around shooting people." Dani motioned to the tie-downs. "Tyson, anchor the plane. Ivy and Seth come with me. I want to know what happened after I left."

The sheriff and his men walked over to where they'd left their packs and pulled them on. "I'll radio any information I get," Sheriff Lindsey said to Dani before they climbed the steps to the lodge.

She waved a hand and led Seth and Ivy into the kitchen. "Mmmm, it smells good. Is there any of the chicken and noodles left that Kitree made?"

Ivy dished up a bowl for Dani and they all sat at the kitchen table.

"Did Kitree make it down okay?" Seth asked.

"Yes. She's with Sage and Tuck at the Kimbal Ranch, along with my horses. Their place is closer to the trailhead than mine to get them back up. Of course, the guests who were taken back want a refund, though they did enjoy the ride." She rolled her eyes. "Now tell me what happened when I left. Why isn't there a prisoner with the sheriff?"

Ivy and Seth between them told her about the stink

and missing food in the ice house and the missing prisoner.

"Bryce is following them," Seth added. "He said he'd be in touch."

Dani studied him. "Do you know where they might be?"

"I know where the crime scene is and that the snare was somewhere near there and the dens are northeast of there." Seth wondered if Dani planned to help out Bryce.

"Tomorrow morning, I'll take you and Ivy up in the helicopter. We'll see if we can't move this capture up a little faster."

Tyson hurried into the kitchen. "What did I miss?"

Dani just smiled. "You'll be hanging out here tomorrow listening to the radio while the three of us do a flyover."

«»«»«»

Hawke sat in the cockpit of Hector Ramirez's helicopter. He'd contacted the pilot and manager of the airport early that morning to make sure he could fly Hawke into the Eagle Cap Wilderness. His head still hurt and he hated leaving Dog behind but he wanted the animal to heal.

"You don't look too good. You sure you should be going into the mountains?" Hector asked him as he started up the rotors.

"I have unfinished business up there." Hawke was determined to catch up to Bryce and the two of them catch the lunatics that were obsessed with poaching a wolverine.

His phone buzzed as he was taking off. Spruel. He turned the device off. He'd left a note on the door for

Wolverine Instincts

Justine to take Dog home with her. Even though the animal would get more rest if he stayed home, he didn't want Dog alone if something they missed kicked in.

"Here are the coordinates we're aiming for," Hawke said, handing the paper he'd written the numbers on to the pilot. He hoped they were correct. He'd still been seeing double when he'd read the numbers off his phone and wrote them down.

"That's around Glacier Mountain," Hector said. "That's all I need to know. You'll tell me the rest."

Hawke nodded and the aircraft rose in the air. He leaned his head back and closed his eyes. Sleep had been sporadic during the night. He kept waking up feeling as if he was missing something.

"Okay, we're coming over the northeast side of Glacier Mountain." Hector's voice woke Hawke.

He scrubbed his face with his hands and looked down. "Head to the south end toward Brown Mountain."

"There's someone else up here," Hector said.

"There should be three people down there on the mountain," Hawke replied.

"No, I mean up here in the sky. Another chopper."

Hawke raised his gaze from the land to the sky and spotted Dani's helicopter hovering above the crime scene area. "Can you contact her? It's Dani."

"I thought it looked like her chopper." Hector flipped some switches and handed him headgear to listen and join the conversation.

Once Hector secured the connection, Hawke asked, "What are you doing flying up here?"

"What the hell are you doing out of the hospital?"

He didn't even flinch from her harsh words. He

knew she was concerned for his health. "I'm here to help Bryce."

"So are we. He said he'd contact us. I thought this would make it easier."

His mind flashed to the word 'we.' "Who is with you?"

"Seth and Ivy."

He would have shook his head but it would make the drums beat harder. They had finally settled to a nice even beat that wasn't too annoying.

"All of you need to go back to the lodge. Hector is going to put me down near Bryce and we'll take care of things."

"How's the concussion?" Dani asked, this time with a hint of caring in her voice.

"Better. I can't sit around while these two are loose."

"I'll drop Ivy off to help you two. Three against two is better odds." Dani's tone said she wasn't taking no for an answer.

"Does she have a pack with food, water tablets, and sleeping gear?" He knew she probably didn't.

"Yes, she does. I made her pack in case she needed to help Bryce." The smugness in her tone made him smile. That was what he loved about the woman. She knew how to assess a situation and prepare for it.

"Watch where Hector puts me down and come in ten minutes later. These birds hanging around this area could make the brothers spook."

"Brothers?" Dani asked.

"I'll fill you in later. I have to find—" his words were cut off when a light flashed him in the eyes. "Hector pull around and tell me what he's saying."

Hector turned the helicopter and started talking. "Down here. They found trap."

Hawke understood. "Can you send a message back? Hawke coming down."

"I need both hands to fly this bird. There's a mirror in that little pocket there. He pointed with his chin.

When Hawke had the mirror in his hands, Hector told him the dots and dashes to make.

"He says, copy."

"You need to find a spot somewhere around there to put me down." Hawke hoped he wasn't going to be a burden on Bryce and Ivy but damned if he would sit home while the killer and his accomplice could be caught.

The helicopter went up over the mountain and Hector snuck back around the side, coming in to the area from a lower level. "If there is someone down there, you don't want them to see you being dropped off, this is the best way."

Hawke was glad the man had thought of that. But then he'd flown helicopters in Vietnam and was an ODFW pilot until he retired.

The aircraft hovered two feet off the ground. Hawke opened the door and hopped out, making his head spin. Before he could reach in for his pack, it landed on the ground beside him.

"Good luck!" Hector shouted and the helicopter left the same way it had come in.

Hawke's head stilled and he picked up his pack.

Bryce stepped out of the trees just enough for him to see.

Hawke walked over and dropped his pack down.

"You look like shit," Bryce said.

"I feel like shit, too," Hawke replied.

"Why are you here?"

"To help you catch these two."

The sound of a helicopter coming in the same way as Hector caught Bryce's attention. "Why is Dani flying around here?"

"She's dropping off Ivy. She thought three to two was better odds."

Bryce peered at him and then shrugged. "As long as she can keep up."

The helicopter hovered in the same spot and Ivy, along with a pack, dropped out about four feet from the ground.

Show off, Hawke thought as the young woman grabbed the pack and ran out from under the blades. Dani waved and left.

Bryce stepped out as he had done with Hawke and Ivy jogged over following him to Hawke.

"Dani says you're an idiot," she said by way of greeting.

Hawke shrugged.

"We need to move. If either of the suspects saw the choppers, they could be headed here to see what was going on." Bryce headed uphill from the drop site.

Ivy donned her pack and followed.

Hawke eased his arms into the pack and walked as fast as his pounding head would allow behind them.

Chapter Twenty-five

Bryce led them to an outcropping of basalt with a boulder on one side. It was like a two-sided cave. A small circle of charred rocks showed that he'd used it as his base camp.

"Put your packs there while we make a plan." Bryce pointed to the side of the boulder.

Hawke was happy to unload his pack. The pressure of the straps on his shoulders pulled his neck and added to his head pounding. He hoped he could concentrate enough to help with the plan.

"Did you see the sheriff and five other guys here?" Ivy asked.

"No. But I've been focused on the two. They must have found the packs with the trap parts. They set up a trap just inside the tree line below the dens." Bryce pulled out his canteen and took a drink. "Before I spotted the helicopters, they had the trap just about together and were spreading something that looked like scent around."

"Do they have a camp?" Hawke asked.

"They don't have any gear with them other than the trap stuff that I've seen. They seem to be able to be sustained by things they find in the forest and I'm thinking pills of some kind. There is no way they can keep going without sleep unless they're on something."

"Zach did act overly agitated and his eyes were crazy when he picked me up on the pretext of buying me breakfast." She shuddered. "I can't believe I went out with him four times."

"You said it, there aren't many eligible bachelors in the county," Hawke tried to help her see it wasn't anything she didn't pick up on.

"And the last time?" Bryce asked, his gaze intent on her.

"I knew he might be a suspect and wanted to see what I could learn."

The man gave one quick nod. "Do we wait until they are occupied with the wolverine in their trap or do we try to catch them separately?"

Ivy motioned to Hawke. "In his condition, I think we'd do better to try and get to them separately."

"I agree. While I'm here to help, I can't deal with one of them on my own. It would be better if you two get one and bring him to me to watch. Then go after the other one." Hawke knew he had pushed himself to the limit by coming back to the mountains. But he felt he owed it to Bryce and Ivy.

"Okay, you sit tight and we'll get closer and keep an eye on the two." Ivy dug something out of her pack.

"By the way, they're twins. I researched while I was in the valley. Zeke, the one who shot the hiker and Alex, was in juvenile detention for attacking a girl who

Wolverine Instincts

wouldn't be his girlfriend. His grandfather never talks about him. Shamed the family, I guess. But it seems Zach is willing to help his brother. They will most likely do anything for each other. Be careful."

Bryce nodded and Ivy studied Hawke for a few minutes.

She finally said, "That makes sense. Zach said something to me once that I shouldn't pretend I wanted something when I didn't. He got this weird look in his eyes and I hurried out of his vehicle and into my house." She peered straight into Hawke's eyes. "The thing was, I never once flirted or came on to him like I wanted anything more than friendship. He didn't give me warm and fuzzy feelings."

Hawke studied Ivy. He'd known her long enough to know she would have admitted if she had come on to Zach. "Do you think maybe he's the one that hurt the girl and they arrested his brother because they look alike?"

She nodded. "Could be. That would make so much sense about the way he treated me when he made us carry the packs."

"Let's go," Bryce said, still wearing his pack. "If you see the cops running around up here, let them in on what we plan."

Hawke nodded, pulling binoculars out of his pack and a small walkie-talkie. "Here, use this so we can communicate. It's set on the same frequency as mine. And just in case the suspects have the Sat radio still and might be flipping through channels, we'll use Morse code."

"Copy. Move out," Bryce said, motioning for Ivy to get moving.

Hawke wasn't sure whether Bryce was upset he had a woman for backup, or if he was upset that Hawke had come back and couldn't be of help.

He lifted the binoculars to his eyes and watched the two until he lost them in the trees. Twisting his position, he could see up the side of the alpine slope of the mountain. He spotted something moving. Focusing the binoculars, he had his first glimpse of one of the full-grown wolverines. It had a triangular head with a fierce expression. The animal stretched and yawned, showing large sharp teeth.

He could see the appeal of having said you caught or killed a wolverine, but they couldn't tell anyone. It was illegal. So why do it?

The animal sniffed, walked around urinating near his den, then faced downhill, sniffed, and took off at a trot.

Hawke hoped the animal avoided the trap. Just as the creature came to the tree line, he stopped and sniffed the air again. His nose remained tipped up as he continued into the forest.

Hawke thought of what Bryce said about the suspects scattering scent around the trap. He didn't know what kind it could be, but it was evident the wolverine picked it up and was interested.

He started forward then shoved his binoculars in his pack, shouldered the canvas pack he'd made sure was light, and after taking the shells out of his shotgun, he used it like a walking stick to head down the mountain, hoping to stop the wolverine from being lured to the trap.

《》《》《》

Seth stood beside the helicopter at the lodge

Wolverine Instincts

arguing with Dani. "But we know where they are. Why not take the two horses and go up and help them?"

"Because we would only be in the way since we don't know their plan." Dani motioned for him to help tie the helicopter to the concrete blocks.

"Did you see the sheriff and his crew anywhere around there? I think they got lost. Why else wouldn't they be there helping?" Seth was frustrated. He could tell by Trooper Hawke's voice he wasn't well enough to be up here. And yet, Dani, who was his girlfriend, didn't seem to be worried.

"I'm going to get on the radio and go find out. Find Tyson and help him." Dani strode toward the lodge.

Seth kicked the pinecone by his foot and dragged his feet toward the barn. He wanted to help. This was his fight as well. He was here to get revenge for his brother. Sitting around the lodge waiting to hear what was going on wasn't what he wanted to do.

He didn't find Tyson in the barn but the two horses were sleeping in stalls. Tyson must have thought they'd be safer in the barn than out in the corral.

Seth turned to leave and spun back around. He walked over to the horse he knew was Dani's. He figured she was the less accomplished rider of her and Tuck, so her horse would be the easiest for him to control.

He grabbed a blanket and the saddle closest to the stall where the horse was. He had the saddle on and was trying to put the bridle on when Tyson walked in.

"What are you doing?" He grabbed the bridle out of Seth's hands and shook it at him.

"I want to help." He heard how whiney his voice sounded and that shook him to think he was being childish.

"Quit acting like a little kid. If Hawke had wanted you down there, he would have asked for you. With Tuck, Sage, and Kitree gone, it's good to have one more person here helping. We may not have guests but these horses need tending and it gives me time to work on some of the repairs. Come on. I can use your help."

Seth uncinched the saddle and pulled it off the horse's back. He placed the blanket over the saddle and led the horse back into the stall. He was glad Tyson saw his childish behavior and not his father or any other adult. He'd learned if you wanted to be treated like an adult you had to act like one.

"What did Dani learn about the sheriff?" he asked as they exited the barn.

Dani walked toward them. "Someone told the sheriff and his group to return to the valley." She raised an eyebrow.

"Bryce said he believed the killer had Hawke's satellite radio," Seth said. "So, they don't have any help coming, do they."

Dani shook her head. "But Hawke is resourceful and this Bryce sounds like he could be too."

"And Ivy?" Seth asked.

"She might be small but she's mighty," Dani said too brightly and with too much teeth to her smile. She was worried too.

《》《》《》

Hawke leaned against a fir tree, catching his breath and waiting for the pounding in his head to ease. He knew it wouldn't go away, but just a lighter version would allow him to think.

A brown flash between bushes caught his attention.

Wolverine Instincts

He shoved away from the tree and slowly crept to the spot. The odor was unmistakable. The wolverine was walking downhill not fifty feet in front of him.

He followed at a distance, to keep the animal from seeing him and hopefully the brothers if they were keeping watch on their trap. The wolverine had his head down, sniffing the ground.

Hawke scanned the area and saw the metal cage dangling from a large branch on a pine tree. His gaze followed the rope holding the cage in the air. It went down behind a bush a good thirty yards away from the cage.

Someone had to be holding the end of the rope to watch when the wolverine was under the cage.

Hawke didn't like the setup. If the animal tried to run out from under the lowering cage, he could be hurt by the heavy metal falling across him. It was apparent the poachers weren't thinking clearly. They had to know this could potentially injure the animal.

He wondered where Ivy and Bryce were. Could they be getting ready to apprehend the guy holding the trap? Or were they following the other one, wherever he was?

Hawke's first thought was to scare the wolverine but that would direct attention to him and he wasn't in any shape to get away from the poachers. He didn't want to contact Bryce by walkie-talkie if he were sneaking up on the poacher.

He decided to sit where he was and if the wolverine went near the trap, he'd shoot his gun to scare him.

《》《》《》

Where was Zach? He said he'd be right back. The

rope was tied to a tree but now that the wolverine had walked into the area, he had untied the rope, holding the heavy trap in the air ready to let it fall over the wolverine. Nothing could stop him now. He knew this creature would soon be his. Just like he and Zach had dreamed of as kids. They'd own a wolverine. They'd be bad-asses with a pet like this. No one would mess with them ever again. Grandfather would be impressed. He'd never trapped anything as ferocious as this.

A grin tugged at his lips thinking about letting the animal loose in a room with Grandfather. Teach him what it felt like to be terrorized. Teach him to give some respect to me. He laughed at the thought.

《》《》《》

Crazed laughter exploded through the forest. Hawke jumped to his feet, starting the pounding, but he was reassured when the wolverine took off at a lope away from the trap and up the mountainside. The poacher had chased his prey away with his laughter. What was he laughing at?

Hawke's feet carried him in the direction of the laughter. Had he captured Bryce or Ivy? If so, he needed to find a way to get them loose.

His walkie-talkie beeped. He quickly ducked behind a bush and held it close to his ear as he listened to the dots and dashes. *Stand down. Stand down.* Was the repeated message.

He clicked back, *copy*.

Bryce must have him in his sight. If he was communicating, then he wasn't caught.

He clicked dot, dash, dash, dot. Dot, dash, dot, dot. Dot, dash. Dash dot. *Plan*.

Bryce appeared in front of him and sat down beside

Wolverine Instincts

him. "Easier to talk than do code," he whispered.

"Where's Ivy?" Hawke asked.

"In a tree watching." Bryce grinned. "She's some climber."

"Who is she watching?"

"The poacher. He's holding the rope on the trap. A couple more minutes and his arms should be good and tired. We'll get him then."

"Where's Zach?" Hawke kept his gaze on the forest around them.

"He took off over Brown Mountain toward Blue Lake. I followed him to the top and watched him go down, then came back. The poacher is all alone." He stood. "Let's go."

Hawke accepted the offered hand to help him to his feet. Once he was steady, Bryce raised his hands to his mouth and a bird call rang through the air.

There was one short reply.

"Okay, Ivy says she'll meet us there." Bryce grinned and Hawke followed.

They made a wide half-circle around the area where the trap hung. Bryce whispered, "They have a camera set up so he could see when the animal is in the right spot to drop the trap."

Hawke nodded and thirty feet before they would encounter the killer, Ivy appeared.

"He just tied the rope to the tree again," she whispered.

"Let's get him," Bryce said, and the two advanced quickly and quietly through the forest. Hawke followed, holding his reloaded shotgun at the ready.

"Hey!" came a shout from the area before Hawke broke through the bushes.

The killer's eyes were wide, round, and wild. He flung his arms and kicked out with his feet. Hawke noticed his rifle was leaning against a tree, but he pulled a knife from his belt.

"State Police, drop your weapon!" Hawke shouted, raising his shotgun as he stepped between the man and his rifle.

The killer roared and lunged at Hawke.

Bryce grabbed him around the legs, tumbling him to the ground as Ivy jumped on the man's back and beat the man's hand on the ground forcing him to drop the knife.

Hawke walked closer, but out of reach of the man's arms and cocked his shotgun. "Drop the knife or I'll blow your head off."

The killer glared at him and dropped the knife. Bryce and Ivy pulled the man's arms behind his back and used the handcuffs Hawke tossed to them.

Up close there wasn't as much of a resemblance to Zach, especially when Hawke saw the sores on the man's face under the whiskers. And when the killer smiled, he had black and missing teeth. He was on meth. No wonder he could go for days without sleep. But where was he getting his hits from?

"Now what do we do?" Ivy asked as she and Bryce hauled the killer to his feet.

Hawke dug around in the packs that were strewn about the ground. He found packets of meth and his Sat radio. "We call Dani to pick him and you up." He glanced at Ivy. "Are you up to transporting him?"

"Yeah." A grin spread across her face.

Hawke turned the radio on and put it on the frequency the lodge used. "Hawke to Charlie's Lodge, do you read me? Over."

After repeating that twice more, he heard, "Charlie's Lodge, this is Dani."

"Need prisoner pickup at the location of drop off. Over."

"Copy, be there in twenty. Over."

"Copy. Over." Hawke turned off the radio. "Let's get him moving."

Bryce had dropped the trap and cut off enough rope to tie around the killer's waist and lead him.

Hawke and Ivy walked behind. Hawke had his shotgun ready, and Ivy had pulled out a handgun.

The helicopter was on the ground waiting when they arrived at the open area. Seth hopped out and Hawke groaned. They didn't need him taking up space in the helicopter.

"What are you doing here?" Hawke asked him.

"I thought you'd need help." Seth glared at the man in handcuffs.

Hawke glanced at Dani. She shrugged.

"You'll compromise the arrest by being in the helicopter with the suspect." Hawke handed Seth his pack and shotgun. "Just stand here."

Bryce and Ivy already had the killer in the back seat of the helicopter. Bryce had tied his feet and was buckling him into the seat.

"This is uncomfortable!" the killer shouted.

"Too bad." Ivy closed the door on him and climbed into the passenger seat beside Dani. "Where do we take him?" she asked.

"County jail until I can get back and write up my report. You go ahead and write up the arrest report. I'll get ahold of you when I get back to the valley."

"When will that be?" Dani asked, leaning around Ivy.

"Hopefully soon. But I have to walk out of here."

"Head to the lodge. When I get back from dropping these two off, I'll fuel up at the airport and come get you." Dani motioned for Ivy to close the door.

Hawke, Bryce, and Seth walked out from under the barely moving blades and they began whirling so fast he couldn't see them. Then the helicopter lifted off the ground and disappeared out of sight.

"We need the camera down by the crime scene," Hawke said. "It could have the fingerprints of the person I think took it from ODFW."

Bryce took off down the mountain.

Seth and Hawke followed slower.

When they were in the area, Hawke pointed out the camera. Bryce gave Seth a leg up to the first branch and he climbed up. Using the bottom of his shirt to handle the camera, he put it in the evidence bag that Hawke had given him and climbed down.

"Put that in my pack," Hawke said, happy to have something that could link Shelly to the camera and help to perhaps get her to turn on Zach.

"I'll take that Sat radio," Bryce said. "I'm going to see if I can find Zach." When he had the radio, he said to Seth, "Get him back to the lodge before he collapses."

Hawke would have taken offense to his comment if he didn't feel like crap and knew it would be a struggle for him to walk back to the lodge.

Bryce disappeared before he could reply and Seth shouldered Hawke's pack. "Come on. We'll go slow."

Chapter Twenty-six

Hawke sat on a downed log drinking from his canteen and Seth stood beside him, staring out into the forest. His body wouldn't go any further. He knew Seth was trying to figure out a way to get him back to the lodge.

"You can go on. I'll be along when I get rested," Hawke said.

"Dani told me to get you to the lodge. I'm not leaving you."

Several groups of hikers had gone by as Hawke sat resting. They all gave him a pitying look as if they thought he shouldn't be up here hiking at all. This was his mountain. The mountains of his ancestors and if he hadn't bashed his head on a tree, he'd be with Bryce following Zach's trail.

The cadence of trotting hooves came up the trail toward them. He raised his gaze and found Tyson riding Tuck's horse and leading Chief.

"Dani radioed and said to come pick you two up." Tyson dismounted and led Chief over to Hawke. "Looks like you could use a lift."

Hawke nodded. His pride was taking a hit today. He stood, grasped the saddle horn, and raised his leg into the stirrup. His head started booming as he struggled to pull his body into the saddle. He felt hands shoving him up and his leg swung over the horse's back. "Thanks," he said quietly.

"You mount up behind him. Chief is better at taking two people than Ramrod is," Tyson said to Seth.

Hawke pulled his foot out of the stirrup so Seth could use it to swing up behind him.

Four hours later, Hawke slid off Chief and walked into the lodge, straight to Dani's bed, and fell asleep.

«»«»«»

Seth and Tyson went out to the landing pad when they heard the helicopter coming about twenty minutes after they'd returned.

"Hawke has only been asleep about twenty minutes," Seth told Dani.

"Let him sleep. If he knew I was here he'd insist on me taking him home. I'll wait until he wakes before I do that. He needs his rest. He's just too stubborn to admit it."

"Let's go work on the cabin that needs repairs," she said.

Tyson and Seth grabbed tools from the barn and followed her.

Seth wasn't sure what to do now. The man who'd shot his brother was arrested. What he'd wanted was done. But he felt like he owed the people at the lodge. They had been more than helpful in so many ways. He should go home and wait for the police to get his identification of the killer, but he also knew Tyson could use his help here. And he wanted one more chance to visit with Kitree.

"When will Tuck, Sage, and Kitree come back?" he asked.

"I called them when I was in the valley. They'll head up with the string of horses tomorrow. Then I can call the people with reservations and let them know we are ready for business again." Dani studied him. "You know you'll have to go down and pick out the killer."

"Yeah. But I can stay here and help until I need to go back for school." His gaze drifted to the forest outside the window. "I like it here. I feel useful."

Dani patted him on the back. "You've been a big help around here. We'll miss you."

"Maybe you can come work here next summer," Tyson said.

Seth glanced at Dani, "Would that be okay?"

"We can always use more help around here." She turned from where she was scrubbing a wall and stared at the doorway.

Seth turned and saw Hawke standing in the opening.

"Where's that ride you promised me?" Hawke asked, taking in the cabin and the camaraderie of Dani and the two young men.

"You look better than the last time I saw you," Dani said, handing the scrub brush to Seth and walking toward him. "I'll get you something to eat and then take you to the valley."

Hawke's stomach growled. "That sounds like a good idea." He followed her to the lodge and while he ate a sandwich and drank coffee, he asked her how the flight went.

"He was so trussed up we didn't have any problems with him. Trooper Shoberg met us at the airport. It was a good call to let Ivy get the arrest. It gave her more confidence." Dani picked up her cup of coffee. "I also think she has a crush on Bryce."

Hawke grinned. "That's interesting. I think she made an impression on him as well."

"Now, what are you going to do? The guy who shot Tuck is still loose," Dani asked, her tone sobering.

"Bryce is following Zach. And I'll lean on his grandfather and see if I can learn anything. If not, I'll stake out the house and do more digging on Zach's girlfriend. He needs to be brought in for shooting Tuck and kidnapping a state trooper." Hawke finished his sandwich and stood. "I'm ready if you are."

Dani stood up and put her arms around him. "Be careful. This case has already knocked you loopy. Be sure you don't wind up like that hiker." She kissed him and he hugged her tight. "I'll be careful."

They left the lodge and climbed into the helicopter. As Dani maneuvered the aircraft up and away from the lodge she said, "Justine said to tell you Dog is doing well and you are on her shit list for running off when I asked her to keep you still."

《》《》《》

Hawke said goodbye to Dani at the valley airport and debated on whether to call Herb or Justine to pick him up. He decided even though he wasn't in the mood to get chewed out by Justine, he wanted to see Dog, so he pulled out his cell phone and texted. *Come pick me up at the airport, please. And bring Dog. Thanks.*

Wolverine Instincts

I can't. Working.
Okay.
He dialed Herb.

"Hello. You shouldn't have taken off like you did," the man admonished him as soon as he answered.

"I needed to get back up and help. Anyway, I'm back in the valley and could use a ride from the airport to home." Hawke understood that people cared, but he was annoyed that they were all telling him something he already knew. They were pissed that he'd not listened to the doctor.

"I'm working on a tractor. But I'll call Darlene. She's shopping in Alder and can swing by and get you."

"That will work. Thanks." Hawke stood out on the tarmac where Dani had dropped him off. The August heat was making him sweat. He walked toward the small building that was the office and welcomed the burst of cold air when he opened the door.

"Hawke, did you get the guy?" Hector asked, from behind the desk and a cloud of cigar smoke.

"We did get one of them. The other one is still loose." Hawke sat down in a chair and set his pack beside him.

"Is he down here?" Hector leaned forward.

"I don't know. My friend is following his tracks. Hopefully, I'll know more by tonight." Hawke leaned back in the chair. "I'm waiting for a ride. Do you have anything cold to drink?"

"Help yourself to whatever's in the small fridge over there."

Hawke hadn't noticed the small Frigidaire that looked like one his mom had when he was a boy. He pulled the handle down to open the door and ran his other hand over the large round corners. He found a bottle of iced tea and grabbed it.

"You've been keeping Dani busy the last few days. Flying people to the hospital and then her bringing that big guy out today and then you." The man grinned around his cigar. "You need a helicopter pilot on the state payroll?"

Hawke smiled. "It just happened her lodge was in the middle of the stuff going on and she offered to fly."

"I heard that the little girl brought out the guests and horses earlier. There were so many stories flying around…" he leaned forward, with his forearms on his desk. "Any chance you want to tell me what happened so I can set people straight?"

Hawke shook his head. "We still have one more suspect to catch. I'm not divulging anything until he's caught."

The crunch of tires on gravel drew Hawke's gaze out the window. Darlene pulled up to the office in her SUV. "My ride's here. Thanks for the drink." Hawke picked up his pack and met Darlene halfway to the car.

"Hawke, why on earth did you take off like you did?" she asked, already in mom mode.

"I had to keep people safe. I just want a ride home, not to be told what I shouldn't have done." He peered into her eyes to let her know he wasn't being harsh, just truthful.

"Ok. I'm done shopping so that works well." She put the car in reverse and drove out of the airport. "How's Dani?"

"Well."

"Did you get the bad guy?" she asked, turning onto Hurricane Creek Road and heading toward Alder.

"One of them, yes." He wondered if Colby Durn would be forthcoming about his grandson, knowing one was in jail and they were after the second one.

"There was more than one?" Darlene glanced over at him and then back at the road.

"Unfortunately, yes. Brothers."

"The Durn twins? Herb told me you were asking about them. Nasty little boys who grew up into awful men." She frowned. "It's all their grandfather's doing. He was a horrid man. I still believe he killed his wife. She was a sweet woman. We went to school together. She was shy and I never understood why she married Colby until a baby arrived seven months after they were married. Later she told me he'd raped her and when her father confronted him about it, Colby said he'd marry her. That was enough for her father. Men!"

Hawke let this information sink in. The grandfather had been abusive to women. Had he taught the grandsons the same thing? Or at least one of them? He wondered if Colby hadn't given up the weaker of the two grandsons to the police saying he was the one that hurt the girl when it was really Zach.

His mind was reeling with all kinds of scenarios when Darlene said, "You're home."

He pulled out of himself and saw his house sitting in front of him. "Thanks for the ride and not badgering me too much. I know I should have stayed home but I couldn't let others deal with the killer by themselves."

Darlene smiled. "Your need to protect everyone is charming, but it could get you killed."

He slid out of the SUV and walked to the house. That was pretty close to what Dani had said to him before.

Chapter Twenty-seven

Hawke stepped out of the shower and heard the ham radio making noise. He pulled on a pair of sweats and hurried to the office where the radio sat.

"Hawke, it's Bryce. Over."

"Bryce, I'm here. Where are you? Over."

"At Two Pan Trailhead. An older man picked up Zach. Over."

"You want me to come get you? Over."

"Negative. My dad is picking me up. Over."

"Thank you for all your help. Keep in touch. Over."

"I plan on giving my statement at the D.A.'s office tomorrow. After shower and sleep. Over."

"You've earned both. Over."

"Copy."

The radio went dead and Hawke heard tires crunching on the gravel in front of the house. He glanced up and spotted Justine's vehicle. Dog jumped

Wolverine Instincts

out and ran to the house.

Hawke was just as happy to see him and strode to the door to open it before Dog could bark. Dog's paws landed just above the waistband of Hawke's sweats when he hopped up on his hind legs.

"Hey, boy, good to see you too," Hawke said, scratching the dog's ears and smiling at him.

"I came over here to give you a tongue lashing but seeing how happy you both are to see one another it took some steam out of me," Justine said, standing on the porch.

"Come in," Hawke walked backward, with Dog following still on his hind legs.

Justine entered and studied him. "You shouldn't have left the hospital or gone into the mountains."

"Maybe, but I couldn't let someone else get hurt. We got the man who killed a hiker and wounded another person." He stopped scratching Dog's ears and the mutt dropped to all fours and walked over to his bed by Hawke's chair.

Hawke asked, "You want something to drink?"

"Just water. It was a long day at work and I feel dehydrated." Justine sat in the chair opposite Hawke's.

He went down the hall to the bedroom to put on a shirt and slipped his feet into the moccasin slippers Dani had given him for Christmas the year before. In the kitchen, he grabbed a glass, filled it with ice and water, and returned to the living room.

"Thanks," Justine said, taking the glass. "Who did you get?"

He had a feeling she might be able to shed a little more light on this suspect. "This is all confidential."

She nodded and made the motion of zipping her

lips shut. Which he knew was as good as her word since she had helped him in similar situations and never breathed a word of it to anyone. That's what he liked about Justine, she wasn't a gossip and didn't spread rumors. But she would tell him what she'd heard.

"Have you ever encountered Zeke or Zach Durn?" Hawke asked.

She shivered when he said Zach. "I've never heard of Zeke but Zach is a woman-hating male who shouldn't be allowed to walk the streets."

"Tell me how you came to this conclusion," he said, leaning back in his chair.

"For starters, when he comes into the Rusty Nail, he thinks he can put his hands on the waitresses. I've slapped him twice and he raises his hand as if to slap me back but someone always comes to my rescue. Merrilee had him banned from the café about a year and a half ago. He was harassing a young woman who is a regular. Merrilee wanted him gone and the young woman to feel safe in the café."

"What about the grandfather?"

"Colby?" she snorted. "He's a lecherous old fart. I hear the nasty things he says when I walk by and I've spilled hot coffee on his hands more than once when he started to grab my leg. I asked Merrilee if she could ban him from the café too, but she got a scared look in her eyes. I think he has something on her. They are about the same age."

"Does he ever mention his boy, grandsons or his wife?"

"He's married! Oh, that poor woman. She's either a saint or he keeps her chained up." Justine sipped her water.

Wolverine Instincts

"Someone told me today that he raped the woman he married and when she told her parents he said he'd marry her. But she later died."

"He probably beat her to death," Justine said, her eyes narrowed, glinting with anger.

"That was this person's thought as well. Have you ever seen the grandfather and Zach together?" Hawke was trying to figure out the family dynamics.

"No. I don't think I've seen them together." Justine finished her water and stood. "I'll let you get some rest. And stay off the mountain unless you are going to the lodge for some rest."

"I don't think I'll need to go up there again for this investigation. The person I'm after is back in the valley. Thank you for bringing Dog home."

"You're welcome. Take care." Justine walked to the door and let herself out.

Hawke remained in his recliner. He tipped it back, put his hand on Dog's back, and fell asleep.

《》《》《》

Banging on the front door woke Hawke. He scrubbed his hands over his face and watched Dog walk to the door with his tail wagging.

"Come in!" Hawke called out, figuring it was either Herb or Darlene.

To his surprise, Spruel walked through the door. His first thought was *Shit, he's going to ream me for taking off into the mountains*.

"Is that where you spent the night?" Nathan asked.

"Yeah. Justine brought Dog home and we were talking. When she left, I didn't have the energy to walk to the bedroom." Hawke put the footrest down and sat up. "Want some coffee?"

"Only if it isn't any trouble." Spruel followed him into the kitchen.

"I need some. Why did you come here? I planned to come in and write up my report about the arrest of Zeke Durn." He spooned the coffee grounds into the coffeemaker.

"Ivy told me you should be home and filled me in on what went down during the arrest of Durn." Spruel sat at the table.

Hawke turned from filling the coffeemaker with water and studied his friend and boss's face. His hands were clasped on top of the table. He had something to say that Hawke wasn't going to like.

As the coffee brewed, he sat down across from Spruel. "Spill what's up."

"You were not medically discharged to return to duty and disobeyed my order to stay put. Word got to Titus in La Grande and he put you on administrative leave pending the doctor's release."

The coffeemaker stopped burbling. Hawke rose to fill the cups. "For how long?"

"However long the doctor told you not to work."

"Technically, he didn't say how long not to work." Hawke grinned, "So I didn't really do anything against his orders."

"But you did go against mine." Spruel's tone was one Hawke had rarely heard and never used on him.

He spun around and stared at Spruel. The man wasn't joking. "Paid or unpaid administrative leave?"

"He thinks just keeping you from working would be punishment enough." Spruel grinned. "We all know what makes you tick. You don't do this job for money. You do it to protect."

Wolverine Instincts

Hawke wanted to be mad, but he couldn't get anger burning in his belly to stoke even indignation. Deep down, he knew he should have stayed off the mountain. He hadn't helped that much in the apprehension of Zeke. But he was still going to find Zach and bring him in. It was obvious he'd treated Ivy poorly when he'd kidnapped her. She was part of his team, his family. As was Tuck. He was going to put that woman-hating, trigger-happy suspect behind bars.

He nodded and set the cup of coffee on the table in front of Spruel. "I understand. I could have jeopardized Ivy and Bryce. They did the take-down. I just backed them up."

Spruel sipped his coffee and peered at Hawke over the rim. He set the cup down. "You're up to something. You don't give in this easy."

"No. I realized while sitting on the side of the trail willing my head to stop pounding and my vision to stop being blurry that I shouldn't have been on that mountain." Hawke stared back into his superior's eyes. "It was the first time, I realized, I'm not that thirty-something officer who took this job and could be in the mountains for a week at a time and chase poachers for forty-eight hours and catch them."

"Are you talking about retiring?" Spruel's eyes widened.

"I'm saying, I might need to train someone else to go up in the mountains and chase poachers." He had been thinking about retiring more and more but he wasn't ready to hang up his badge just yet.

"What about Dani's nephew, the one that works at the lodge in the summers? I heard he's taking Criminal Justice courses."

Hawke grinned. "That was who I was thinking of. He knows the area around the lodge well. I just need to take him on the other mountains and trails."

"How soon can he get into the academy?" Spruel asked.

"I'm not sure. I'll ask the next time I see him." Hawke liked the idea of having Tyson Singer replace him. It would keep a Nez Perce presence on the mountain.

He shoved that to the back of his mind and said, "I heard from Bryce this morning. He said Zach Durn came out of the mountains at Two Pan and an older man picked him up."

"Colby," Spruel said.

Hawke nodded. "Someone needs to go around and talk to him and see if Zach is staying there. Also, get a warrant written up to arrest Zach for kidnapping a State Trooper, a civilian, and for shooting Tuck Kimbal."

"Your leave is making a lot of work for me," Spruel grumbled.

Hawke just shrugged.

"Write up your reports here at home and then rest." Spruel finished his coffee and stood. "I think Ivy is capable of taking over with help from Steve."

Hawke nodded, glad that Ivy would be on the case. He'd be able to get information from and to her.

As Spruel walked toward the door, Hawke spotted his pack. "I have something that needs to go to forensics." He walked over and handed Spruel the evidence bag with the ODFW camera. "This is the camera the SD card came from. No one at ODFW checked it out. I'd like to know whose prints are on it."

"I'll send it to forensics in Pendleton." Spruel took

the bag.

After Spruel left, Hawke walked out to the barn and pasture with Dog trotting along beside him. When he walked up to the pasture gate, he realized Dot was still with the lodge horses or at the Kimbal ranch. He patted Jack and Horse, handing them each a hay cube and then wandered back to the house. He picked up the phone to call Tuck. When the wrangler didn't answer, he realized Tuck probably went back up to the lodge with Sage, Kitree, and the horses. He looked up the number of Tuck's brother.

After a short conversation with him, Hawke learned Dot was at the ranch outside of Eagle and he could pick him up whenever he wanted.

He wanted to head there now, but knew if he didn't write up his account of the arrest of Zeke, Spruel would think he was out doing something he shouldn't be. Which was his plan when he picked up Dot.

Chapter Twenty-eight

Hawke and Dog sat in the pickup hooked to the horse trailer a half a mile from Colby Durn's house. Spruel must have gone straight to the D.A. for a warrant to search the Durn property. Two state police and three county vehicles were parked in front of the house.

Hawke had planned to have a chat with Colby, but from the looks of things, he wouldn't be in the mood. Putting his pickup in drive, Hawke headed to the Kimbal ranch to pick up Dot.

After his reunion with Dot, Hawke decided to go to Al's Café in Eagle to see if Lacie had more info about Zach and Shelly.

He was surprised to find a large enough spot for his trailer and vehicle in front of the café. By the time he parked and walked in, Lacie stood at the counter with an iced tea and a menu in her hands waiting for him to pick a seat. It was easy to do since only half a dozen people were in the place.

"Are you headed up to the mountains since you're

in civies and pulling your horse trailer?" Lacie asked, placing the glass on the table he chose.

"Nope, just picked Dot up from Kimbals and was hungry."

She studied him. "The Rusty Nail or Blue Elk would have been on your way home."

He grinned. "But then I wouldn't get to ask you questions."

"About?" She pulled her pad and pen out of the pocket of her apron.

"Have you seen Zach Durn and the girl with the green hair in here lately?" Hawke picked up the menu and studied it even though he knew every item they made.

"Funny you should ask. They met outside here as soon as we were opening this morning."

Hawke raised his gaze from the menu. "What vehicle were they driving?"

"The girl was driving. Zach pushed her into the driver's seat and then got in the passenger side. They headed toward Winslow." She pointed the clicker end of the pen at Hawke. "Are they in trouble?"

"Just interested. I'll have two cheeseburgers, one with pickles, and fries to go." Hawke closed the menu and handed it to her.

When she walked away, he pulled out his phone and texted Ivy. *Zach is riding around in a car with a woman named Shelly Smith, who is the receptionist at the La Grande ODFW. Get her car description and license. They were last seen headed to Winslow from Eagle.*

Her reply. *Searching at Durn place now. Will forward to Sergeant Spruel.*

Don't forward. Tell him. I'm on administrative leave. Hawke didn't need Spruel thinking he was already disobeying his orders.

Copy.

Hawke waited for the food, paid, and walked out to his pickup. There wasn't anything he could do other than take his horse home and do some digging on the computer. He'd like to know more about the woman Zach was using and figure out where the man was hiding.

Dog ate his burger in three bites and burped.

"Good to know you enjoyed it," Hawke said, patting the animal's head and opening his burger. He ate as he drove back to his place. As he passed the State Police office in Winslow, he slowed down to see if the troopers were back from serving the warrant. It didn't look like it.

He continued on home and after putting Dot in the pasture with his buddies, Hawke went in and jumped on his work computer. He wanted to know all about Shelly and everything he could find about the Durns.

«»«»«»

His head was pounding after two hours of looking things up on the computer. This was going to be a slow process if he couldn't focus and keep from having a headache. The crunch of tires on the gravel out front sent Dog to look out the window. His tail started wagging after a car door closed.

"Must be someone we know," Hawke said, standing and walking to the door. He opened the door as Ivy stepped up onto the porch.

"Thought I'd come over now that we're through with the warrant search and see what kind of trouble you're in." She walked through the open door and into the kitchen.

Hawke followed and asked, "You want coffee or something cold?"

"Ice water is fine." She sat, tugging on the duty belt to sit as comfortably as possible.

He filled a glass with ice and water and placed it in front of her. Then he poured himself a cup of cold coffee and microwaved it.

"Spruel was here bright and early to tell me I was on administrative leave for as long as the doctor said I should rest." The microwave dinged and he took the cup out, sitting down across from Ivy. "That's why I didn't want what I sent you forwarded. I'm not supposed to be on this case anymore." He grinned at her over the rim of the mug.

"I see. And that was you not being involved." She picked up her glass and drank.

"Yeah. I was hoping I could send you everything I come up with and you would use it and not say where it came from." He studied her. She was a by-the-book officer but also a pit bull when it came to finishing what she started, so she understood why he couldn't keep his hands out of this.

"I can respect your need to help bring in someone who hurt your friend." She nodded.

"And who kidnapped you, one of my colleagues," he added.

"I'm not letting that color how I deal with him," she said a little too quickly.

Hawke knew from experience you can never be completely unbiased when you have been used or manipulated by the person you were after. "I did some digging. Shelly Smith is the woman Zach has been using to gain information from the ODFW and now I believe has coerced into helping him either hide or run." He told her what Lacie had seen outside the restaurant.

"He is a user. What did you learn?"

Hawke explained how the young woman seemed to be alone but had a connection to the valley. "She had a great-grandmother who left her a piece of land here. I planned to do a drive-by now that I know her car make and license."

Ivy shook her head. "Give me the address. I'll do it."

He pulled out his phone and texted the address to her. "You shouldn't go alone in case they are there."

"Says the man who does nearly everything alone." She picked up her water and drank.

"I either have Dog or I call in backup." He didn't like this young woman telling him what his sergeant had hounded him about for years.

To change the subject he asked, "Did you find anything incriminating at the Durn place?"

"There were remnants of the materials used to make both the traps. Which pretty much puts someone in that family in the mix of poaching and the vicinity of the shootings. We have the eyewitnesses to the shootings. And Bryce will testify about the poaching."

He noticed her cheeks pinked when she said Bryce's name.

"What about Colby? Did he say anything?"

"Not really. He just clamped his mouth shut and glared at us." Ivy put the glass down. "I think he knows something. I watched him when the searching was going on and he would get nervous when someone would walk by the chicken coop. I went in and it was just a chicken coop. No place to hide anything. It might have just been my misreading something."

Hawke didn't think so. He'd take a little trip out to Durn's place tonight and have a look around.

Ivy stood. "I'll go take a look at this address."

"Let me know what you find," Hawke said, following her to the door.

"I will. You stay out of trouble," she said before walking down the steps and out to her car.

Hawke glanced down at Dog. "Now what fun would it be if we stayed out of trouble?"

The dog's tongue hung out of his mouth and it looked like he was smiling.

《》《》《》

Hawke spent a couple more hours digging through newspaper archives looking for information about the Durn family. Then he called Darlene.

"Hello?" she answered.

"Hey, Darlene, it's Hawke. I have some more questions for you about the Durn family."

"Well, come over for dinner. I made a pot roast and that usually lasts the two of us several days."

"Thanks, I'll be over in an hour." Hawke's mouth started watering thinking about having some of Darlene's cooking.

"See you then."

"We got invited to dinner," he told Dog. The animal made a circle with his tail up in the air and Hawke was pretty sure he had some drool at the corner of his mouth.

Not wanting to intrude empty-handed, Hawke

found a bottle of wine that someone had given them. He and Dani weren't wine drinkers. He also found what he figured was the bag it was given to them in. He knew Darlene liked wine but Herb was a beer man.

He and Dog used the four-wheeler to drive the connecting road between their place and the Trembleys'. It was how Herb kept an eye on the place when Hawke and Dani were gone. He pulled up to the front of the house.

The front door opened and Darlene stood in the doorway a smile on her face. "This is like old times when you lived in the apartment over the arena."

He nodded. "This is one of the things I miss." He handed her the gift bag with the wine.

"Oh! I like this kind," she said, her cheeks flushing with color. "Come in. Herb's in the shower. He was working on equipment all day. Everything always breaks down in the middle of hay season."

He knew all about it from having lived in their apartment for over fifteen years before he and Dani met and got a place together.

"How did the first cutting go?" Hawke asked.

"Good. He managed to get it all up before that rain a few weeks ago. But in the rush, he had to use baling wire on a couple of the pieces so he's fixing them properly now."

Hawke nodded as she handed him a glass of iced tea. The aromas as he entered the house started his stomach flopping and his mouth watering. "Do I smell apple pie?"

"Yes, baked this afternoon. It's still warm."

"Did I hear the pie is still warm?" Herb asked as he entered the kitchen. "Hawke good to see you looking better than the last time I laid eyes on you."

"I feel a lot better. But I've been put on administrative leave, so you'll see a lot of me for about three weeks." He said it with more enthusiasm than he felt. He didn't want to be out of the loop of this investigation. He'd started it and he wanted to finish it.

"When has something like that kept you down?" Herb asked, pouring himself a cup of coffee.

"It came from higher up than Sergeant Spruel. I'll have to abide by it or get even worse consequences. But you're right. I'm still helping from the sidelines."

"He wanted to pick my brain about the Durn family," Darlene said, placing the pot roast in the middle of the table. "Let's eat and talk."

Hawke was more than happy to dig into the roast, potatoes, carrots, macaroni salad, and celery sticks with cream cheese. When his plate was heaping, he asked, "You said you thought he killed his wife. What made you say that?"

"Because she just disappeared. She was in the backroom of a PTA meeting one night and the next meeting someone said they'd heard she had left Colby. He said she'd gone to visit a relative and never came back. Several times, I'd see her pull down the sleeve of her sweater to hide bruises. He is an awful man and I believe he killed her." She set down her fork and stared at her plate. "I wish I had tried to reach out to her more. She always pushed me away but I could tell she needed someone to talk to."

"It's not your fault," Herb said, patting his wife's arm. "You have helped many women over the years. But some just don't want to be helped or are so scared they fear retribution from their spouse for talking to you."

"How old were the twins when she disappeared?" Hawke asked.

"Oh, they weren't born yet. Clyde, her and Colby's son, must have been about ten or twelve, I'd say." Darlene looked at her husband.

"Yeah, around that," he added.

"I wonder if he knew what happened to his mom?" Hawke sliced his meat as he started thinking of how to find someone who might have been in Colby's confidence back then.

"If Clyde saw it, I can't imagine him keeping quiet. He loved his mother and despised his father. Unfortunately, his health wasn't very good and when the twins were eight or nine, he passed and the wife handed the boys over to Colby," Herb said.

"Zeke has been doing meth. What do you think would start him using drugs?" Hawke asked, peering around the table at the husband and wife. "Ivy thinks Zach was high when he kidnapped her. They both had a wild look in their eyes when confronted."

Darlene shook her head. "I'm glad Clyde isn't alive to see the mess his father made of his boys. Clyde was always kind and considerate, a lot like his mom. Those boys are the spitting image of Colby, from looks to their temperaments."

"Can you think of anyone Colby might have confided in before his wife left him? Or when he got the grandsons?" Hawke asked. "Or someone that his wife might have talked to?"

Darlene picked up her dishes and then Herb's and set them in the sink before turning to the table and saying, "I saw Mrs. Durn talking to Helen Peebles.

Back then she was the minister's wife, she's a widow now, in her eighties. She might know something. She was known for being the person to go to if your husband was being abusive."

"Thanks, that's a start." Hawke studied Herb. "What about friends Colby had as a teenager or young married man?"

"I can only think of two people. Mrs. Van Hoosen's son, Richard. He doesn't live around here but she might have some insights and Otis Powell. He and Colby were friends in high school." Herb filled his coffee cup as Darlene set the pie in the middle of the table.

"That looks delicious," Hawke said, not even concealing how excited he was to take the first bite.

Chapter Twenty-nine

Hawke and Dog left the Trembleys' with full bellies. Hawke couldn't remember when he'd eaten so much. The woman was the best cook he'd ever encountered. Every food she touched was delicious.

He wanted to sit in his recliner and let the food digest but he also wanted to go snooping around the Durn place. Dismounting from the four-wheeler, he glanced at his pickup. This was something best done at night but it would be even better if he had some information that he could use to put Colby off if the man came across him trespassing.

Hawke waddled into the house and straight to the shower. He'd get a good night's sleep and question the people Herb and Darlene had given him and check out the chicken coop at the Durn property tomorrow night.

《》《》《》

The following morning Hawke looked up the three people he wanted to question in DMV records and found their residences. His first visit was to Mrs. Helen

Peebles.

"Hello?" she questioned through the screen door of her small home on the east side of Winslow.

"Mrs. Peebles, I'm Senior State Trooper Hawke." He held up his badge. He had it clipped to his belt today. "I'd like to ask you some questions about a woman you knew."

"State Police you say? I'm sure I can't be of any help."

"I'd like to ask you about Mrs. Colby Durn." He waited as the woman searched her mind for the name.

"Oh, that poor woman! Come in. I'm not sure what I can tell you but I never for one moment thought she left him on her own." She opened the screen door and motioned for him to enter a house that was cluttered with furniture and knickknacks. "Coffee or tea?"

"Coffee but only if you have it already made," Hawke said, moving stacked boxes of puzzles to sit in a chair.

"I just made a fresh pot." She continued talking as she walked into the kitchen. "I get up early and have coffee and sweets while I work on a puzzle. They say it helps keep the mind fresh." She walked into the small living room with a tray holding two cups of steaming coffee, two spoons, a sugar pot, and a little pitcher.

"Thank you, I drink it black." He took the cup offered to him and sipped. It was good.

"What did you want to know about Thelma?" She put sugar and cream in her coffee.

"I was told she would confide in you. Could you tell me what that was about?" Hawke sipped the coffee and smacked his lips, tasting every drop.

Mrs. Peebles smiled. "I've been told for years I

make the best coffee."

"I would agree with that. About Thelma, what did you two talk about?"

"She's been gone for nearly forty years, why are you asking me about this now?"

Hawke studied the woman. She seemed to know something and he really needed leverage to get information out of Colby. "Her grandsons are caught up in illegal activities and I need to find a way to get their grandfather to tell me where they could be hiding. I thought maybe if I had some information about what happened to his wife, I could persuade him to help me with the grandsons."

She snorted, very unladylike, and then said, "He made those boys into what they are. Just like he killed his son and wife."

"Tell me about the family before Thelma disappeared." Hawke leaned back in his chair, holding his cup of coffee.

"Thelma and Clyde were gentle souls. You could see it in their faces and how they treated people. Thelma told me how Colby had raped her when she was seventeen and when she told her father he made them get married or he'd turn Colby over to the police." She shook her head. "Can you imagine what that child must have felt like being married off to her rapist?"

Hawke couldn't. But he knew the meanness in Colby and feared he knew what kind of life the woman lived.

"She came to me a couple of times just to have someone to talk to that wouldn't spread her troubles all over the county. I took pride in listening to the women who had no one else they could turn to. My husband was a compassionate man but men don't understand the hold they have on women when they become their husbands. Especially back then. She feared the wrath of our savior if she divorced him, and the wrath of her husband if she tried. She feared him yet felt bound to him by the marriage vows."

"Did she ever tell you she feared for her life?" Hawke asked, understanding what the woman was saying about a man not fully understanding the woman's point of view in marriage and many other matters.

"The last time I saw her she said she'd intervened between Colby punishing Clyde and Colby told her he'd kill her if she tried to stop him again. That Clyde had to learn to be tough." Her eyes glinted with anger. "His form of toughening up boys was to knock them around. I know he did the same thing to those grandsons. Zeke was a gentle soul until he became a teenager. By then he'd been beaten on enough that his anger lashed out at everyone he came in contact with. Poor boy ended up in Juvenile detention."

"What about Zach?" Hawke asked.

"He seemed to take the beatings with stride and smile. Like he was proving to his grandfather that no matter how much he was beaten, he'd not let anyone know it. Tough kid. But a bitter man, I think."

"Have you seen him lately?"

"The last time was at church. He sat in the back with a thin woman with green hair."

"When was this?" Hawke asked, wondering what the two of them had been doing in church.

"About three weeks ago, I think." She thought a moment. "Yes, it was the day we had cake afterward for the minister's birthday."

"Which church was this?"

"The Methodist church here in Winslow."

"Thank you, Mrs. Peebles, you've been a great help." Hawke finished his coffee, said goodbye, and headed to the Methodist Church. Perhaps the pastor could shed some light on why the two were at a Sunday sermon.

At the church, a young man told him that Minister James was out visiting parishioners who were housebound. Hawke left his card and asked that the minister call him.

On his way to visit Mrs. Van Hoosen, Ivy called. "What did you learn?" Hawke asked.

"Not much. I drove by and didn't see a vehicle, so I staked it out until midnight and no one came. I think it's a dead end."

He heard disappointment in her voice. "Okay, thanks."

"Are you getting anywhere?" she asked.

"I'm interviewing people about Colby's wife who disappeared. I want to have something on him before I talk to him."

"Remember you're not supposed to be doing all of that," Ivy said.

"Only you and I and Spruel know that." He ended the call as he pulled up to Mrs. Van Hoosen's house on the outskirts of Winslow on the way toward Eagle. Her large Victorian farmhouse always impressed Hawke when he drove by. He wondered how the ninety-something woman kept it up.

At the door, he knocked and waited. When he didn't hear anything after five minutes and knocking again, he walked over to the garage that was once a stable and found her car there, but that didn't mean anything. Mrs. Van Hoosen wasn't supposed to drive anymore. Her doctor had taken her license away from her. Her cousin, Merrilee, the owner of the Rusty Nail, usually took her to town to do her errands.

He had one foot in his vehicle when Merrilee's car pulled up to the front of the house. She wrinkled her brow at the sight of Hawke. Exiting the vehicle, she walked around to the passenger side and opened the door, helping Mrs. Van Hoosen out.

"Trooper Hawke, what do I owe this honor?" Mrs. Van Hoosen asked.

"I have a few questions I'd like to ask you about someone who was a friend of your son's." He followed them up the walkway to the house.

"Do you mind if I stick around to hear these questions?" Merrilee asked.

"Not at all. You know the person I'm asking about and might have some information too." Hawke settled into a chair across from Mrs. Van Hoosen. "I was told that your boy Richard was friends with Colby Durn."

The old woman's face puckered up in distaste, doubling her wrinkles. "That boy turned into a nasty man. He and Richard were friends until they were seniors in high school. I'm not sure what triggered the mean streak in Colby. When he started bullying people and treating girls poorly Richard didn't want anything to do with him."

Hawke tried to wrap his mind around what could have made someone snap like that. "Did you ever figure out what made him change?"

"His mother died his junior year of high school.

But you wouldn't think losing his mother at that age would have caused such a change in him," Merrilee said.

"What about the dad?" Hawke asked.

"He was never in the picture. No one really knew who his dad was," Mrs. Van Hoosen said. She shook her head. "Though there were rumors that his mom had been working in one of those houses outside of Reno before she became pregnant. She ended up in the county because she came to stay with an aunt when she was pregnant."

Hawke was starting to see why the man hated women. He'd more than likely been lied to by his mom until her death and then she must have told him the truth and it was more than he could bear. Finding out the mom he'd adored was a prostitute who conceived him with someone she couldn't even name. And if people started talking about her past profession once she died, that could have fired him up.

"Any idea why he seems to treat his grandsons so poorly?" Hawke asked.

"I know that Zeke wasn't top of the class. He was a sweet kid when he was small but as he grew, he became angrier," Merrilee said.

"What about Zach?"

"He's always been an asshole."

"Merrilee, your language!" Mrs. Van Hoosen admonished her cousin.

"I'm sorry, Georgie, but it's the truth. I can't think of any other word that describes his behavior." Merrilee gave him a conspiratorial wink. She'd said the word to goad her cousin.

"Yet, I heard their father was a nice man. What

about the mother? Is she still alive?" Hawke wanted all the dirt he could get on this family.

"Clyde was nice. Always kind to everyone. He would come to school with bruises and say he fell down but I know it was from his dad. You could tell by the dullness in his eyes." Merrilee's eyes were moist with sympathy.

"Was that before or after his mom went missing?" Hawke asked.

"After. Before I think his mom took all the hits," Merrilee said.

"And did he ever talk about his mom leaving?"

She shook her head. "He only once said something like, she's still here just not with us."

Hawke leaned forward. "Like his dad killed her and hid her?"

Merrilee nodded. "He didn't come right out and say it but we all kind of understood what he meant. We all knew his dad and knew his temper."

"Do you have any idea where the twins' mother is? Or what her name is?" Hawke wanted to see if Clyde had ever confided his thoughts about his father killing his mother to his wife.

Mrs. Van Hoosen stood. "I'll call Richard and see if he knows."

Hawke was confused. Richard was friends with Colby, not Clyde. "Why would he know?"

"Because he was the attorney who wrote up Clyde's will. He didn't like Colby but he liked Clyde and helped him out now and then." She shuffled down the hallway.

Hawke studied Merrilee. "Did you know Thelma Durn?"

She nodded. "Sweet young woman. After she left, I heard how she ended up with that monster for a husband. Life is cruel."

He wondered if she was thinking about her husband leaving her and then losing her children. One to a car crash and the other to a birth caused by being raped by a preacher.

"It definitely has it's downer days," he said in sympathy. "Did you know Thelma well?"

"I met her at their wedding. My husband worked with Colby. Then we chatted a time or two in the store when she was first married. After Clyde was born, I rarely saw her. When I did, I didn't like the look in her eyes. Fear."

Mrs. Van Hoosen shuffled back into the room. "Richard said her name is Rhoda Greenly now. She lives in Pullman, Washington."

Hawke smiled at the old woman. "Thank you. I appreciate all of your help." He faced Merrilee. "Thank you for your thoughts. Please don't repeat what we talked about. I need to catch Zach and the best way to do that is to figure out his grandfather and him."

Merrilee nodded.

Chapter Thirty

Hawke was on a roll. Now to talk to Otis Powell and see if he could shed some more light on Colby. After that, he'd give Rhoda Greenly a call.

As he drove to Otis's place, his phone buzzed. A quick glance at the name and he pulled over. "Minister James, thank you for calling me back," Hawke answered.

"I'm not sure why you need to talk to me Trooper Hawke," the man said.

"I'm curious about a couple who attended the Sunday sermon the day of your birthday. Zach Durn and Shelly Smith. What can you tell me about them?"

"Zach and Shelly? Why are you interested in them?" His tone was noncommittal. He knew something.

"Have they been to your church before?" Hawke decided to start with the easy questions.

"Shelly has been coming at least once a month

since her great-grandmother passed and left her the house near the lake. She started bringing Zach a couple months ago. They talked to me about marriage counseling."

This wasn't the picture Hawke had painted in his mind. "Marriage? Do you think they are a good match?"

"I think Shelly puts more into the relationship than Zach. Until that is equaled out, no, I don't think it's a good match for Shelly. But Zach is a lot like his father. He feels he has to dominate people rather than let them like him for himself."

The minister had figured Zach out. "I agree. Thank you for calling me back."

"Is that all you needed?" the minister sounded skeptical.

"Yes, thank you." Hawke ended the call. It appeared Shelly was thinking of marriage and Zach was playing along to get what he wanted. Access to the information at the ODFW. They had to be staying at her great-grandmother's place, but why hadn't Ivy seen anything?

He continued on to speak to Otis. Though the thought on his mind was staking out where Shelly and Zach were most likely staying.

At the Powell farm, Hawke stopped in front of the house and waited for the two old cow dogs to waddle out to the pickup and sniff him. Once they approved of him, by wagging their tails, he walked up to the front door and knocked.

A woman slowly made her way to the door. Hawke watched her through the open door and screen door.

"Yes?" the woman asked, standing on the other

side of the screen.

"Mrs. Powell?" he asked.

"Yes. Are you trying to sell something?" She glared at him.

"No. I'm Trooper Hawke." He held up his badge. "I would like to speak to Otis if he's around."

"You'll find him out in the barn repairing things." She turned around and walked away.

Hawke said a quiet, "Thanks," and strode off the porch and over to the old barn. As he walked closer, he heard banging.

Inside the barn, Otis was bent over a wooden box nailing.

"Otis," Hawke said to get the man's attention.

The small man threw his arms in the air, causing the hammer to fly and hit the barn wall. "Hawke, you nearly scared me to death!"

Shaking his head, Hawke walked over and picked up the hammer. "All I did was say your name." He handed the tool to Otis.

"I was deep in thought as I nailed this feeder back together. What are you doing here?"

"I heard you were friends with Colby Durn. Could you tell me something about him and his wife?" Hawke leaned back against a pole.

"Colby and I haven't been friends for a long time. He turned too mean for my liking. And then when Thelma disappeared, we all knew he probably killed her but didn't have any way to prove it. She conveniently went to stay with relatives on a weekend when Clyde was staying with a friend. Thelma wouldn't have left her boy. She would have taken him with her." Otis's face darkened with anger. "Are you looking into her disappearance after all these years?"

"That, and I need to find a way to get to the grandsons." Hawke didn't want to say too much.

"Because of their poaching? Everyone knows they take what they want and don't give a damn about anyone else."

"That and shooting people." Hawke watched the man.

Otis nodded. "I figured it was only a matter of time before they started taking human lives for granted just like they do animals." He picked up his hammer. "I wish I had more to tell you but like I said, I haven't had anything to do with that family for a long time. But I'd sure like to see them get what's coming to them."

"What you've told me is enough to hopefully get the information I need. Thanks." Hawke left the barn and walked to his pickup. With the information he'd gathered, he could do some pretty good bluffing if he was caught by Colby tonight while snooping around.

«»«»«»

Hawke returned home and made a call on the ham radio. "This is Hawke calling Bryce, do you read me?" He repeated it a couple of times and then left the frequency open.

Next, he called Ivy.

"Hawke, did you learn anything new?" she asked.

"I'm headed to the Durn place tonight after dark. I want to snoop around the chicken coop and beyond. Just thought I'd let you know in case you heard of an altercation on the radio tonight."

"Is this your way of asking for backup?"

"I'm trying to get hold of Bryce for backup since I'm not supposed to be working."

"Call his dad's. He's been there the last couple of days." And the call ended.

Hawke grinned. She was either staying in contact with him or keeping tabs on Bryce.

He found the number and called.

"Hendrix residence," answered Solomon.

"Solomon, this is Hawke. Is Bryce around there by any chance?"

"He told me how he's been helping you. This is the most spark I've seen in him in years. Thanks!"

"Is he there? Can I talk to him?" Hawke had a feeling it wasn't helping him that put that spark in Bryce. It was a small feisty female trooper.

"Hey, Hawke," Bryce said.

"Hi. I need backup tonight. In case Ivy didn't tell you, I've been put on administrative leave but I think I can figure out how to get Zach if I sniff around the Durn property."

"Yeah, Ivy said you'd been put on leave and you weren't giving up on the case. What's the address?"

Hawke rattled off the address.

"That backs up to public land. I'll come in from that direction. What time?"

"I plan to get there about midnight."

"Copy." The line went quiet.

Hawke now had backup and a bit of a plan of action. He took a nap, ate a good dinner, and then dressed all in black to keep from being seen. He had a small pack with a flashlight, folding shovel, and a first aid kit. He had his knife in his left boot sheath and his backup Glock in his right boot sheath. He didn't plan to use either of them but it didn't hurt to be prepared. He also had three hamburger steaks with a sleeping drug to feed to the three dogs.

At eleven-thirty, he and Dog loaded into the pickup and headed for the Durn property. He switched off his lights and rolled into a side road that was across the road from Colby Durn's. Exiting the vehicle, he shouldered the small pack and headed across the road onto Durn's property.

When they were close to the house, Hawke put the steaks in a paper bag and tossed it toward the place he'd witnessed the dogs diving under the porch when he was last there. One dog woofed, then came out and sniffed. He picked up the bag and ran back under the porch.

Hawke could hear the bag tearing, scuffling, and growls. About fifteen minutes later all was quiet. He sent Dog out in front of the porch.

Nothing.

He hoped that meant the dogs were sleeping.

He gave a soft whistle and Dog ran back to him.

From visiting one time Hawke had an idea of where the chicken coop sat. He headed straight for the old building. The wood was weathered and shingles were missing from the roof. It appeared the building hadn't been used in years.

The door creaked when he slowly opened it. Glancing toward the house he waited to see if a dog would come running or a light would come on. When neither happened, he entered the ten-by-fifteen building. The nesting boxes were precariously hanging from the east wall. The roost was three poles tethered unevenly. It was the ground he was interested in. If the man had buried his wife here, the ground shouldn't be as compact in that area as the rest of the floor. Using a pointed metal rod, he started at one end of the area and shoved it into the ground seeing where it was hard to push and where it was easiest. Under the nesting boxes it appeared to be the easiest.

He put the rod away and pulled out the folding shovel. The first couple of shovels were hard but after that the digging became easier.

"What are you doing?"

The whisper sent his heart racing and his hands clenching the shovel. He glanced down and saw Dog's tail making dust where it wagged on the floor.

"How did you sneak up on my dog?"

"I didn't. We made eye contact and he knew I wasn't your enemy. What are you doing?"

"I think Colby killed and buried his wife here years ago."

"What does that have to do with this case?" Bryce asked.

"I thought if I could prove it, he would give up his grandson, thinking it would serve him well." Hawke shrugged.

"I found something better in the trees," Bryce said.

Hawke peered through the darkness. "What?"

"A meth lab."

"Really? Why didn't they find it when they did the search?"

"It's not on Durn land. It's on that public land I told you about. Come on." Bryce disappeared from the doorway.

Hawke folded his shovel, put it in his pack, and said, "I'll be back Thelma," and then motioned for Dog to follow Bryce.

Out of the chicken coop, Hawke glanced toward the house. It looked still. He followed Bryce into the forest. They went fifty yards and crossed a fence.

"This is the public land," Bryce said, walking to the left. "Even if this had been on the Durn property, they probably wouldn't have noticed it. I only did because I caught a whiff of something off and followed the smell."

Hawke sniffed and noticed the smell as well. Not what one would usually encounter in the forest. In the dark, he saw a mound ahead of them. It wasn't the shape of a house. It looked more like a boulder covered in dirt.

"You might want to cover your mouth and nose," Bryce said, pulling up the bottom of his facemask to cover his mouth and nose.

Hawke told Dog to stay and watched Bryce move brush to the side to reveal an opening in the mound. They stepped into a twelve by twenty earth cave that stunk of chemicals. Hawke turned on his flashlight and did a sweep of the area. It looked like a typical meth lab setup. Except for the green hair sticking out from under a dirty blanket in the corner.

Hawke dove down on the ground and pulled the blanket back. Shelly had bruises and blood trickling from cuts. Her eyes were shut. He felt and found a thin pulse.

"We need to get her out of here," he said to Bryce, who picked the young woman up as if she weighed no more than a child. "I'll call Ivy to get an ambulance and a forensic team here."

He dialed Ivy and stepped out of the meth lab.

"What are you doing here?" shouted Zach. He held a bright flashlight on Hawke's face. It was the voice that gave him away. And this was similar to what he'd

Wolverine Instincts

done before shooting Tuck. Always a bully. Make the other person vulnerable and then strike.

"Looks like you and your brother were doing more than poaching and shooting people," Hawke said, keeping his voice loud so that hopefully Ivy would hear through the phone what was going on. She knew approximately where to find him. "And now you beat up a woman. All Shelly wanted was your love and you nearly beat her to death."

"She was nothing. Always going on about getting married and getting me away from my nasty grandfather. Grandfather understands me." The hand holding the flashlight wobbled.

Hawke was stalling, but he didn't know how Bryce could come to his aid when he filled the doorway. He started to ease sideways.

"Don't move. I'll blow your head off if you move. I gotta think. No one will miss you. I heard you were put on leave. They'll just think you went off into the woods and didn't come back."

That's when Hawke realized Dog wasn't waiting for him at the door. "What did you do to my dog?"

"What dog? I think you're going nuts. There was no dog here."

Zach's smile churned Hawke's gut. What had he done to Dog?

Hawke decided he was done waiting for the young man to explode. He'd make the first move. He dove to the side of the mound, scrambling to hide in the shadow and pull his Glock out of his boot.

"Freeze, police!" Ivy's voice rang through the trees like bells at Christmas.

Boom! The echo of the rifle was punctuated by two

taps of a revolver.

Hawke walked out of the shadow of the mound.

Ivy stood over Zach, her weapon drawn.

Bryce stepped out of the mound carrying Shelly.

Ivy grabbed the radio on her shoulder and called in the attempt on her life, the need for an ambulance, and a team to go through the meth lab. When she finished the call, she peered into Hawke's eyes. "You need to get out of here before the others show up."

"Get forensics to finish digging in the chicken coop. I think they'll find the body of Thelma Durn," Hawke insisted.

Just then Dog came running out of the woods and jumped on Hawke. "Where have you been? I thought that lunatic killed you." Hawke hugged his friend.

"I managed to get him away from here before Zach saw him." Ivy stepped up and ruffled Dog's hair. "You two get. Bryce and I can finish this. We'll come by tomorrow and tell you what happened."

Hawke nodded, whistled for Dog, and walked through the woods back to his vehicle. As he drove away the ambulance siren rang in the air.

Chapter Thirty-one

Hawke and Dog went home. Hawke gave Dog a treat and then he went into the office and used the radio to call Dani.

"What's up? Over," Dani asked.

"I've been put on leave. Thought I might come up and help out at the lodge for a couple of weeks. Over." This would be a good trial to see if he could stay busy enough with helping at the lodge to not miss work.

"What did you do? Over."

"By going up to the mountains while still suffering from a concussion, Titus put me on administrative leave with pay until the doctor okays me to work. Over."

"What about the case? Over."

She knew him too well.

"It's being wrapped up tonight. Ivy and Bryce are handling it. Over."

"And you stayed out of it? Over."

He laughed, she knew he didn't. "Let's just say my name won't come up in the report. Over."

"When will you get here? Over."

"I'll either leave tomorrow afternoon or the next morning. Over."

"Make it the next morning. Here's the list of food we need." She read off the list and he wrote it all down.

"Looks like I'll be bringing Horse. Over."

"Bring Jack too. We could use another good kid's horse. Over."

"I'll see you day after tomorrow. Over."

"Looking forward to it. Over."

Hawke was smiling as he went to bed. He'd be in the mountains enjoying himself for two weeks instead of chasing someone.

《》《》《》

Hawke had a pot of fresh brewed coffee and a pan of Darlene's cinnamon buns waiting when Ivy and Bryce pulled up to his house. Ivy was out of uniform and Bryce wasn't wearing a mask.

Ivy had a smile on her face as she practically skipped up the walkway to the house. Bryce had a silly grin that wasn't hindered by the puckered-up skin on the right side of his face.

"Good morning. Are you here to give me an update?" Hawke asked, letting the two in and leading them into the kitchen.

"Yum! How did you know we haven't had breakfast yet?" Ivy asked, plopping into a chair and digging out a cinnamon bun.

"I thought even if you had, no one can resist Darlene's cinnamon buns." Hawke placed cups of coffee in front of each of them. He waited for Bryce to grab a bun before he asked, "What happened after I left?"

"When the ambulance arrived, Colby came charging out of the house with a shotgun. I had to arrest him for threatening the paramedics. They took Shelly and from what I learned this morning, she's going to be okay. Breathing in all that nasty air at the lab and then the beating she took, she's lucky to be alive. And she knows it. She feels stupid to have fallen for Zach's good-guy act. She said the last week he started showing his true colors and by then she thought she was in too far to get out without being killed. Which is what he tried to do." She took a bite and chewed. "Man, these are good!"

"Darlene wins a blue ribbon for them every year at the fair. What about Zach? Was he dead or alive after you shot him?"

"Dead. I'll have to go before the board, but I shot in self-defense. They'll probably call you to testify." Ivy took another bite.

"Are you okay?" Hawke asked. He knew what it felt like the first time you killed someone in the line of duty. You knew it was your job and duty but it was still something hard to get over. Until the next person shot at you and you had to discharge your firearm.

"Yeah." She glanced over at Bryce and then sighed. "I'm not worried about the investigation. It's the psych eval I have to go through. I don't like people making things out of what you say."

"You'll be fine," Bryce said, patting her arm. "You got rid of someone who would have gone on hurting and possibly killing people."

Hawke decided to change the subject. "We have the brothers' testimony about Zeke killing the hiker and shooting Alex. He will go to prison for a long time.

What about Colby? Can you get him on anything?" Hawke really wanted the man to go to jail too. It was evident in how his grandsons turned out and the comments by the people he talked to that the man had anger issues and took them out on everyone around him.

"Your instincts were spot on. Where you were digging about five feet down was the body of a woman. I'm sure we will discover it was Thelma Durn. He will go down for her murder." Ivy licked her fingers and dug in the pan for another bun.

Hawke smiled and glanced at Bryce. "How did you know to stay inside last night when I was confronted by Zach?"

"I'd called Ivy when I found the meth lab. I figured she'd be showing up. So why give him two people to shoot if help was on the way." He grinned and grabbed another bun.

Hawke studied him and laughed. "I radioed Dani this morning. I'm going to spend the rest of my leave at the lodge. Did you manage to get all the reports written and your signature on them?" Hawke asked.

"Yep, your name isn't mentioned. Bryce called me about the meth lab, I got there to find Zach holding a gun on him. When I called out 'Police,' he turned and fired at me. I shot him twice in self-defense found the woman in the lab." She grinned. "Thanks to your leave, I have my first homicide collar."

"I wouldn't have wanted anyone else to get credit for it. You deserve it after what you went through at the hands of Zach." Hawke meant it. He was glad Ivy was getting the credit for the arrest.

"How did you conclude that there was a body

buried in the chicken coop?" Bryce asked.

Hawke smiled and said, "Wolverine instincts, I guess."

《》《》《》

Thank you for reading *Wolverine Instincts*. I became enamored with the wolverine as a child when I read a book about the animal. As I ran through the animals on my list to use in titles for the series, I decided it was time to write about a wolverine.

I hope you enjoyed Hawke's latest adventure. Please leave a review where you purchased the book. You can also leave them at Goodreads and Bookbub too. Reviews are how an author's book gets seen.

If you would like to stay in contact with me or know more about my books, or even purchase ebook, audio, and print books directly from me, you can go to my website: https://www.patyjager.net or subscribe to my newsletter https://bit.ly/2IhmWcm

Murder of Ravens
Print ISBN 978-1-947983-82-3
Mouse Trail Ends
Print ISBN 978-1-947983-96-0
Rattlesnake Brother
Print ISBN 978-1-950387-06-9
Chattering Blue Jay
Print ISBN 978-1-950387-64-9
Fox Goes Hunting
Print ISBN 978-1-952447-07-5
Turkey's Fiery Demise
Print ISBN 978-1-952447-48-8
Stolen Butterfly
Print ISBN 978-1-952447-77-8
Churlish Badger
Print ISBN 978-1-952447-96-9
Owl's Silent Strike
Print ISBN 978-1-957638-19-5
Bear Stalker
Print ISBN 978-1-957638-64-5
Damning Firefly
Print ISBN 978-1-957638-82-9
Cougar's Cache
Print ISBN 978-1-962065-49-8

While you're waiting for the next Hawke book, check out my Shandra Higheagle Mystery series or my Spotted Pony Casino Mystery series.

About the Author

Paty Jager grew up in Wallowa County and has always been amazed by its beauty, history, and ruralness. After doing a ride-along with a Fish and Wildlife State Trooper in Wallowa County, she knew this was where she had to set the Gabriel Hawke series.

Paty is an award-winning author of 50+ novels of murder mystery and western romance. All her work has Western or Native American elements in them along with hints of humor and engaging characters. She and her husband raise alfalfa hay in rural eastern Oregon. Riding horses and battling rattlesnakes, she not only writes the western lifestyle, she lives it.

By following me at one of these places you will always know when the next book is releasing and if I'm having any giveaways:

Website: http://www.patyjager.net
Blog: https://writingintothesunset.net/
FB Page: https://www.facebook.com/PatyJagerAuthor/
Pinterest: https://www.pinterest.com/patyjag/
Goodreads:
http://www.goodreads.com/author/show/1005334.Paty_Jager
Bookbub - https://www.bookbub.com/authors/paty-jager

Windtree
Press

Thank you for purchasing this Windtree Press publication. For other books of the heart, please visit our website at www.windtreepress.com.

For questions or more information contact us at info@windtreepress.com.

Windtree Press
www.windtreepress.com
Corvallis, OR